The Dark Strip

The Dark Strip

Judy, keep or give to a friend — good book ☺ — Elizabeth

a novel

Journey with Christ Jesus — on His Path — for His glory —

Elizabeth Barnes

Elizabeth Barnes

Had I not written this book myself, I would wish that I had. I like it. With no claim to literary eminence, it is nonetheless both serious and funny, fiction and fact, imaginative and well written, profane and true.

iUniverse, Inc.
Bloomington

Its truth belongs to the One who is Truth. All glory to Him!

January 6, 2020

The Dark Strip
A Novel

This is a work of fiction. All of the characters, names, incidents, organizations, and dialogue in this novel are either the products of the author's imagination or are used fictitiously.

iUniverse books may be ordered through booksellers or by contacting:

iUniverse
1663 Liberty Drive
Bloomington, IN 47403
www.iuniverse.com
1-800-Authors (1-800-288-4677)

ISBN: 978-1-4620-4909-7 (sc)
ISBN: 978-1-4620-4908-0 (hc)
ISBN: 978-1-4620-4907-3 (ebk)

Library of Congress Control Number: 2011915115

Printed in the United States of America

iUniverse rev. date: 09/19/2011

for my father and mother, Terry and Annie Mote Barnes,
who lived some of this story and inspired much of it,
ere I had dreamed it

Acknowledgments

Rebekah Barnes Horrell, my daughter, and Christopher, her son, my eldest grandson, have made the submission of this book possible, with cheerful work and intelligent expertise in cyber technology which I do not have. Thank you, Chris and Rebekah.

Ethelene Russ Barnes and Judy Schlegel are excellent friends whose helpful contributions made this a better book. I thank them.

In memory of Doris, I am grateful for her, kinswoman, lifelong friend, and muse.

Others helped in the telling of this story in generous and lovely ways. I am thankful for, and to, each and all.

Especially, I now believe that Mac and Gabe offered to me and daily embodied as my grandson companions, a gift of Spirit, which created this story. Like Temperance in this novel, they helped when they didn't know they were helping and when they had no conscious aim of it. Thank you, my boys.

Elizabeth Barnes
March 5, 2011

We conclude that in the field of public education the doctrine of 'separate but equal' has no place. Separate educational facilities are inherently unequal.

Chief Justice Earl Warren, ruling
in the case of *Brown versus Board
of Education of Topeka*, May 17,
1954

PART ONE

Journeying on the Edge

Prologue

I *understand and relate to the position of the weak in the world, and* I *feel much more comfortable around those people than around the powerful.*

Paul Watson

People talk about defining moments. It's safe to say that the dark strip incident was such a moment for Temperance Green Smith. On a hot, humid Saturday in July of 1954, in a small, textile town in North Carolina, Temper and Rhonda Edwards, best mill hill friends, went to the seven o'clock showing of that week's movie at the Paramount, probably to see Clark Gable or Marilyn Monroe or another star.

They hadn't gone to a movie alone that late in the day before then. Instead, they were getting out and heading home at seven. When they walked out of the air conditioned theater, Temper was startled to see how close to dark it was. But she was not yet worried, not at all alarmed. The warm evening air had lulled her. Besides, they had taken their customary way home along Savage and Blount many times. Though not so late, almost nine o'clock in the evening. Still, their familiarity with the route and the balmy, summer twilight itself kept anxiety at bay. Until they were two-thirds of the way down Savage.

As they passed Howell's Lunchroom, two men staggered from the alley running between the closed grill and Sasser's Tobacco Warehouse on its north side. So abrupt was their appearance, the men nearly collided with the girls. Shocked by their drunken look,

3

Temper identified Craven Herbert and Butch Morris, millhands she recognized as two of Stedman's employees. Partly through surprise, partly through fear, she said nothing, but pressed on faster, more deliberately.

Morris and Herbert, both of them "three sheets in the wind," staggered and shuffled and tried to focus their blurred vision on the girls hurrying up the sidewalk. Herbert managed a wolf whistle and a few salacious grunts and wiped his mouth on his dingy pocket handkerchief. A sour smell of sweat and cheap liquor hung on them.

"Hey, ain't that Stedman Smith's girl up yonder?" Temperance heard one ask the other.

"Yeh, she's a heartbreaker . . . stuck up, though."

The first muttered a response she couldn't make out, but the sound of their laughter unnerved her more and she thought she heard the word "split-tail." She picked up obscenity, in any case.

The girls quickened their pace and hoped the men had turned and gone in the opposite direction, but they did not look back to see. Twilight had deepened to "that blue time of day," Temper's name for it; and it would soon be pitch dark. All the stores, along with Howell's Lunchroom and Fox's Ford dealership, had closed at five. The streets were deserted. Daylight would be completely gone before they were halfway home, Temper realized, a grab of fear now clutching the muscles in her stomach. She wished they hadn't wasted time window shopping. When she and Rhonda turned the corner off Savage onto Blount, she saw that the men were following them.

Ahead, a strip of sidewalk about the length of a house, shrouded and dark, lay midway the block, the longest block they would travel. Temper and Rhonda called it the dark strip, although they'd never walked through it at night before; it was shaded and cool in the daytime, and noticeably darkened on sunlit days as well as cloudy ones, owing to Miss Mattie Cannon's thick, climbing roses covering a fence enclosing her backyard, on one side, and a dense row of overarching trees meeting along the street, on the other. Curiously, Lenoirville had never put street lighting along that strip of walk. It would be hard for anyone to see what was going on in there when light was gone.

On the way to town and back, Temper habitually walked along the outer perimeter of the sidewalk. Uptown, she switched to the inside, closer to the store entrances and theater box office. It was in her nature to make subconscious calculations which maximized her range of motion and access. Rhonda, nearly two years younger and of a different personality sort, made no complaint, if she noticed it. Now, Temperance had done it again without overt deliberation, moving smoothly to the outside of the walk as they had turned off Savage onto Blount.

Just as seamlessly, without turning to look at her, she whispered in a stage whisper to Rhonda, "When we get to the edge of the dark strip, start running as fast as you can."

Rhonda breathed in a hyperventilated voice, "Okay," and waited for further stage prompting.

Shaking, they kept their brisk, but even, pace toward the now-dreaded strip of sidewalk, strong hearts hammering their ribs and adrenaline pumping their muscles. The instant they stepped inside the shadowed, outer edge of the dark strip, choreographed by trust and close friendship, both girls in perfect synchrony took off in a headlong dash,

"Now! Run!"

Both men started running, too, aiming to catch up to them where there was no light.

Immediately, a tall, lean figure crossed the street diagonally ahead of them and dissected the space between the girls and the pursuing men. Temper and Rhonda never saw their rescuer, but Craven and Butch did. In the fading, last light, Gabriel Laughinghouse had observed the incident from the other side of the street and acted.

"What's got you fellas in such a hurry?" Gabriel called out loudly, intending to alert others who might also be within earshot.

Had others heard? No evidence left in the darkness would answer that question.

When Gabriel Laughinghouse had stepped out of the back of the Greyhound Bus in Lenoirville some weeks earlier, he already knew what he wanted, no matter his youth. Twenty-two years old, a lifelong native of Detroit and a transplanted graduate student at Morehouse College in Atlanta, he was grandson to Native American, Negro, and White forebears, and at least a half millennium of America's blood flowed in his veins. Two years earlier in Chicago he had heard Paul Robeson sing and orate on the subject of racial oppression. About a month prior to his odyssey of research and inquiry to Temperance Smith's hometown, Gabriel had marveled over, and excitedly discussed with Morehouse and Spelman College friends, the surprising and momentous decision handed down by the United States Supreme Court on May 17. Like most college students, Gabriel was not until then aware of the *Brown vs. Board of Education of Topeka* case which Thurgood Marshall had argued in December and for which he was, that spring of 1954, awaiting the decision from Chief Justice Earl Warren and his high Court. Some of Spelman's women students now worried that a federal ruling striking down school segregation could mean the end to schools like theirs. A *New York Times* editorial had scolded the Court for its decision and objected that it had detoured from jurisprudence into sociology. But sociology was Gabriel's academic field, and he saw in the ruling a prescient value. It meant the highest court and constitutional law of the land had outlawed all attempts to keep Negroes "in their place." With Thurgood Marshall and others of the NAACP, Gabriel recognized that individual rights would never again be legally tied to race or color. Discrimination named by the euphemism of "separate but equal" policies and practices had been exposed and correctly named. More, it had been declared unconstitutional, outlawed.

A political and cultural paradigm had shifted. Thurgood Marshall's mighty voice had prevailed. The old paradigm *would* be displaced. A new one was forming.

Someone has said that what a person wants determines that person's story. Gabriel Laughinghouse knew what he wanted. He wanted to name his place. He knew that the Supreme Court's decision implicitly supported the basic human freedom to say for oneself what one's place is. That decision had given legs to the Declaration of Independence and had cemented legal, constitutional clout behind the "self-evident" liberty of the individual.

A culture of White supremacy since Reconstruction had named the former slave's place, and an adamantine legacy had passed it to every generation of America's slave descendants. It had enshrined it in America's laws and customs. "White Only," writ large over water fountains, public toilets, lunch counters, and front row seats on vehicles like the Greyhound Bus on which Gabriel had ridden into town signified it. Jim Crow until then had designated his place. And the place of all people of color.

Cotton mills, too, had a "White Only" policy. Negroes need not apply. Must not apply. Nobody could remember the last time a Negro had. But the day Gabe arrived, that fact was about to change in one cotton mill town, in Lenoirville, North Carolina.

When Gabriel climbed the front porch steps of Stedman and Mae Smith's white, mill village house, he had gone there to find his grandfather's childhood friend for whom he himself had been named. First and middle names. He had experienced a fair amount of difficulty tracking the old gentleman down before he learned that he was living with his daughter and her family in Lenoirville. Gabriel's grandfather, Seth, had told him stories about his boyhood best friend, a White boy named Gabriel Lewis. Their friendship was half his reason for coming to Lenoirville; the other half was that it was a cotton mill town. He meant to conduct a sizeable portion of his thesis research there.

Temperance Green Smith, named for a great-grandmother who had marched for suffrage in 1919, was intemperate in audacious measure, as she imagined her grandmother also to have been, and was, that July, a few weeks shy of her sixteenth birthday. She was the only child of parents descended from untallied numbers of generations of poor, but land-owning, farmers and preachers, the lot of them proudly White. Pretty enough to nurture the fantasy and smart enough to know it was no more than that, Temperance secretly yearned to be as beautiful as Elizabeth Taylor and Marilyn

Monroe combined. Her black hair, classic features, and eye-catching figure (although her legs were too skinny, she thought) fueled the fantasy, as did the movie star magazines she picked up at Standard Drug on her way home from the movies. Plenty intelligent enough to achieve it, Temper (the family nickname fit her better) considered a college education a possible goal, and if she decided to do that and got one, she knew, she would be the first in her family to do so. It was growing into an indistinct but emerging dream. Beyond that handful of disparate and half-formed fantasies and goals, she didn't know what she wanted. Except that she wanted to get married and be a mother someday.

Gabriel Laughinghouse stayed six weeks in Lenoirville that summer. The dark strip assault shook the Lenoirville community but did little to overhaul its established conventions. Nonetheless, the incident's trajectory, with events and trauma devolving from them, changed foundationally Temper's perspective and formulated what she wanted irreversibly. Linked with other influences farther back in time, redolent yet with power, they forged in her a lifelong ambition, a goal worthy to stand as companion to Gabriel's.

Gabriel wanted to name his place. Temperance wanted to oppose all forces keeping him in his place.

Chapter One

"What if Rhonda and I had gone to the *five* o'clock movie, the way we had *always* done before, instead of to the *seven* o'clock movie?" Temperance nearly shouted into her cell phone.

Fredericka recognized this pattern of emphasizing every fifth word as Temper's stressed-out, getting-nowhere habit of going repeatedly back over everything, *everything*. Heck, now she was doing it herself, repeating and italicizing her thoughts, Fred worried.

Temperance persisted, "Freddie, I *know* things would have been *different*. Almost certainly."

Fredericka gave no reply. The question had been rhetorical. It was Fred's role to listen, mainly that. The Listener, that's who she was. She knew it; they both did. Their friendship had evolved that way. Maybe it had started that way, too. Many, many years were a long time to remember. In any case, she and Temperance had been over this before, gobs of times. Temper seemed obsessive-compulsive about this matter, Fredericka realized.

"Two more hours of daylight would have guaranteed it, I believe."

A difference of safety, she meant. The chance encounter would not have occurred so early. The tired sound had swamped Temperance's voice. God! She'd said it enough to be tired of it, or from it, whichever it was, Fredericka thought. Her old friend was beating up on herself again, but Fred had long ago learned that she could do little to head it off, once the battle had started, and little to keep it from heating up and getting underway. The best she could do was to listen. Maybe no one else could do more than that, actually. Perhaps not even Jeffrey Singer. Dr. Singer.

"What if I had read my mental Rorschach test another way the day I went to McLelland's, and suppose I had chosen another seat?"

Temperance had moved on to another regret, another thorn of affliction.

Temper knew she could have. Why hadn't she? What was to blame? Was it her lifelong, confrontational stance whenever anything stood in her way? There was good reason her ancestral name had been shortened to "Temper." Temperate was a modifier and attitude hard for her to manage, typically.

"I'm gonna' go, Fred. Thanks for hearing me out again. I know you've got a lot to do. See you next Tuesday. Bye, bye."

"Bye, Temp. Loosen up. You're back at it again. It wasn't your fault. None of it. Goose egg. See ya'. I love you." Fred's clipped manner of speaking took matters in hand and soothed her.

Temperance snapped her cell phone shut and jammed it back into her pocket. She'd called her friend to tell her something she'd read that morning in Juan Williams' Marshall biography. Statements in *Thurgood Marshall: American Revolutionary* had led her down her hard-beaten path again, as civil rights histories generally did whenever she read anything about that era in which she and Fredericka also had lived. (Had it been long enough ago to call it an "era"?) She hadn't marched in Selma, nor traveled out of North Carolina in those days, but Temper's history and story overlapped that time as well, a time before hardly anybody knew the South was changing. And how it was changing. And before most Southerners thought it needed to change. Gabriel Laughinghouse had been victim to that nearly forgotten preamble to civil rights history.

But what *about* her unleashed, confrontational disposition? Had *she* changed at all, even now? What about *maturity*? Temperance asked herself. She couldn't help a whimsical, self-satisfied smile when she remembered something Mae once had said to her in a rare moment of pique:

"Temper, I declare, I believe you would argue with a signpost!"

"Yes, I *would*, if it had the wrong thing *written* on it!"

Poor Mae, her poor, dear mother, she had had to put up with a lot of that kind of thing from her, Temperance regretted. At least in part, she regretted it. Still, she was even now a little too amused by her smart-aleck, adolescent retort and the characteristic side of her from which it came to think she had changed much.

Temperance's thoughts sobered. She was a female Lear, she'd concluded in Norma Johnson's Shakespeare course at Meredith. That conclusion came out of another melodramatic idiosyncrasy of hers, the assigning the King Lear moniker to herself. Maybe her life just hadn't offered room and opportunity for dramatic expression sufficient to what she had in her, Temperance mused.

Back to the recriminations. What role had sheer luck, *dumb* luck, played in it all? Would it make a difference, now, if it were called fortune? Shakespeare's characters seemed to have had a lot of trouble with bad fortune. The question had been coming up more and more often lately. She was tempted to pick up the phone (she remembered it wasn't "pick up" but "dig out" the phone, now) and call Fredericka again, but she resisted the urge. Fred had things she needed to do. But what *about* luck? Or fortune? Was she responsible for that, too? How *could* she be? This soliloquy was getting her nowhere, but she couldn't turn it loose just yet.

She couldn't blame luck that it had been her idea to go to the later movie that fateful Saturday in 1954. She was sure it had and imagined she had talked Rhonda into it. She didn't even know how Rhonda had gotten permission to go, or if she had. Maybe her grandparents had thought Rhonda was visiting late at her house, or Rhonda had simply counted on their thinking it. While her memory was not clear on these facts, she took the lead, more often than not, and Rhonda had followed it that day, she believed.

And McLelland's. It had been her choice to sit at McLelland's lunch counter on *that* particular stool. Another one at the end of the counter, five seats away, had been vacated the minute she had sat down. She could have moved there. Why hadn't she? It could have, probably *would have,* changed everything, she was convinced. She wished she didn't believe it; her soul would have more peace if she could change her mind about that one conviction. At least, Rhonda wasn't there for the McLelland's incident. She could be thankful for that much, in any case.

Damnation! Her head was throbbing and a bright light zigzagged across her field of vision. Temperance didn't suffer full-bodied, migraine headaches, but Dr. Philip Evans had told her these episodes were related to migraines. She generally backed off and gave herself a little rest from whatever she was doing, whenever the warning symptoms flashed. She could do that. Temperately, she added, with annoyance. Temperance both disliked and valued her great-grandmother's name. Generations meant something to her. But the name was a lot to live up to, and she could seldom pull it off. Not to mention the sheer contradiction between the name and her personality. Still, she and her great-grandmother had one important thing in common besides family genes and a name. They both *gave* a damn. Grandma Temperance Green had marched for women's right to vote, for suffrage. Temper had written a dissertation about social justice and tried to make some waves of her own, at least in the classroom and at a few pivotal times outside it. Had her activism been enough? It seemed anemic, at best, to her now.

The incident yesterday had nearly guaranteed a visitation of the light stabbing her vision. The jagged, zigzagging line heralded the return of Gabriel Laughinghouse, and with him, memories she would struggle to repress again. Like Captain Marvel's lightning bolt, the light behind her eyeballs portended an event of moment. This serial drama was a weary, five decades old. Did she have energy now to do that, to repress the memories, to stop the momentous event, one more time? Talking with Fredericka helped. Somewhat. Talking with Jeff Singer helped, but not enough. The young graveyard assistant had looked too much like Gabe. He was catalyst. She hadn't seen it coming. What could she have done, if she had? She wasn't omniscient; she couldn't have anticipated the effect he would have on her, how much he would resemble Gabe, and in how many other ways he would be like him.

———〰●◖◗◉◖◗●〰———

The doorbell jarred her awake. Temper was relieved to discover the nap had worked. Her vision had cleared and the jagged line was gone, and unless she just didn't remember it, the nightmare had not returned. However, it waited for dark. She knew that. Fredericka stood at the side door, looking into the kitchen.

"I finished the few errands I had to run. The others can wait. I'm here. Talk. I'm listening." Fred pulled back a chair from the kitchen table and sat and rested her elbows, both hands cupping her mouth and chin. The body language bespoke patience and attention.

Could there be a more faithful friend? Temperance wasted no time.

"It was the young man who helped me yesterday, Fred." She paused long enough to take a deep breath and expell a loud sigh. "He was Gabe Laughinghouse all over again. Isn't it uncanny how features of totally unrelated persons get passed along from generation to generation—as though nature runs out of patterns—even *mannerisms*, so much alike you can't believe it? I mean, of people who never even saw each other!?"

She paused again and thought about this arresting phenomenon a few seconds longer, before she forged ahead, "His resemblance got me thinking about it all, all of it, again." Temperance expelled another deep sigh.

The explanation was plausible. Still, Fred and Temper, both, knew it took far less than that to get her started. But here was the worst part:

"The dream, that god-awful nightmare, has returned. I dreamed it again last night, Fred. I thought, I hoped, it had ended. I don't think I had dreamed it for over a year." She sighed heavily again, pulling her breath up from a place of dark weariness.

"But there I was, slogging through black, hip-deep water, not deep enough to drown me or pull me down, but too deep to pull out of, with the mud sucking at my feet. I woke up exhausted and hopeless—helpless—hopeless—both. Take your pick," she finished, with something like sarcasm in her voice. Or self-pity. Definitely, agitation. And regret.

Temperance reached for a cigarette and lit it. God, Stedman had certainly modeled that one enough times for her. And given her the genetic blueprint for it, too, no doubt. How many times had she tried quitting? Damnation! Who was counting?!

Who was she kidding? *She* was. This time, she had lasted fifteen days. Last attempt, it was three months and two days, and not a single day had passed when she hadn't died for a smoke. What had made her think her advanced degree would help her kick this addiction? At least she could admit it *was* one. She'd made that much progress, anyhow. Maybe her smarts *had* helped a little, Temperance thought, with a modicum of satisfaction. But nothing had helped enough, so far.

She had blamed Carson for her smoking a full, two decades after the end of their nine-year marriage. Eventually, she had laid the blame at Stedman's feet. Needy and insecure, certainly, but guilty as hell nonetheless, Carson had impregnated a college student, one of his own freshmen, while Temperance was working night and day on her dissertation. She had nearly hit the wall when he told her about it, ("she's getting an abortion; we're okay"), but Virginia Slims had calmed her down enough to carry on and finish her degree. With the cigarettes fortifying her, she had early kicked the King of Sleaze out and with little looking back since that day. And damn! The cigarettes were good!

Time passed and Temperance eventually forgot about finding or being found by someone else, not that she had given much thought to it anyhow. Those years with Carson had been a sad mistake before adultery and a baby on the way gave her decisive reason to divorce him. She still thought so. Besides, the single life suited her more than she would have guessed. Back then, most women thought they had to have a man in their lives, a husband and children, and she had thought so, too. She had discovered it wasn't so, thank you very much.

"Want a Coke, or somethin' else, Fred? Let's go into the family room."

"No, thanks; I'm good," Fredericka answered as she stood up from the table.

Settling into their usual chairs, they faced each other across a butler's tray table laden with assorted books, including the Marshall biography, an Oxford English pocket dictionary, outdated copies of *The New York Times* (she received them through the mail), snapshots of relatives, a *Newsweek* copy showing a cover picture of John McCain and Sarah Palin, last month's *Harper's*, and an oversized, green, ceramic ashtray. Temper thought it curious how many people went outside to smoke at their own houses, and not just in the warm summer months, but when it was cold enough to freeze the ass off a brass monkey!! Ludicrous! she thought.

She didn't light up indoors either, when she had a visitor who minded, and she asked. That was common courtesy. Fredericka didn't. Mind.

Temperance's long hallway to three modest bedrooms, her office, and the rest of her house, was lined with Wal-mart bookshelves (Fred teased her for buying them there) and served as a room (now it was "more than wasted space," not a "mere passageway") for the library she still used as an ethics professor emerita. Later, she meant to give it to a third world school needing books as much as money. For now, she didn't want to part with them. Her walls in every room except the two small baths constituted a portrait gallery exhibiting family likenesses spanning seven, maybe eight, generations. The oldest was a portrait of her maternal grandfather's paternal grandparents. She sometimes searched their faces and imagined she saw some faint resemblance to Pa Gabriel in them.

"Fred, I've been thinking about Jeff's recommendation that I write my memories and thoughts. In a sort of diary or journal. He's insisted that repressing my memories, *my* preference and habit, is not what I need. I've tried to journal before and not lasted long with it, but maybe he's right." She stopped and lit another cigarette, like Stedman, with the one she was already smoking.

"Maybe I'll try a more challenging art form than journaling; that rather bores me—something like a combination of fact and fiction. Maybe I'll write it the way it was and the way it should have been, or the way I wish it had been. Something imaginative, to insulate me, on the one hand, and inspire me, on the other." She was clearly working it out. Thinking out loud with her friend. And constructing a sarcastic buffer already.

"What the devil! I'm not testifyin' before a court o' law! Wha' d' ya think? Are you willin' t' listen t' me read it back t' you?" Temperance relapsed into colloquial, sub-standard English, sloppy and natural, when she joked around with Fred, and she was trying now to lighten up a bit. Still, her professorial habit kept her a bit stiff at it. Not least because language meant a lot to her. As it had to Pa Gabriel. And to Gabriel Laughinghouse, his namesake.

"Sure thing, Temp! I think Jeff Singer's idea is a good one." She backed up a little. "I guess I'm a smidgen concerned you might bog down with it, though. If the headaches and zigzags get worse, maybe you'd better let it be."

Not given to finishing on a down note, Fredericka pressed onward and upward, "But I'll bet they improve, instead. Yes, Sir! I'll bet it helps! Go for it, Temperature! I *need* a good thousand page book to read!" she whooped, arms flailing every which way.

Fredericka could be depended on to encourage her, often with laughter, usually that way. Her comic improvisations lifted Temper's spirits, her Lear episodes. And nobody could do a better Carol Burnett than she could. Or a better Mama or Tim Conway, for that matter. Her repertoire was current, as well. Fred was as good at Tina Fey's Sarah Palin as Fey herself. Moreover, Fred could do Tina Fey *as* Palin. That one *really* cracked her up. There was no doubt about it, Fredericka had missed her calling, Temperance allowed. Mostly, however, Fred just listened. Her timing, like that of all good comic artists, was precise and sensitive. And like good people generally, she'd made of her best qualities a craft.

"Thanks, Freddie." Picking up a leather-bound copy of a Barnes and Noble journal tucked underneath a pile of newspapers, Temperance smiled weakly and said, almost too softly for her friend to hear it, "I think I'll start with Gabe's application for the summer job." She added, more inaudibly and hesitantly, "in the cotton mill."

Perhaps because she was an academic, and no doubt to buttress herself against the bad memories, Temperance chose to write from a third person point of view, in an expository, dialogical style, as if writing a serial story for publication in a literary journal. Holding the story at arms' length that way, she cushioned herself for what she knew was coming. For what she did not remember, or remember having been told, she reached into her soul and her imagination boldly, ambitiously erasing the line between what she could plausibly have witnessed and what she could not possibly have known. She would not write it any other way. Only so, could she bring together her conscious and her subconscious minds, and only so was she willing to undertake this inauspicious challenge. In point of fact, Temperance knew truth lay somewhere on the mysterious interface of event and interpretation, and getting to it was not commonplace, she had observed. Moreover, interpretation itself was married to imagination, she knew, and many a divorce had occurred when cold, single fact tried to rule meaning apart from imagination's complement. As if there were any uninterpreted facts at all, the literalist's folly was just that insistence on discovering and adhering to those nonexistent facts. If she touched truth, Temperance was convinced, she would do it by embracing the glorious ambiguity of inseparable event, imagination, and interpretation, that inextricable triad and its gift and serendipity.

She embarked on her narrative journey midway, with incidents surrounding Gabe's applying for a job in Glen Rivers Cotton Mill that summer of 1954. The episode had involved Stedman and, ineluctably, other people, as events ripple in unpredictable and unmanageable ways naturally. She felt like Odysseus, but whether headed home, or through treacherous waters to inhospitable and dangerous places, or, like Homer's protagonist, finally to both, she could not tell. Her preface began:

Individual, unsung deeds and accidental and chosen roads met in a timeless convergence in the summer of 1954 in a sleepy North Carolina town—before Rosa Parks was arrested for refusing to surrender her seat to a White man on the Montgomery city bus—before civil rights marchers faced down police dogs and fire hoses—before M. L. King, uninitiated pastor at Dexter Avenue Baptist Church, became Dr. Martin Luther King, Jr., acclaimed champion of the American struggle for racial and social justice. Accounts of the struggle for equality and place in the last half of the twentieth century have been told many times over, by historians, biographers, and poets and storytellers extraordinaire. Depression-era and post-World War Two socio-political and cultural and spiritual currents, and the moral violence of those blind forces, came first, historical prologue to the Civil Rights Era. We know too little of that earlier time and its stories. They yet await their turn at telling and being told.

Here follows a narrative of certain of those stories, each an odyssey in search of place. Together, all, a march to Canaan.

Temperance wasn't sure, but this process felt authentic, natural, to her. A kind of exhilaration and wonder began to form, mixed with her dread of the inevitable reappearance of Gabe's ghost, and gradually, she started to anticipate what she had avoided, the writing itself. Just as she expected, Jeff Singer saw it as progress. She was synthesizing early memories and recent events, combining them as she thought them and they emerged, materializing independently of her control. Was this the way writers experienced their ideas? she wondered.

Temperance continued with the story of Gabe's job application at the mill:

On Monday morning, according to his customary practice as general overseer, Stedman went out to the mill superintendent's office to talk over the week's work plans with Bill Foster. Orders for cotton thread were short, he found; thus, he decided he would send five workers on each shift home to "rest" for a day apiece that week.

He would pass those instructions along to Gene Brewer and Marvin Swindell, second and third shift overseers. Both Stedman and Bill tried to be as fair as possible about deciding who would be assigned to "rest" whenever orders were slack. They played no favorites. When orders were plentiful and heavy, everybody worked the full, five-day week and, occasionally, they got the chance to pull some overtime on Saturdays. Most millhands dreaded to be sent home to rest; they needed the full week's wages. Temperance remembered how Mae complained when she was sent home, and this from a long-suffering woman who rarely complained about any situation, but bore up under all conditions stoically.

Just as he was picking up his half-filled Chesterfield pack off the corner of Bill's desk, Stedman saw Gabriel Laughinghouse come through the outer mill office door and heard him greet Nora Winters, Bill's secretary. Gabriel asked to talk to Mr. Foster and, seeing that Stedman was about to leave, Nora pointed him courteously, but curiously, toward the superintendent's door. Stedman walked into the outer office, spoke to Gabe while wondering what his purpose for being there was, waved to Nora, and hurried on over to the mill, leaving the younger and older man to their meeting, still puzzling over Gabriel's reason for a visit with Bill. He hadn't mentioned that intention at home last night.

Stedman would hear soon that Gabe Laughinghouse ("some Colored boy") had applied for a job. In the cotton mill. And that Bill Foster had told him that work was slack at the mill just now, orders being down as they were, and that no jobs were open. Nora had heard it all. A few of her friends knew most of what occurred at the mill. All of what Bill had said was true, as far as it went.

"Mr. Foster, with all due respect, Sir," Gabriel had persisted, but tactfully, "is it not the case that there would be no jobs open to a person of my color, even if there were a vacancy and orders were high, Sir?"

Mr. Foster took the question and its challenge with equanimity. "Perhaps so," he admitted, "we don't ordinarily hire Colored folks except as truck drivers. Can you handle a rig? Would you be interested in that? If you are, I can check that out for you."

Bill Foster had sized up the well-spoken young man in his office, now, and knew that he was well-educated, over-qualified, and probably fresh out of college, with better prospects available to him in the Negro community.

"No, Sir," Gabe responded, "thank you, but my interest is in a job inside the cotton mill. Are there policy specifications which deny my eligibility for employment inside the mill?" He could feel himself trembling slightly; he hoped not perceptibly.

Gabriel had pressed the issue. He had felt some reluctance to do so, because he, too, had sized up the man sitting behind the desk. Bill Foster, he inferred, was a basically decent man whose own sense of fair play chafed at the strictures of Jim Crow policies, but he was enmeshed in and benefited from a poisoned social system. He was part of it.

"It is true," Bill said, a red splotch brightening the skin on his neck, "that Colored folks are hired only for driving the big rigs. That's company policy," he finished grimly, faintly apologetically. "Except to fire the boiler," he added.

"Thank you, Mr. Foster," Gabe replied, standing and sticking out his hand, "I appreciate your time. I'll be on my way. Good day, Sir." He would not labor his point.

One of the world's oldest cliches holds that news travels fast, especially bad news. Nora Winters had lunch at Howell's Lunchroom with two of her closest friends that day, and by two-thirty that same afternoon, most in the mill village knew that a Negro had asked for a job at the cotton mill. *Inside* the mill. Already, rumor had embroidered the report to say that he had applied for a job in either the carding room or the spinning room. Was he so ignorant that he didn't know that only women worked in the spinning room? He'd even asked for a job there, scorned some. Craven Herbert and his sidekick Butch Morris got wind of it soon as the news got out.

"We oughta teach 'is black ass a lesson," Butch sputtered, cleaning his fingernails with his pocketknife and eyeing the blade with an obscene smirk.

"Yeh," agreed Craven, "don't he know niggers ain't got no place inside a cotton mill?"

Feelings were running high all over the village when Stedman got off work a few minutes after three and headed home. Outside the mill, he ran into Butch and Craven as they lumbered out of their worn-out, Chevy pick-up, the license tag caked with river mud and hanging by a single, rusted bolt. As usual, they were several minutes late for their second shift jobs and Stedman thought he caught a whiff of liquor on their breath, but he let both infractions pass. Stedman didn't nit pick. People's jobs mattered too much and the wolf was constantly at the door, for millhands and a lot of other folk besides them.

"Mr. Smith, d'ya know dat Colored boy what ast fer a job hyer t'day?"

They'd heard talk he'd been seen hanging around Stedman Smith's house on the overseers' block across the street from the east end of the mill. Coming out the front door. And everybody knew there was a young, White girl lived there, Smith's girl.

"Yes," Stedman answered evenly, making steady eye contact with, first, Craven and then, Butch. "He's a good boy, I think, a college student just wantin' a summer job to make 'im a little money, a temporary thing, I'm sure."

Studying them a moment silently while he lit his Chesterfield slowly, almost languidly, Stedman let them take in the image of authority he knew he presented, before resuming his pass at damage control, "He didn't know no better. It won't come to nothin'."

He blew a long stream of smoke in their direction. They got the message: don't stir up trouble. (Decades later, Clint Eastwood would remind Temperance of her father, the same unflappable toughness, the same stare.)

With one, last, deliberate gaze, Stedman turned and walked straight and tall, shoulders back, the way he characteristically did, and now more so, toward his house, not too hurriedly, but definitely with purpose. Stedman's intuition caught most things, and he had recognized better than anyone else on the mill hill would, the explosive mess they were in; this kind of thing hadn't happened before at Glen Rivers, to his knowledge, but it didn't have to for him to read the signs. Ironically, he would turn out to be the one who forgot what his intuition had shown him, when events barreled out of control and erupted closer to home.

"Ef you ast me," growled Butch, when Stedman was in his yard and too far away to hear, "Smith's nuttin' but a nigger-lover hissef."

Lowering his voice to a gruff whisper for extra measure, Craven stoked the fire, "Someb'dy needs to teach 'im a lesson, too. Nigger-lovin' 's as bad as bein' one."

Both men had a sore spot toward their bossman. Several times, he had gotten onto them about laying out drunk, or sleeping off a hangover, one or the other. He'd warned them sternly he'd have to let them go if he couldn't count on them. All the work force, all three shifts, knew their general overseer, second only to Mr. Foster in authority and command, to be a fair bossman. He'd give you the benefit of the doubt, just as he'd done that day, to Craven and Butch. A millhand himself all his adult life, Stedman Smith knew what it was to be hungry, broke, and worst of all, powerless. He lived the same story Craven and Butch did, as a hired hand. But he wouldn't excuse sorriness and put up with it. They knew that, too.

Blessed with something like an innate homing device for justice and fair play, Stedman possessed, as well, an abundance of life experience to fortify his natural inclination toward just treatment of others. And not because he had escaped unjust treatment himself. Some of it still rankled, and he often reminded others he'd been to the College of Hard Knocks. Still, he'd call anybody's hand who tried to take advantage of his good will. Butch and Craven had reason to step lightly around him. They resented him for that.

Temperance wrote the last line and slumped in her chair. She couldn't remember when she'd felt as tired. She picked up her cell and called Fredericka and got her voice mail, "Fred, I forgot to remind you that I'm reading *The Lorax* this Thursday. Can you come to Story Hour again and make it interesting and accessible to my little kids? Thanks. I'll see you there. Ten-o'clock, remember? Thanks, Fred. Make it really fun and funny; the story's a little above these pre-schoolers' heads, you know. You can make ecology fun and funny. You know I'll make it serious. Bye, I'm gone now."

Chapter Two

And where is Thurgood Marshall?
> Temperance Green Smith

If slavery is not wrong, nothing is wrong.
> Abraham Lincoln

"Lilly Ledbetter, Jeff. Can you believe that story?! In the 1990's, and now, the 21st. century?! We're not talking about thirty-fifty-years ago!"

It was fortunate for her that Jeff didn't charge Temperance for her counseling sessions with him. As one of his parishioners, she qualified for free counseling. (Others who weren't members of his church got free or next-to-free help, too. For Jeff Singer, little of value was about money.) Temperance consumed large portions of their time with matters like the Lilly Ledbetter case. Lilly's story of having been paid only sixty percent as much as her male counterparts for the same work was an old but still shocking one. An "infuriating" one, Temper fumed. A "damnable" one, she judged. Temperance was now on a tear, churning out adjectives and expletives at a white-hot pitch and pace.

"And the Supreme Court, for God's sake, Jeff! This Court is backing us into the wilderness! We could use Earl Warren's Court today! And where is Thurgood Marshall?!"

Jeff concurred and said so. He knew, as well, that Temper could avoid her own issues. He tried to guide her there.

"How's it going with the journeling?"

She ignored his effort. "I heard on National Public Radio recently that Helen Thomas has asked every new president she has covered, ten of them, at their first press conference the same, first question,

'When are you going to free the slaves?' I *love* that!! It's the only question, Jeff!"

"'When are you going to free the slaves?'" Jeff repeated, savoring its meaning and sound as much as Temper, "the Unfinished Emancipation," he pondered, "I like it. That is the central question, isn't it? Still that one."

"I can't imagine a better tone-setter for a new administration than Thomas's question. How I admire that woman! Too bad they haven't taken her up on it. Perhaps Johnson did. I'll come back to Lilly Ledbetter, Jeff. At least, the new administration has set that one right. You're not going to derail me that easily," Temperance answered him finally, scolding him mildly, but acquiescing in his ploy to get her on track with her narrative.

"Here goes," she sighed and jumped in, "the nightmare's back, worse than ever. I'm dreaming it often now, maybe every few days; I doubt I remember it every time I dream it. I try to, as you instructed me to do, but I don't think I can always bring it to recall—and I know I don't really want to," she confessed.

Was it different? Was Gabriel in the dream? She still didn't know.

"If writing is supposed to help, something's not working, I'm afraid."

"Maybe it is, Temper. Progress doesn't always feel or look like it. You've begun with some threatening aspects of your story. Now, your father's threatened, as well. Maybe going back to an earlier chapter in your life will help you process those threats. It might give you some psychological distance from the violent episodes you're recalling now. Let's try that method. Write about a time before this pivotal conflict.

"Okay. I also know that it's all one story; we both do," Temperance complied. They talked about Stedman's encounter with Morris and

Herbert and her feelings and impressions, and then she arose and stuck out her hand. "Thanks, Jeff. I'll see you Monday."

———⁓•◦⊙⟊⊙◦•⁓———

Jeffrey Singer's doctorate was in religion generally and pastoral care specifically. He was senior pastor of Walnut Grove Baptist Church and, while home again in Bladen County only a little over five years now, he had become widely recognized for his skill in pastoral counseling. Many trumpeted the help he had given them. Jeff's thoughtful sermons, more intellectual than some cared for, too academic they thought, but not so in Temperance's view, had influenced her to move her church membership to Walnut Grove. Those, and his perspective toward and stance on the subject of homosexuality. Homosexual Christians, in particular, but not exclusively. She had her own strong ideas on such matters and had made them a focus in her teaching. Owing to Jeff Singer's influence, Walnut Grove was the one Baptist church in a tri-county area which fellowshipped with gay and lesbian men and women. Or, more precisely, the only one which declared itself open to doing so, according to the published policy stated in its church bylaws. It was not known for sure whether there were any gay folks there or not. To be sure, Walnut Grove was the single church of any denomination in that area with an open policy toward homosexual persons. Jeff Singer's leadership got the credit. And the blame. His outspokenness could have messed up a lot of things. Like Jeff's counseling reputation, but so far, it didn't seem to have done that. Still, Temperance had reason to worry about his safety, she knew. And she did. Whatever grace had achieved on that score had been won "in territory held largely by the devil." Flannery O'Connor had it right; she was certain of that. The realization kept her vaguely uneasy constantly, and sometimes it made it hard for her to sleep at night without Xanax.

"When are you going to free the slaves, Mr. President?" *Indeed*, Temperance thought. But the question was for others besides the president; it was for everyone.

Jeff had returned home to Bladen County from New Haven and Yale Divinity School (probably the only person from Bladen ever to attend an Ivy League school, since Duke didn't count) because he was a Tar Heel. Not a Carolina fan-Tar Heel (he was that, too), but a North Carolinian with turpentine and resin glued to his feet and zeal and grit sticking to his soul, Temperance liked to think. A particularly prized legend was the one claiming the popular name got its origin in the Revolutionary or Civil War, she couldn't remember which, and described not men on a basketball court but men who refused to retreat from the hottest battle, the thickest fighting. Instead, they stuck it out and fought like dogs, the last to leave the field. Jeff, like most Carolinians who knew that heritage, was proud of it. Having been born in Bladen and brought up there, he had come home with his Ivy League ideas and erudition, back home where he wanted to grow them among home folk—in Tar Heel soil and society. His was that tenacity which had won the respect of military men, and civilians as well, back then and since then; he would stick it out and fight where the battle was hottest.

There were other concerns, and maybe they were distractions mainly. The faithful at Walnut Grove were unprepared for Wallace and Mary Singer's overachieving, eldest son to fill their pulpit as a seminary-trained minister, and said as much when Tom Merritt first proposed Jeff's candidacy, some of them did. Ben Norris, chairman of the deacon board, was afraid the divinity school might have "took away" Jeff's faith and said so outright. Others were troubled the same way. Whether such education had destroyed his faith or watered it down, that was their worry. Watered down faith was as bad as no faith at all in the common opinion; even the unchurched agreed with that, and colleges in general tended to subject young Christians to a watering down process, most folk were convinced. Some felt Satan just plain out destroyed young students' faith through atheistic professors and their teachings on evolution and science.

But a fair number, like Miss Effie Middleton, who had known the Singer family fifty years or more and the solid reputation Miss Mary and Mister Wallace had throughout the community as strong believers and faithful workers in the church, were less suspicious of the effects their son's education might have had on his faith. That boy had been raised, Miss Effie pointed out. At last, they took a chance on him.

Jeff was aware of the ambivalence still in his congregation. He had grown up in it. But home had called him back and that was where he had cast his lot. The Walnut Grove pastorate for five years had been his core ministry. There he exercised the full panoply of his gifts and skills in preaching, teaching, writing, community activism, and caring for the pastoral needs of his people. He especially looked forward to his pastoral visits to the half-dozen elderly members of Walnut Grove no longer able to get about, those either too chronically frail to get out to church or too acutely ill to rise from their beds or chairs. He tried to make regular calls on Miss Margaret Sweetwater, weak with congestive heart failure, and Mister Ira Gordon, afflicted with gout and diabetes, on Wednesday mornings. At Walnut Grove, Jeff taught the children, elders, too, the importance of "neighboring." Having reclaimed the older verb form of the word, he enjoyed hearing the children talk about neighboring, as if the word had been in continuous usage all along and never fallen into long disuse. As had the practice itself. He visited Mister Wade Graham and Mister Arlie Matthews, both suffering from metastatic cancer, lung and prostate, on Thursdays, and on Saturday mornings, sweet Miss Clementine Owens, ninety-six and nearly blind from macular degeneration and irascible Mister Henry R. Pickens, ill as a hornet and with a right to be, considering his pain from osteoarthritis and ravaged hips and spine. They balanced each other, Miss Clementine and Mister Henry R. (he preferred the initial be spoken, too), and for that reason, Jeff bookended his Saturday mornings with calls on them. Mr. Henry R. last; the visit braced him for the rest of his weekend. Three of these old folks, when he was a boy, had been his Sunday School teachers, surprisingly, Mister Henry R. the most memorable one of them. The old malcontent's energetic view of the gospel had stayed with Jeff and energized and shaped his own. Jesus's scourging of the temple profiteers "with a cat-o'-nine-tails" was a favorite text of Mister Henry R.'s and became a favorite of his. With Mister Henry R.'s help, Jeff had seen that Jesus, meek and mild, was no wimp. The lesson had stuck.

Jeff's other field of ministry was the Southeastern Carolina Ministry and Counseling Center he directed in Elizabethtown. The name was a mouthful, but the acronym worked, if he dropped the last "C," which he commonly did. Along with Jeff, five other pastoral counselors, three with masters of divinity degrees and two with doctoral degrees in religion, all with concentrations in pastoral care, staffed the SCMC. Its renown had spread in just half a decade throughout the southeastern counties surrounding Bladen and across the state line to Myrtle Beach and that area of South Carolina. The staff's expertise accounted for most of that recognition, but there were other reasons the Center was popular in the economically depressed area it served. Fees were graduated according to ability to pay. All fees, moreover, were substantially less than those of private psychiatrists and clinical psychologists in Fayetteville, Wilmington, and North Myrtle Beach. Nonetheless, the Center managed to be self-supporting and to sustain a modestly reasonable pay scale for counselors and staff. No one at SCMC, however, and certainly not Jeff, who founded it for reasons of ministry, expected the clinic to show a profit above sufficient operating capital. The SCMC was first and foremost a ministry, not a business. Marsha Singer, Jeff's wife, deserved the credit for its smooth and successful operation; she was office manager, a very able one.

"Temperance—Lilly Ledbetter—I cut you off too fast, I'm afraid. I apologize. We'll get back to her, okay? You asked a question: 'Where is Thurgood Marshall?' I've been thinking about that one all afternoon. I've a notion President Obama has asked that same question. Perhaps he'll find him and answer it. Sorry I didn't reach you directly. No need to call me back. Just wanted to say these things. See you Monday? Bye."

Chapter Three

The child is father to the man.

William Wordsworth

Her parents' marriage seemed to Temperance a safe and hospitable place to begin again. She wrote:

When Stedman Lemuel Smith married Mae Johnson Lewis on May 10, 1934, she wore a blue-flowered dress with cap sleeves and accordion pleats, and he wore a gray suit with a white dress shirt and a dark tie. Stedman, in particular, enjoyed dressing up in those days, perhaps largely because, before he went to work in the Bennett Cotton Mill, he didn't have much to dress up with. And Temperance recalled hearing Mae say once, in a rare moment of self-revelation, that she had gone to work in the mill because she wanted some money with which to buy herself some pretty dresses and shoes. The Lewis's had plenty to eat, but not much money for store-bought clothes. The Smith's had less.

In the black-and-white picture postcard Stedman mailed to his favorite brother, Jacob, four days after his marriage to Mae in Dillon, South Carolina, just across the state line between the Carolinas (there was no waiting requirement for blood tests in South Carolina), Stedman is decked out in what Temper assumed to be his wedding attire, the dark gray suit and a lighter gray fedora. A cigarette, a Chesterfield, no doubt, dangles rakishly from the left corner of his mouth. (Stedman was lefthanded and leftfooted, too.) He looks a little like a Mafia hit man, until you look more closely. Then you see that his face is thin and smooth, with only a light

29

beard possible underneath his careful shave, and his gut is tucked in close, hungry-close, to his backbone. At twenty-four, Stedman was boy-thin, intent on looking like a full-grown man and a worldly one, if he could pull it off. He nearly did. His postcard, dated May 14, 1934, the penciling faded but legible, if you look hard, reads:

Dear Brother,

Will write you a few lines. I am married now to Mae Lewis. Hope you all are well. I am liable to come soon.

A Bro.
Stedman

Stedman wears a ring on his left ring finger, but it is not a wedding band. He and Mae did not exchange wedding rings; few country folk did in those days. Perhaps because it seemed wasteful to spend money on jewelry and sentiment, when there was barely enough for necessities. Or maybe because they didn't have it at all. But Stedman had bought himself a ring, presumably, Temperance figured, at an earlier time. Though she couldn't tell for sure, it was probably a birthstone, a ruby, she guessed, although Stedman was not born in July. She remembered how he favored the deep red stone. He seldom splurged, so far as she could tell. Her father could manage money. But he also knew how, and when, to enjoy it.

After Temper was born, Stedman splurged on her. He and Mae, Temper was sure it was his idea, took her to a portrait studio in Lumberton for a sitting there, first, when she was just beginning to crawl and pull up, and again, when she was five. They were the only family on the cotton mill hill with formal studio portraits on their walls. Stedman had prevailed on Mae to go with him to have one made of her soon after their marriage, and the beautiful portrait of Mae, painted in soft watercolors, already a family treasure, hung over the fireplace in every house in which they lived. Of Stedman, however, Temperance had only the picture postcard (which she later enlarged and framed) and a few snapshots. This was a major regret.

In her own portrait made when she was five, Temper wears a gold locket and a small sapphire ring, her birthstone. Both are real. She misplaced, or lost, the ring and the locket while still a child.

Here, Temperance stopped her narrative and realized she needed to go back to an earlier time, two years before Stedman's marriage to Mae. She wrote:

Walking into the Bennett Company Department Store in downtown Pineboro, Stedman had smiled respectfully and amiably at the saleslady who offered to help him.

"Good Morning, Ma'am. I wonder if you could help me find two of your white cotton shirts."

As they headed toward a glass-encased counter, he asked, "You wouldn't know if the thread was made right here in Pineboro, would you? The thread for the shirts, I mean."

Stedman thought maybe she would have that information, since the store and the cotton mill both were owned by the Bennett family, Pineboro's first family, by everyone's accounting.

"No, Sir, I don't," she replied matter-of-factly, in an uninterested tone which suggested that she wondered why anyone would want to know.

"Oh, I hope so. I like the thought of wearing shirts made from our very own thread. We do a good job over at the mill, you know."

It was hard to tell whether the saleslady did, in fact, know that. Not bothering to reply to Stedman's remark, she pulled out of the long, glass case two Arrow shirts, 100% cotton. "What size do you wear?" she asked.

Stumped momentarily, Stedman recovered and blurted agreeably and a little shamefacedly, "Well, Ma'am, I don't rightly know. You see, these will be the first store bought shirts I've had."

Warming a little to Stedman's open and genial charm, the saleslady responded with a hint of a smile, one which Stedman was glad to see, "Well, let's just try a couple of sizes on. You look like a 32 neck and a 32 or 33 sleeve length to me. Here, let's try these two."

Handing the shirts to Stedman and taking off briskly across the large room to the back of the store, she pointed him to a men's fitting room. Everything here was a first for Stedman, and he was grateful for this woman who knew something about shirt sizes and even gave him a room in which to try the garments on, before be bought them. He'd do his best not to mess them up.

When he left Bennett Company Department Store that Saturday morning, he carried in a large paper bag the first true wardrobe he'd ever owned—two 100% cotton dress shirts, size 32 neck, 33 sleeve, and with them a pair of gray dress pants and a pair of navy ones. On his head he sported a 100% woolen, gray fedora like those he'd observed gentlemen, men of substance, wearing in Elizabethtown. In the bag, he carried, as well, a red-and blue-striped necktie and a solid yellow one. In two weeks, when he got his pay envelope again, he planned to return to Bennett's and purchase a new pair of dress shoes and a sterling silver tie clip which had caught his eye, a good eye for nice things. He strode toward the mill hill a half mile west of town, whistling softly under his breath and glancing now and then into his wardrobe bag, watching all the while to see how many people noticed his new fedora.

The next day, a bright Sunday afternoon, Stedman sat astride his ladderback chair and leaned it against the porch railing, inhaling deeply the leveling draft of nicotine from the Chesterfield between his fingers. This was a habit, already an addiction, he now had money for, and it had been a lack of money alone which had delayed his smoking until then. Enjoying his cigarette and the bulge in his shirt pocket the three-fourths-full Chesterfield package made, he warbled in a muffled, satisfied tone,

"Precious mem'ries, how they linger; how they ever flood my so-o-oul." His thoughts were of Addie. The move to Pineboro and independence had not been without a fair amount of homesickness, mainly for his mother's dependable, loving presence. She had been his best influence and truest friend.

Other memories were hard. Numerous had been the times Addie had rescued Stedman from Samuel's irrational temper and abrupt, merciless whippings by hiding him behind her apron and repelling her husband's grasp for him with a sharp swipe of her dishrag and a coquettishly aggravated smile,

"Aw, go on, Samuel! He's just a boy. He didn't mean no harm. I'll take care o' him."

In time, Addie's *double entendre* became one of Stedman's "precious memories." And take care of him she did. Holding him close to her soft bosom, Addie looked down into his frightened, tear-filled eyes and said to him each time,

"It's all right. It's all, all right, Stedman."

———

Temperance paused her story and opened her cell phone. "Hi, Fred. What's up?"

Fredericka had Anderson Cooper's interview of Barack Obama on her mind. "Did you see Anderson Cooper and the President on CNN last night?"

That was all she got a chance to say. Temperance catapulted headfirst into her own thoughts on what she had heard.

"*Why* don't they leave the President *alone* about his *smoking,* for God's sake?! *Let* the man smoke! *He* knows he needs to quit—for his health, example to his children—and the nation's children, and all that. The man's got the hardest job in the world and the biggest load on his shoulders!"

She hadn't finished. "Of course, he shouldn't do it publicly and influence teens and children that way. He wouldn't. Does anybody seriously think he would?! But leave him alone! Let him handle it! We've elected him to handle everything else, all of it more pressing than his own personal habit of smoking; now, let's give this man some peace! Stop nagging him!"

Her mind zipped ahead to another topic. "Whistleblower, Fred, Harry Markopolos. Etch that name in your memory. God! How I admire that guy!"

Temperance was as intemperate in her acclamation, when she deemed it deserved, as in her denunciation, when she thought it fit. Maybe enthusiastic was what Temper was; in any case, passionate.

"Markopolos did his best, for *nine years*, to blow the whistle on Bernard Madoff and his Ponzi scheme. What does that tell you about our system? The way they ignored him, I mean. I can't believe it. Yes, I can, sadly."

Fredericka was as comfortable with Temper's kaleidoscopic movement from one subject to another as with her own comparable views on those matters. "Exactly; I hope the Securities and Exchange Commission gets the once-over it needs. How it failed to pick up on Madoff's house of cards, especially in light of Markopolos's efforts to inform them, is beyond me. I agree with you."

She thought of Temper's memoir. "How's the writing going?"

"Okay. Jeff's decision to send me back to earlier parts of my story has led me all the way back to my father's boyhood. I'm discovering this narrative is as much about him as about Gabe, I think. Or maybe it's about something common to them both. I don't know yet, though I think I do know in part where this is leading me. It's more of a discovery than I imagined it would be. I think I'm on the edge of making some connections I wasn't aware of 'til now. I'll let you know what I find," she said in her thinking-aloud tone.

"I'm not surprised to hear how much this has set your analytical wheels to turning, Temp. In fact, if it didn't, that would be the surprise. Bye. I'll let you get back to it."

"Bye, Fred, thanks for calling."

"It's all right. It's all, all right, Stedman," Temperance resumed her story.

Addie's comforting reassurance of a Reality ultimately sane and steadfast, despite apparent evidence to the contrary, she made sure to set in him early. And until he was too long-legged to hold in her aproned lap anymore, she rocked him and calmed his fears in her creaky, armless, kitchen rocker, and hummed or sang to him her favorite hymn:

"On Jordan's stormy banks I stand, and cast a wishful eye

To Canaan's fair and happy land, Where my possessions lie . . . ."

Stedman sensed that his mama was calming herself, too, centering her soul in her faith before she said anything else to him. Sniffing and kissing his head and forehead in her customary, affectionate and maternal way, she collected herself for what Stedman knew came next.

Addie had a short Bible lesson she generally repeated to him at those frightening, sad times.

"The Bible tells us that 'perfect love casteth out fear,' Stedman. Do you know what I think that means? God's love is perfect, and He loves you perfectly. And my love ain't perfect, but I love you maybe as perfect as anybody can love another person, so don't you be afraid, Stedman. Don't you be afraid of nothin'. It's all right. It's gonna be all, all right. You'll see."

As she spoke these fervent words to her young son, Addie's strained voice modulated from weary, determined concern to a soft, comforting litany of love, divine and human. As sure as Stedman could count on his father's angry outbursts and brutal beatings ("spare the rod and spoil the child" seemed to be Samuel's favorite Bible verse), he could count fully as much on Addie's efforts to protect him and limit those attacks. More than he knew, he relied on her faithful paeon to overcoming, transforming love.

When he grew much older, he wondered if she had believed her own words. He knew she had, but in what way had she believed them? he probed. One thing was sure, she meant them to be true, and she trusted God would make them true in a reliable way. God intended his well-being, Stedman knew his mama believed. How it would all come to pass depended on God's mysterious ways. Addie trusted those. Her theology was simple and unassailable.

Stedman puffed his Chesterfield down to a glowing stub, mashed it out against the railing, flipped it over the porch banister, and drew another from his shirt pocket before thinking to remind himself to save his matches by lighting it with the butt, a practice he was working on. "A penny saved is a penny earned," he mumbled absently. The old aphorism made good sense.

Family scenes, good and bad, played and replayed serially in his thoughts. Blessing and bane, they gave him a fair amount of work to do sorting them out and making sense of things. His good memories of his mother were mixed up and messed up with the bad ones of his father, he judged. One, especially, tormented him.

In late winter, throughout his childhood, Stedman had searched through the woods for Addie's favorite flowers, yellow daffodils. Wild and lacking cultivation, the small handful of blooms he hunted and found each February was exquisite still, each yellow cup shining brilliant and hopeful in the drab pine straw. Like manna in the wilderness they were to Stedman and Addie, sustenance on the long journey to Canaanland, the place his mama sang about when she rocked him in her rocking chair. He plucked them quickly and ran home as fast as he could, hoping his absence wouldn't be noticed. Stedman typically arranged the flowers in one of Addie's prized drinking glasses which her mother and aunts had given her as a combination birthday and wedding gift when she and Samuel married on her sixteenth birthday. Stedman filled it with a dipper of water from the enamel water bucket beside the stove and admired the floral cutwork as he pressed his fingers against the pattern and enjoyed its touch and sight, the delightful sensations of both.

Once, his papa walked into the kitchen just as Stedman placed the dipper back into the dented bucket. Seizing him by the arm, Samuel demanded to know why he wasn't watering the livestock, instead of wasting time hunting and watering flowers. The worn and dry-rotted fabric of Stedman's too small, homespun shirt gave way under Samuel's hard grab and ripped off the shoulder seam. His skinny arm was already starting to bruise darkly under the tight clamp. But his father had more punishment in mind. Just then, Addie's light footfall sounded on the doorstep to the kitchen porch. Appearing in the doorframe with a mess of fresh collards under one arm, she quickly assessed the situation. Daffodils, cutwork drinking glass, Stedman's torn sleeve, the bruised arm, and Samuel's tall frame towering over the terrified boy, all of it. Addie grabbed Stedman out of Samuel's grasp and wrapped her feedsack apron around the convulsing child. Stedman was going into some kind of spell!

"What have you done to him!?" she fairly screamed at her husband. Barely five feet tall, she glowered upward into Samuel's bearded face, eyes flashing with scared rage, "I *sent* him to pick those flowers, and I watered Old Bessie while he was gone! He ain't done nothin' but what his mama tol' him to do! We don't whip boys for mindin' their mamas, do we !? Look at him!" she wailed, her anger turning to panic, "He's havin' a fit!"

Bursting into tears, she blurted desperately, "Here, Stedman, here, Baby, it's all right. It's all right. It's all right, Sweetheart. It's all right! It's all, all right!"

Addie fell into the rocker and squeezed him to her heart so tightly and furiously they both were shaking with the convulsion's force. Willing him to be all right, she lifted her heart and voice to the Lord and interceded mightily on behalf of her precious child, all the while rocking and squeaking in the old chair and kissing and crying and holding him bound in her arms such, that the warmth of her body and the strong rhythm of her heartbeat suffused his own. And, gradually, the spasms slowed and halted. Stedman nestled wan and motionless, at last, in the sanctuary of her lap, drained and weak and scared still, but calm and recovered.

"Don't fret, Stedman," Addie repeated, turning her attention now to his bruised arm and deciding it was not too badly hurt. "It's all right, Baby. It's all, all right."

Pulling nervously on his tobacco-stained beard, Samuel turned, wordless, and left the kitchen.

Stedman had gained another window on the world. Addie had lied to protect him from further harm. In truth, he had disobeyed her that morning and not minded her at all. She had told him to fill the hog trough with the dishwater she had left over from washing the breakfast dishes and to "stay out of them woods this morning," before she went to the collard patch. Rather, Stedman had left the chore undone and headed to where the daffodils grew. Her capacity to forgive him was matched by her unconditional love for him; that much he knew. Now, he had learned something more. If need be, his mother would violate her own conscience for his sake.

Stedman's reverie took him to another block of his story and its influence on the way things seemed to him to be. He had left school, not of his own choosing, four years after the daffodil incident, at thirteen, and as the oldest boy still at home, he had been set to farming his papa's meager acres of cotton, corn, tobacco, and soybeans. Samuel Smith had kidney trouble, kidney stones, with high blood pressure. And frequent, ass-kicking attacks of kidney colic had left him weak and unable to farm his land. The scourging pain made him unbearable to live with for everyone in the family except Addie, who bore up under his bad disposition with uncommon grace, despite an overload of stress.

Taking his oldest boy out of school to work the fields had not been an unusual act on Samuel's part. It happened in more farm families than not. Besides, that was what Sam Smith had raised his houseful of boys for, at least in large part. With eight, living boys and only one, spoiled girl, Samuel figured the Lord had blessed him more than his brothers, Jesse and William, whose combined progeny were nine girls and just four boys. When his kidneys were not messing up, he stood a little taller and a lot prouder over that and enjoyed real status in the community, on account of it. The reason was clear. If a man could "get" boys, he was more of a man than others, folks believed. Those who were suspected of being "no good," that is, sterile and unable to "get" either boys or girls, could hardly claim full manhood at all. Unless they could put out a longer and harder day's work than men who did beget offspring. Some men worked themselves into the grave proving their manhood that way.

That kind of hard, manly labor was where Samuel fell short, and he worried it whittled him down in the eyes of his kin and neighbors. God knows, when the boys were all little, he had tried, although often not physically able to handle the work he managed nevertheless to do to keep food on the table and a roof over their heads. Nobody knew how difficult it had been. But he could no longer trudge behind a mule-drawn plow through stubbled earth with all the strength that plowing a big mule and guiding a heavy, iron plow in a straight furrow demanded. Twice, he had hemorrhaged after a day's work at that. The great amount of blood in the slop jar had frightened Addie, and he had tried hard not to let her see how much it had scared him. When his first son, Hector, left home three days after his eighteenth birthday to get a job in the pulpwoods with Rufus Medlin, Samuel harshly ("don't you git no notions 'bout leavin', too') informed Stedman that the obligation (he hadn't fed him 'all these years for nothin") was now his to keep the farm going and feed the Smith household.

They were all doing the best they could, Addie comforted her son, with something like shame in her eyes.

With help from his younger brothers, for eight years and two months, Stedman did what he could to meet the responsibility which had fallen on his then childish shoulders. They didn't remain the shoulders of a child long, however. The heavy work broadened them and toughened him up fast. Giving up schooling had been harder than he imagined it would be. While he couldn't say he had liked everything about school, he had enjoyed figuring and world history a lot. He had learned he had a real head for numbers and figuring. It all seemed more like a puzzle or a game than actual work to him. And even his papa had said he was good at it and depended on him to keep the farm's simple accounts after Hector left. The study of history had shown him an older, bigger world than he knew existed before then, and Stedman meant to find out some more about it.

For that reason, and others, when he reached the official age of manhood, and Joe and Jacob and Winthrop were all older and bigger than he had been when Hector left for the log woods and freedom, Stedman itched to turn over the job of farming the land and feeding their crowd to his brothers. Besides, Clement and Harvey and Willie had grown big enough to help out, too, by then. It was not like he would be leaving his folks with no help. And he meant to buy his mama some nice things he wanted her to have, like a tall, handsome Philco radio to stand beside her easy chair in the front room. One like his Aunt Emily across Colly Creek had gotten recently.

But Stedman knew Samuel would not take well his intention to leave. Hellfire! He knew he'd be lucky to get away without gettin' his ass busted. But he'd considered that threat and made his plans soberly. He had decided he wouldn't fight his own papa, but he had resolved just as strongly that he wouldn't take anymore beatings, either. His father's frustration and abuse would have to be delivered another way, and Stedman expected that he would find one. Samuel knew a bunch of ways to hold his family in line, though a merciless whipping was his preferred punishment for all his boys except the two littlest ones, but their day was coming, too, Stedman hated to think.

Surprisingly, the dreaded leave-taking turned out not to be a physical one at all. Perhaps because Samuel had realized that he had taken his cracked, leather belt off to Stedman the final time. He took another tack. In stern, intimidating tones, Samuel warned his tall, lanky son whose eyes met his on a level now, about the wiles of the devil awaiting him outside the farm's property lines. Wild horses at the gates of hell couldn't have persuaded Stedman to change his mind, though. He had made his hard decision. Besides, he knew the devil's territory was not reserved for lands across that line of trees which marked the farm's supposed horizon and his own. He reckoned he'd seen some of Lucifer's diabolical work right there at home. It had set up a powder keg inside him. No doubt about it. It was fortunate he was self-aware enough to recognize it. The strain of cynicism his father's harsh treatment had implanted in him, however, he might not have identified so readily. That would surface later; already, there were early signs of it.

After Temper's birth, on the occasion of Mae's and Stedman's first visit to introduce their baby daughter to their families, Samuel took Stedman into the backyard for a talk.

"I'll tell you how to raise that girl of your'n," Samuel began, spitting tobacco juice in what seemed a dismissive manner, one which Stedman knew well, "When she needs a beatin', you jus' take off your belt and give her a good whippin', an' she'll thank you fer it when she's growed," Samuel advised.

His voice tight in his chest, Stedman looked straight into his father's eyes and said, "I don't thank you for a single whippin' you ever gave me."

—⁓∾⊶⊙⊷∾⁓—

Temperance returned to Stedman's initial decision to seek a job in the cotton mill in Pineboro and how that had developed. She recognized that she was searching for something important, its identity still unknown:

Stedman had heard from Tommy Jackson about the good wages to be made at Bennett's Cotton Mill in Pineboro, just twenty-six miles away. It was the spring of 1932, and the country was reeling from the Great Depression, groping its uncertain, tentative way forward. Still, the textile industry in the South had already begun clearing its path toward a looming, wartime boom which few, if any, could yet see coming. (A recovered, flourishing economy funding the Second World War would last through the forties and fifties until Stedman and Mae had returned to Bladen County from Lenoirville. In that regard, Temperance was thankful for her hard-working parents' good fortune. It had not lasted for others; a boom-and-bust capitalism on the rise would wreak disaster for many, on into the twenty-first century.) But in the thirties, as in the twenties, young men like Stedman and Tommy, and young women like Mae and her cousin Thelma, continued to pull up their farm roots and leave their homesteads to go to mills all around the Southland. Southeastern North Carolina had its share of those ubiquitous factories, harbingers of an economic recovery on the way, and Stedman was fortunate to live reasonably close to one of them, he had felt.

It was uniquely salutary that Stedman did not expect to hear words of appreciation and godspeed from Samuel, because he didn't get any. As he climbed into Tommy's old car, nervous but expectant, his ears hummed with Addie's soft weeping and pleas to "watch out for yourself," but Samuel had walked off. He had no words of farewell for his second son.

Trips back home to see his mama and brothers (Effie had married Grover Singletary in '29 and moved near Clinton; he had missed her like thunder) would be worked out with Tommy every few weeks or every month or two, he hoped. Or maybe he could eventually save up enough money to buy himself a used Ford or Chevrolet, if not a brand new one. That acquisition would become a primary goal and, in a few years, a successful one, but it would require patience. Stedman had that kind of patience. Addie had instilled that attribute in him and nurtured it through example and exhortation.

In Pineboro, Stedman had found a job at the mill but not at first what he had hoped to land, though any job at all was a coveted prize. Everyone understood that. The only job open the day he arrived was one sweeping the floors. He had hoped to be hired and trained in the carding room where cotton husks, seeds, bits of leaves, and other debris, were carded, or removed, from raw cotton at the initial stage of the process of manufacturing cotton thread. Already, Stedman's goal transcended the more immediate ones of earning sufficient money to live on and get himself, maybe, an automobile. He determined to learn the entire process of thread-making—*quality* thread-making. In the beginning, his natural curiosity and intelligence had impelled him to learn so much. Two decades later, his commitment to his chosen work had fueled his successful rise from the lowliest job in the mill to the highest he could attain without a college degree. He was thankful to begin, that first day in Pineboro, with a job paying a regular wage. He said so to the Lord, and he cultivated distinct, named gratitude in his heart, as Addie had taught him to do, for his job and a number of things.

Mill work had that one, big advantage over farming. Payday rolled around every two weeks and workers could count on it. It took Stedman several months to get over the excitement (he wished he could have retained it) he felt, when he looked inside his pay envelope and saw those paper bills and the handful of change it contained. When he pulled the bills out and poured the coins into his open palm, he felt pure joy, he thought. Not because he coveted riches. Temperance was confident she never saw that in him. But he wanted to be able to pay his way with money he had earned with honest work. That was it, and it was all of it. Being able to do that made him feel competent, responsible, resourceful, and smart. Those, too, were qualities Addie had nurtured in him, and not for his sake alone, but for the good of the family he would head someday, she hoped, and for the neighbors he would have. Most of all, for the Lord she prayed he would serve.

To Stedman, fifteen cents an hour seemed like a pot of gold. Those wages added up to more than a dollar a day, and lodging, along with two homecooked meals, at the house where he and Tommy and a third millhand, Jake West, shared a room, cost him less than two dollars a week. Besides, pushing a wide broom across floors littered with discarded cigarette packs, Juicy Fruit chewing gum wrappers, cotton balls, fragments of thread, coastal plains sand, a few sandspurs, and other assorted trash, was a lot easier than cropping tobacco in the boiling sun of July and August and clearing new ground with frostnumbed hands in January and February. While the lint-laden air inside the mill was often hard to breathe, indoors work guaranteed that Stedman stayed dry and warm in the winter and tolerably cool enough in the summer, despite the high heat and humidity inside the mill. That was mild compared to the blistering sun of a southeastern Carolina August. Most members of the Smith family had never had that kind of work. He was grateful for it and intended to do all he could to keep it.

In less than six months, an opening in the carding room was offered to Stedman and he was on his way, learning what he had set out to learn and now earning a wage of twenty cents an hour. Stedman had more money in his pockets than he had reasonably expected to earn and some to help his folks when they needed it. And enough to impress his brothers and cousins whenever he told them how much he was making. On Christmas Eve, Stedman hauled a tall, gleaming Philco radio out of Tommy's backseat and, with his assistance, carried it into the house and set it by Addie's chair. He would never make another purchase which would give him as much satisfaction as buying that radio for her had done.

The Smith heritage and its store of family memories included these memories and anecdotes, passed along year after year through repeated tellings around kitchen hearths and on front porch swings, each a burnished heirloom, bestowing context and adding meaning by giving stories to the few tangible heirlooms Temperance owned. Her favorites of those concrete treasures were a delicate kerosene lamp Stedman had given Mae early in their marriage and an embroidered muslim wall hanging Addie had made when Stedman was a boy and hung over the tall radio on that Christmas Eve he brought it to her from Pineboro. The lamp's glass shade and base were each adorned with handpainted, yellow daffodils. Perhaps the lamp first had caught Stedman's attention because the flowers' golden brilliance reminded him of the daffodils he had picked for Addie every winter. Temperance was sure it had. The fragile gift had survived four, separate moves, and Temper was nearly obsessive about protecting it from damage. The embroidered, muslim piece her grandmother Addie had worked and framed originally to hang over her kitchen fireplace, and it had hung there for many years, until she moved it to its final, proper place above the radio that Christmas Eve. It heralded one word: **CANAAN**.

Stedman, with other textile workers like Tommy Jackson, Jake West, and Mae and Thelma, would not be aware, in the years just ahead, of the hard road social activists would travel to achieve a mandatory, minimum wage for low-income workers like them, blue-collar folks invisible to those who lived up the pyramid. The poverty and limited circumstances, socially and educationally, which Stedman had come out of would make it difficult for him to see his situation clearly. When President Franklin Delano

Roosevelt signed the National Industrial Recovery Act on June 16, 1933, Stedman had no knowledge that the Supreme Court brought down its elitist, iron fist and ruled the legislation, with its promise of a legal, minimum wage, unconstitutional. Unaware of how his representative democracy worked, Stedman did not even know that President Roosevelt had signed such an act, crafted by a Congress with the plight of people like him in mind.

Five years later, in 1938, when Congress passed the Fair Labor Standards Act, a more progressive Supreme Court upheld the bill and, before long, Stedman was drawing a mandated wage of thirty cents an hour. Because the national minimum wage was not inflation adjusted, and an act of Congress would continue to be required to raise it, however, factory workers like him and Mae would remain at the mercy of politics and economic tides over which they had no say. Furthermore, powerful voices on the sides of both industry and labor unions had argued persuasively, and would argue still, that keeping working class people in their place on the lowest level of the economic pyramid, (although they seldom used such revealing language), was ingredient to maintaining a strong economy. The labor unions feared workers would be harder to convince of the value of the unions' agenda if federal government itself guaranteed a mandatory wage and improved labor standards. And captains of industry deployed their considerable power and influence to keep wages low and profits high. Temperance realized, in a way her parents had not, that the Fair Labor Standards Act of 1938 almost didn't happen at all.

It would take a patently crass and brutal act by one of those "captains of industry" to jolt Stedman out of a somnolent state and into awareness and action of his own. It would occur at the mill in Martinville after they moved there when Temperance was seven. And lived there just two months. The extremely short tenure would be directly related to that singular incident. The wake-up call and Stedman's vigorous response to it would toughen him for Gabriel Laughinghouse's fight in Lenoirville and his own unsought, but collegial, role in it. What happened in the halls of power in

Washington was unknown to Stedman, but certain kinds of direct, local entanglements of the powerful over the powerless he had had a primer course in, with Samuel first, and with a few others along the way, the incident in Martinville capping the stack.

Part and parcel of the same struggle, Gabriel's journey and Stedman's would coalesce in one march to Canaanland.

"Jeff, I identified a most important piece of the puzzle I'm working on; I knew I was looking for something critically valuable soon after I began writing, reluctant as I was to undertake it."

Here Temper smiled a "you were right" acknowledgment. "Gabe's and Stedman's stories are both about finding their place—their places—overturning social, economic, and political barriers, which keep the weak and powerless in 'their place,' you know."

Her eyes searched his for agreement, aware of the pitfalls of self-deception and how easily we fall into them. Before he could reply, she added, "Color and race add another dimension, to be sure, an invidious level of discrimination and rejection no white person has to experience. I have no intention of diminishing that, for God's sake. Still, I am remembering incidents which my folks had to deal with every day, which were about abject powerlessness, and the injustice which kept them 'in their place,' as relentlessly as segregation inflicted that crime on people of color." She stopped briefly, but wasn't satisfied.

"Nonetheless, I'll admit no white person, to my knowledge, was lynched for refusing to stay on the bottom of the pyramid. That's a major difference," she judged, and concluded, in her characteristically forthright way, stumbling earnestly to make it fair.

"I think you're onto something, Temperance. Where is the story taking you next, do you think?" Jeff nodded to all she had said and prodded her to the next step.

"I'm seeing more clearly all the time that it's one story, Jeffrey. These early years in Pineboro, and certain events in particular there, keep coming to mind for me."

"I had a professor in pastoral care who developed the thesis that the handful of earliest memories we retain, none of us has more than that, are significant and instructive for helping us understand our entire life stories. He referred to the family as the 'cradle of theology'," Jeff recalled. "Stay there awhile. Spend some time with those few, earliest memories, Temperance. I think they'll be revelatory for you. And helpful."

"Okay. I need to tell Mae's story now, I think. That's as far back as I can go with my own memories, since my memories start with her."

Chapter Four

What doth the Lord require of thee, but to love mercy, to do justice, and to walk humbly with thy God?

(Micah 6:8)

Temperance began her story about Mae with what may have been the fulcrum of their family life, an incident which occurred when she was just two years old, about which she had been told and about which she also knew on her own. She wrote:

Sometimes, we've ended up helping people the most when we didn't know we were doing that. And when we had no conscious aim of doing it, Temperance thought. She swatted an aggravating gnat away from her eyes and wiped the sweat off her neck. Like Mae, she got hot on her neck, back and front, when she was outdoors in the August heat and humidity. In the South, you always thought those two together, heat and humidity. Maybe that was where the saying, 'hot under the collar,' got its origin, she reflected. Somewhat illogically, she realized, and poked wry fun at herself for thinking it.

Unexpectedly, her mind looped back to the day at the graveyard with the young funeral home assistant who had looked so much like Gabe. How had it gone? Temperance wrote and recalled:

The young man had left. He had been a great help to her, but now she was by herself again. And that was okay, too; there had been something about him which made her uneasy, and she wasn't yet ready to give her mind to what it was.

Looping again, her distracted thoughts backtracking and weaving, and perhaps exactly to do the weaving work, Temper figured she had helped like that, without conscious aim or thought, most of March and all of April and May, and June and July, and on into the late summer and fall of 1941. When she was two and a half. And then, three years old.

In that year, her mother had given birth to a stillborn baby boy and nearly died herself. Years afterward, Mae would tell, now and then, during her infrequent, talkative moments, how she had felt him move, two or three days before the backbreaking cramps (she would learn it was called back labor) started. She was sure that was when he died inside her, because he thrashed around hard and wild, like he was hurting bad, she thought, or like he was trying to get away from something, or maybe even having a fit, and the idea of her unborn baby in a fit just about caused her heart to stop. Then, she didn't feel him move anymore.

The look on Mae's face at this point in her narrative recapped for her listeners, usually just Temperance and maybe Addie, the lingering desolation of those long-ago days. They had been there, too, Temper and Addie, and Mae's story transported them back to that time and place.

She had been too young to remember much of it, but Temper sometimes wondered if that was when her gentle, quiet mother stopped talking, or more accurately, conversing. Her occasional narration of the birth story showed a side of Mae which folks seldom saw. Mae could tell a story. She could transfix you with it. But except for this one, she rarely did. Had her mother talked a lot before the baby died? If so, Temper no longer could retrieve that memory.

When Dr. Dewey Williams had realized Mae would not be able to deliver the baby, he had said quietly, his strong, clean hand on her forearm, "Mae, you need more help than I can give you here. I'm sending you to the hospital in Martinville."

The direct, deliberate gaze of his clear, sky-blue eyes reassured her, and she knew he was doing the best thing for her and the baby. She trusted him completely. Stedman agreed; Addie stayed with

Temperance, and Mae went to the hospital, although babies were nearly always born at home. That was where they did the operation and took him out. A pitiful, waterhead baby had been taken, a little boy, stillborn, otherwise healthy, perhaps, because he was full-term and weighed around eight pounds without the excess fluid, the surgeon estimated.

My little brother, Temperance thought, it's curious, but every March the fifth, I think of him and how old he would be if he had lived. She calculated by counting back two years from her own age. That way, in some measure, he aged along with her. And some years, she imagined for a moment or two some specific detail or characteristic, like how he might have looked, assuming he had been born normal, or what kind of work he might have done. But those thoughts lasted only momentarily.

Without fail, though, she imagined and let her mind linger on the overwhelming loss and suffering her young parents must have struggled with that terrible, green, and paradoxically hopeful, for the reason of the greenness and something ontologically unnameable, spring. On some level, she experienced again the struggle and a kind of memory of it, and not just what she had been told about it. She was there. With them. All the time.

Mae stayed in the hospital in Martinville five weeks longer, after the caesarian section, owing to the near-fatal infection she contracted, whether from the baby's dying inside her or from the surgery itself, no one offered to explain to her or Stedman. In those early months of the nineteen forties, when the big War was young, there was no penicillin yet. No powerful antibiotics for infectious diseases and contracted infections like Mae's.

"Daddy, I wanta' go home! Let's go, Daddy! It stinks!" Temper had begged, pulling on Stedman's hand.

As much as Temperance needed and missed her mother, she was too young to understand the overpowering stench in Mae's hospital room. The putrid, almost gangrenous odor made her plead to be taken home. Stedman would tell the story numerous times over the years, expressing and eliciting nervous laughter each time. It conjured a mixture of horror, amused relief, and residual pain for them all, and with its brew of black comedy, a feeling of having dodged a hellishly dangerous bullet. They would continue to sort it out in Stedman's serial retellings. Great danger was a feeling they would experience a number of times in the years which lay ahead. It was merciful they couldn't see it all. Or find a way to think it out, perhaps, either in philosophical terms or just plain folks' thinking. Temperance had retained and nurtured an idiosyncratic mix of both.

Finitude has its value, Temperance recognized. Earth creatures evolved for planetary life have no business coveting ultimacy. The error is as old as Eden, she knew. She didn't embrace everything Darwin had said, but evolution through millions of years of struggle made sense to her. Survival. Civilization with its overlay of social veneer millennia old, ever more complex, had made the bottom line, the bare elements, harder to discern. Except in times of stark peril. Not seeing events beforehand made a kind of sense complementary with finitude and offered a singular mercy. Only deity need bear the burden of ultimacy and omniscience, or of perfect memory, for that matter; it was unlikely finite humans would evolve those attributes, she reasoned. She did not miss them.

Temperance thought again of the graveyard incident.

Another cognitive loop pulled Temper's attention back to that incident and the young assistant whose strong resemblance to Gabriel had resurrected his ghost:

"Ma'am," it was the young man returned to get his work tools, "I forgot these," he explained, as he reached to pick up the implements from the grass where they lay. Young enough to be embarrassed by his blunder, he had grinned a kind, sheepish goodbye and turned to go.

Watching his back as he walked away, Temperance saw abruptly what it was about him which had made her uneasy and had brought memories of Gabriel Laughinghouse vaulting back to her. What it was which somersaulted into that mysterious part of her brain which recognized Gabe's lost face, encased in fifty years of shrouded outline and retrieved reluctantly, apprehensively, whenever a similar face, one not yet born in Gabe's lifetime, restored long-faded eyes and nose and mouth, erased, as familiar, even beloved, features fade, inexplicably, within days. Confused and overcome by emotion, surprised by this intrusion of images, Gabe's very face and form, Temperance had sat down hard, flat on the ground, despite knowing the difficulty she would have pushing herself up again. Fumbling for her tepid bottle of Aquafina, she managed a swallow and made herself listen to the cicada castanets in the pines and oaks surrounding her. It was a practice she had learned from her grandfather, this turning to nature to settle her down. Also from Mae. Only then had she let herself remember other details.

Headed to the next assignment on his day's schedule, the young man, Temperance had seen then, possessed other aspects of Gabe's own look, most noticeably, a slightly high-waisted, but not unattractive, body image and type, owing to disproportionately long legs. And, as Gabriel Laughinghouse had been a graduate student in the summer of 1954, this young man, too, was a graduate student, he had told her. Gabe had been a sociologist. This student was an environmental scientist.

He was White. Now was the first time she had capitalized the word in decades.

The cicadas had stopped. In step with them, Temperance had backtracked, as she generally did when memories of Gabe intruded, though never so clearly before, as in this incident, memories distinct, unbidden. She had thought of something else.

———— ·····◦◦◦◦◦···· ————

Temperance had digressed from her early story. Perhaps she had retreated defensively; she didn't know, but if that had been her attempt, it had failed. Gabe's apparition had imposed itself more alarmingly than at anytime before; she was synthesizing early memories and recent events, combining them as she thought them and they emerged, tumbling out of her mind through her pen onto her paper. Was this the way writers experienced their ideas?

Stop; she had already asked that question, in just that way. She was doubling back, as she was wont to do. She had rocketed, or glided, (which?) from one period to another, from past to present, and constructed an amalgam which, astonishingly, seemed natural to her. Was it a mind game? At least, the tombstone the young assistant had placed for her was a concrete element, not an imagined one, which belonged in the story entire and tied disparate parts together in an elegiac way, it seemed now; the baby's death before birth had done that, as well. That is, united elements of seemingly unrelated narratives into a unitary whole, profound in grandeur and mystery, birth and death, natural and tragic. *Had* they done that? The process felt both discordant and astonishingly authentic to her. Something like anticipation, or wonder, might now be welding itself to angst, adhering itself to dread of the inevitable reappearances of Gabriel's ghost, Temperance identified. Even as she admitted the idea, she retched. It was too much. Her body, and mind, protested it. How could she anticipate comfortably what she had avoided absolutely? She wasn't ready for that, even if Jeffrey Singer should read progress where she saw threat and disaster.

She would go back to Mae's early story:

When Mae finally went home, she went home 'in a ambulance on a stretcher,' as Mae typically recounted it. Weeks longer, she lay sick in bed, an invalid, unable to go back to her job as a winder in the winding room of the mill, or to do much to look after her child. Addie had stayed in Pineboro with Temper and Stedman while Mae was in the hospital, but when Mae returned, she had left to care for Samuel and the boys still at home. They had done without a lot of things they needed while she was gone, Addie worried. Stedman cooked when he got off work each afternoon and managed to stir up some pretty good meals after his mother left, though his combination of ingredients sometimes surprised Mae. No matter, she appreciated his efforts and ate a few bites of everything he fixed with no complaints. Besides, food was not something which interested her, one way or the other. Yearning to visit her baby's fresh grave, but neither strong enough, nor yet recovered enough, to walk the short distance to the graveyard set aside on Bennett Cotton Mill land for millhands and their families, Mae lay and looked out of her window to the dark, wooded strip separating the mill village from the cemetery. Waiting for the day when she could go there.

April gave subdued hope, despite Mae's burden and loss and obvious peril, made apparent by the fact that she was, in no way, as yet out of danger. Dr. Williams made regular, after-office-hours visits to check on her temperature and assess her condition. He mandated bed rest.

At the end of April, it rained for three days and nights straight, alternating from pounding, driving downpours to quiet set-ins whose steady, comforting patter echoed from the tin roof overhead through the plaster ceiling and relieved the dreary gloom and gray outside the door, making sleeping at night more relaxed and restful. Temperance sat and played with her dolls and other small toys on the foot of Mae's bed, usually absorbed and quietly, but occasionally talking animatedly to Betsy, her favorite doll. Mae enjoyed her toddler's precocious jabber. On one of those long, rainy days, a day of racking pain, after Mae had prayed aloud, evidently repeatedly, to "my Jesus" for divine mercy, she heard Temper implore,

"Mama's Jesus, have mussy."

Decades later, just a few years before she died, but many years after the mercy had been granted, Mae told Temperance,

"I was the first person you ever prayed for."

Throughout Mae's long, precarious recovery, Dr. Williams kept unflagging vigil over her progress and, unasked, promised to do all he could to see that her job was waiting for her when she was well enough to toil again. He had suspected that her worry over the threat of losing her job was slowing her healing, and he intended to remove that impediment. The woman who was running Mae's winder while she was out sick could not expect to keep it, he reasoned; Mae's complications had come through no fault of her own, and Bennett Cotton Mill had few workers so diligent as Mae, including the woman replacing her. Dr. Williams was a Bennett on his mother's side. The day he assured Mae her job was not in jeopardy, a little pink color began to show on her cheeks and she got out of bed and went to the table for supper that evening. Doctor Dewey had said to her before he left,

"I talked to James Bennett about your job, Mae. He said you don't have to worry about it. 'Just take care of yourself and your little girl, and get well,' he said."

Like Dr. Williams, the neighbors paid regular visits throughout Mae's illness; if not continuously flowing (she would not have wanted that), theirs was a steady stream of calls, bearing homecooked dishes and neighborly compassion to her bedside and table. And the neighbors prayed with her there. Simple folks and simple in their care, they would visit up until they had seen her back at work in front of her tall winding frame, or heard about it, from those who had. When her slight, forlorn figure was noticed again walking the short distance from her home to the mill before seven in the morning and back again after three in the afternoon, the visits on weekdays would cease, but until then, one or the other of her neighbors, Dora Page, Delphie Carter, or another neighbor, would cross the dirt road with a lemon meringue pie lifted out of their wood-burning oven, or a warm bowl of fried okra and a tomato picked from their backyard vegetable garden, and perhaps a Mason jar of sweet iced tea with a chunk of ice from the company store to cool it. In late May, when she felt like sitting on her side porch again and Dr. Dewey approved it, they joined her there in the shade away from the glare of the late afternoon sunlight streaming directly onto the front of the house, and together, in a homely ritual of sisterhood, they dipped snuff and talked a spell while the smaller children, with Temper, played at their feet or in the yard. Delphie and Dora talked; Mae listened, mainly.

On Sunday afternoons of fellowship, occasionally, one or the other of the men brought to neighborhood gatherings, and to the Smith house when Mae was recuperating, a guitar and, feigning reluctance when asked to 'play us a tune,' strummed a gospel number on it, playing 'by ear' and striking the chords vigorously, making up in volume and fervency what he, perhaps, lacked in training or talent. Most of the time, the selection was a gospel country tune, or a church hymn, and nearer the end of the forties, after they had heard Flatt and Scruggs on the Grand Ole Opry, a bluegrass gospel rendition like "Will the Circle Be Unbroken?" It was at those times that beatific smiles relaxed tired, millhand faces, the spiritual melodies and hopeful lyrics lifting stooped shoulders and setting toes to tapping. Then, her mother's face appeared serenely, unself-consciously happy; Temperance remembered that.

Other memories of those vanished days, also, had made Temperance long for their survival and return, something which had not happened, and she knew would not, as the textile era of the early and mid-twentieth century aged and waned, capitulating to more powerful economic and political currents than mill villagers knew about, and the century drew to an inglorious and disappointing close. More than the textile industry, and the cotton mill hill, had become a relic of the past. Tobacco barns and tobacco warehouses, drive-in movies and drive-in grills (not the same as drive-by grills), Remington and Royal typewriters, and houses with used front porches passed, as well, decades before the century, and the millennium, flagged, sputtered, and finally died, and a new century and millennium made what seemed to Temper to be a contrived, media-appropriated, and clumsily gaudy stage entrance. Temperance's store of memories she held, sifted through, and interpreted. Her penchant for analytical thought had plenty to occupy and challenge her, apart from Jeff Singer's assignment to write her story. None of it was theoretical or academic for her, or therapeutic, for that matter. Therapy, also, was incidental, as far as she was concerned. Too much hung in the balance. As Faulkner had said, the past wasn't dead. It wasn't even past.

—⁓•◦⊙◦↶⊙◦↷⊙◦•⁓—

The first Sunday Mae felt strong enough to walk to the cemetery, bolstered by an afternoon of fellowship and hymn singing with her neighbors, she and Stedman left Temper with Addie, who was visiting that weekend, and just before sundown, they went together to see the baby's grave. Mae's legs, wobbly and emaciated from long weeks of illness and bed rest, strengthened gradually and she enjoyed the walk, for the most part, though nothing much was able to get her attention except the hallowed spot toward which she pressed. More than anything, she wanted to see the place where her baby's body lay. There was no ground more sacred to her. As they approached the neglected graveyard provided by the mill, her eyes picked out a handful of thin, stone markers, a mere couple of inches in thickness, the best that surviving loved ones had been able to afford, and a somewhat larger number of decaying, wooden spikes, a few of them still holding metal memorial cards, with others, which in by-gone days supported cardboard memorial cards, standing empty.

Behind those stretched a grassy expanse with no visible markers, stone or wooden, in it. Stedman led her there and paused and looked around, searching for the small spike and its cardboard sign over which he had stood numb and read three or four times, "Baby Boy Smith, infant son of Stedman and Mae Smith, March 5, 1941."

The paper card and spindly, wooden spike were nowhere in view. Stedman searched with pounding heart through the tall broomstraw perennially growing at the graveyard's edge, as if finding the card, or at least the spike, would prove the baby's resting place lay close by, and would indicate, somehow, its very location. Because the tiny grave had not been dug near one of the large, standing monuments and therefore could not be identified by that association, and because new grass had grown to cover it, there was no way for Stedman to recall, or figure out, the exact spot where his baby's remains were buried. Not wanting to show Mae his own rising despair, he tried to say as evenly as possible,

"I can't tell where it is."

The heavy, spring rains had washed it away.

When Mae realized she would not be able to identify where, in the graveyard, her baby's body lay, she sank to her knees, no longer able to bear the weight of her body with that of her anguished soul, and wailed, loud and pitifully, out of a solitary, inner abyss, her heartsick injury, as one mortally stricken. In an observant and analytical part of his brain, as if detached and unthreatened, though responsive, Stedman heard himself say,

"Do you hear that? That's the sound of a mother's heart breaking."

He crouched trembling beside her and rocked her thin body back and forth like a mother comforting her child. He wanted to say what Addie had said to him,

"It'll be all right. It'll all be all right."

But he couldn't. Nothing could make it all right. He wished he had checked on the grave during the rains. When they started, before the heavy downpours, one after the other, had swept the card away and loosened the sodden earth holding the flimsy spike. He had not returned since the day of the simple burial when just he alone with the funeral home worker had borne the little box, an infant's white casket, to this place. If he had, he thought, he might have pushed the spike more deeply and securely into the ground. He was sure he would have. Why had he brought his son here? There were no grandparents lying here to receive him, no baby siblings, dead before they lived, like him, no kin folk of any degree of kinship to place his little body beside. Then, he had been nearly crazed with grief and worry, shock and anger. Now, he felt equally disoriented with regret and guilt, with pushed down, unexpressed disillusionment and rage, and something he had no name for, so hellish it was to him. If only he had thought to check on the grave, he hadn't, he might have pushed the spike more deeply and securely into the earth. He was certain he would have, he repeated. Perhaps he could have had the funeral home to replace the cardboard marker with a metal one. Stedman's thoughts spiraled into a headlong plunge, the acid of his self-denunciation more searingly tormenting than any which others might have poured on him, repeating and doubling back, one accusation atop the other. He felt his mind slipping away, he feared. Yes, he was losing his mind, he felt.

They stayed there, wailing and sobbing their grief and abandonment, their remorse and guilt, Stedman openly crying now, no longer attempting to disguise his own lacerated spirit. Night had fallen about them. Addie and Temper would worry.

———————

Sometimes, we help most when we have no idea we're doing anything like that, Temperance thought again. Actually, it was many long years afterward before she realized the crucial, indeed mind-saving, role she had played for Mae and Stedman, more for him than for her, that spring and summer of 1941. Mae had her faith; Stedman had a much harder spiritual struggle, though Mae never accused him. Temper's brimming perfection and vivacity, her cute and challenging sassiness, each sassy mischief which Stedman pretended he hadn't noticed, and which caused him to modify her ancient, ancestral name to a more appropriate form, a lasting, loving-and-chastising nickname befitting her kick-butt attitude of which he was proud and fond, and also a little apprehensive for her sake, this it was which pulled him up and back into his right mind and kept him sane. Temper herself. Rather, her selfhood principally, kept both her stricken parents grounded and going, kept them swinging their legs over the side of the bed and getting up in the morning, simply going, however disspiritedly, that sad, dangerous time, she knew.

Yes, that was paramount; her chirping, talkative toddlerhood refused to let them give up. They couldn't. They had her.

Temperance knew, when many years had passed, that she had rescued them.

All the same, not even a healthy, thriving and bright, two-year-old could obliterate, or reverse, the losses Mae and Stedman had suffered. Compounding the death of their second child and only son was the black knowledge there would not be another. This knowledge Stedman and Mae had taken to the graveyard with them that Sunday. Temperance would be their only one. The baby's deformity had prompted Dr. Cecil Brownwater in Martinville to recommend sterilization, convincing Mae and Stedman that any future babies of theirs would likely be similarly malformed. He had alarmed and convinced them, numb as they were, because he was, after all, the doctor. They felt self-consciously unequipped to question or challenge his superior knowledge and assumed good judgment. Perhaps they should have asked Dr. Dewey what he thought about it, but second opinions were rarely, almost never, sought in those days. Nevertheless, Temperance asked those questions now, rhetorical and ineffectual, and as damnably hopeless and infuriating as they were.

Did Dr. Brownwater not know about the healthy child Mae and Stedman already had? Had he asked? What scientific evidence indicated a third or fourth child would not be as healthy and beautifully formed as she? And the timing. Did he realize, and care, that such medical advice as he was giving might be too much to bear so soon? What impact had this second blow had on Mae's duel with death? With her weakened immune system's ability to fight the infection which nearly vanquished it?

And this. What influence had the so-called Eugenics Movement then sweeping the medical profession had on Dr. Brownwater's perspective? Had that pernicious, and now discounted, philosophy shaped his medical advice to her parents? How many of his poor, economically desperate patients, both white and people of color, Black and Lumbee Indian, had Dr. Brownwater advised in just that way? Temperance wondered if Dr. Brownwater's medical judgment would have been the same had Mae been the mill owner's wife, instead of his millhand. If Stedman had been a textile entrepreneur, instead of a cotton mill section hand. She doubted it.

As she reflected on these questions, Temperance saw more interface with Gabe Laughinghouse's struggle to name his place than she had expected to find. Economic and social vulnerability, poverty and powerlessness, of persons of *any* color, invited oppression, as she had already said to Jeffrey Singer, and now saw again. Injustice. In truth, she had seen it always. When you lived in it, and you were smart, you saw it early. You swam in it, like a fish in water. If not as naturally as fish do, case-hardened to it and galvanized by it. Tempered by it. The fit of her nickname now, so meant, she liked, if, as in her case, love had intervened and pulled the sting from cold hate's diabolical power to destroy, making survival a likely probability, despite the odds. She had been there; she knew whereof she spoke. When are you going to free the slaves, Mr. President?

———————

Temperance typically assumed, or lapsed into, a quasi-professorial mode of speech when she undertook her sessions with Jeffrey Singer.

"Dr. Singer, Jeff," she smiled, more to manage her own feelings than his, "I haven't dreamed the nightmare since I last saw you, but it's a wonder; I've written some hellishly disturbing memories. I'm surprised they didn't resurrect that familiar ghost, the nightmare, I mean," she said, though Gabe was in her mind, too.

She handed her journal to him and paused and re-adjusted her chair, turning it toward his, "I included the incident concerning the young, funeral home assistant who looked so much like Gabe Laughinghouse," she continued, more matter of factly than she expected or intended to do. "That wasn't easy," she went on, expressing personal feelings more like herself. "Harder, though, was the story surrounding my mother's loss of the baby. And my father's trauma, as bad as hers, I think." Her face conveyed as much information as her words now.

Dr. Singer listened intently, one shoe propped on the toe of the other. He nodded his agreement, "I can understand. I've seen my sister and brother-in-law there."

"I'm sorry," Temperance responded with empathy. She continued, "That whole Eugenics Movement, we can see, targeted the poor and the powerless," Temperance announced in her ethics professor voice again. She moved naturally from professional to personal and back again through multiple revolutions. Those who knew her well had adjusted to this characteristic way of hers. Fredericka teased her about it. She had even created a raucous comedy skit around it. Of course, she performed it for Temper alone.

61

"I probably would have had a sister or brother, or two, if we hadn't been millhands, you know."

The ethics professor and the daughter of white, underclass workers were never more one, Jeffrey saw. It was a combination he identified with; his own family had struggled to put food on the table and pay the doctor bills. "That philosophy has been discredited, you are right. It is, indeed, a sorry and lasting blot on the medical profession, there's no doubt about that," he said with a weariness almost Sisyphean, a match for her own, Temperance recognized. "It harmed a lot of people, like your family."

"Thank you."

Temper paused a moment and then brightened a bit, "I've remembered some good things, too, Jeff. Things I don't want to forget again. And my name, I have a temper, it's true. But I am also tempered, I think. And I have, as well, a capacity for temperance when it counts, I believe. In any case, we'll see, I imagine, don't you?" she laughed.

"We will; you do; and you are," Jeffrey agreed with a thumbs-up response to each of her assertions.

———

Stedman and Mae were not entirely unprepared for their struggle for survival in 1941. They had already met death and its harsh, commonplace fact in the loss of unnamed twin babies in Mae's family, and siblings, Homer, and a year later, Hester, in Stedman's. Every family they had known of their parents' generation, and all those before them, had lost two or three babies, or more than that. Infant mortality was so prevalent as to seem inevitable. Diphtheria and whooping cough had taken the Smith babies, and the Lewis twins, like their little boy, were stillborn. Those deaths, whatever their circumstances, had not been the result of medical error or bigotry, or yet of class warfare, Temperance assumed. They had occurred at home and without professional, medical intervention, or medical interference.

A person who helped and ministered to the Smith family more than most that spring and summer of 1941 was Miss Ethel Thompson. Reverend Mrs. Ethel Thompson. Jeffrey Singer's great-grandmother. Under the auspices of the Free Will Baptist Church, Ethel Thompson was a woman preacher far ahead of her time. While most Christian denominations had long since closed their doors to women in the pulpit, the Free Will Baptists recognized and encouraged God-called women like Miss Ethel. Known across four counties, Bladen, Robeson, Sampson, and Columbus, as one of the best preachers around, not just as one of the best women preachers, she packed the pews when she led revivals in rural and cotton mill communities. Her visits to New Faith Free Will Baptist seldom disappointed the mill folk who worshiped the Lord under her preaching. Heavy set and generously endowed, but nonetheless agile and energetic, charismatic, most importantly, Reverend Miss Ethel electrified her working class congregations with her Spirit-filled evangelism, the "ole time" religion, and she softened their hearts with her own. Shouters hit the floor when she got happy, happy themselves. Happy in the Lord, they called it, they danced like David before the Ark. But they didn't call it dancing. Dancing was frowned upon and flatly prohibited. It wasn't dancing. It was *shouting*. Over the years, Temperance had remembered Mae among the jubilant shouters. The image was among those earliest family memories Jeffrey had encouraged her to notice, but she had needed little encouragement. Mae had been a primary one of those ecstatic shouters at New Faith then. The memory offset the sad ones. The sad one. Sitting underneath the collection table where she scampered for a better view, a pre-school Temper had watched the whirling and Mae's shouting joy with beating heart. The shouting transformed her quiet, doleful mother into an exultant beauty, her thick, black hair tumbling free on one side of its bobby pins straining, and failing, to hold the gleaming mass in a tight, upside-down corona coiled around the bottom of her hairline, a forties style Mae would wear into the sixties. Her face wreathed with smiles and glistening with tears of spiritual ecstasy, Mae's catharsis and beatification left an indelible, if puzzling, impression on her very young daughter, who missed none of it.

Reverend Miss Ethel's preaching, powerfully delivered as it was, wasn't powerful merely because of the way she executed it. It was powerful on account of its substance. The substance was the Christian gospel, and Miss Ethel had something authoritative to say. Truer to the core of that eternal substance than most preachers Temperance had heard from that day forward, Jeff Singer excluded, Reverend Miss Ethel didn't waste precious time and limited opportunities on minor sins like drinking, smoking, and cussing. She went after big sins like hate and greed, real transgressions. Maybe that's why she never got her own pulpit, Temperance wondered and surmised. And Miss Ethel went after big troubles and burdens. Like unmerited suffering, the kind Mae and Stedman bore that spring and summer of '41. Not presuming or claiming to see any more clearly through that biblical "glass darkly" than the Apostle Paul himself had done, Reverend Miss Ethel wasted no time trying to explain suffering, but she had some clear notions about how to face and bear it. And she understood from practical experience that good things could come out of tragic circumstances, thank God. Theodicy was a word she didn't know and a philosophical and theological concept with which she was unacquainted. Any notion that God's power and love needed harmonization with the facts of suffering and evil was an idea foreign to her understanding and one which she would have rejected out of hand, if someone had suggested it. But she knew something foundational and ingredient about faithful Christian discipleship, and she was well-versed in matters of theology, on those grounds. She stood on firm ground.

Reverend Miss Ethel's theology met Mae's need on a specific Sunday. The first time Mae was able to get back to church after the baby's death and hers nearly, Miss Ethel was the guest preacher that day at New Faith. She took her text from the first chapter of Colossians, where Paul proclaims the startling, severe notion that God expects Christians to be faithful stewards of their suffering. Not just of their blessings. That one gets preached a lot. Their sufferings, too. The whole shootin' match. Mae knew about being a faithful steward of her blessings and had tried to do that. She had regularly untied her knotted, embroidered, white handkerchief and poured the improvised change purse's silver coins into the offering plate as it was passed up and down the pews. Just as regularly, she had passed her mustard biscuits out the back porch screendoor to the hungry Clark children, the rest of the week.

"Miss Mae, can I have a mustard biscuit?"

The answer was, "Yes," unfailingly.

"Of course, Sweetheart. How's your mama today?"

"Here, Sugar. Tell your mama to come to see me."

And so it went. Mae had practiced sharing her food and her money. The blessings part wasn't hard for her. But this idea of being a good steward of sufferings which she could hardly bear herself was a puzzle to her. At one and the same time, it was both unsettling and hopeful. As Reverend Thompson preached on, Mae's eye fell on Lizzy Sessoms sitting across the aisle from her and Temperance. Lizzy and her husband, Roscoe, had lost three babies to miscarriages and another soon after birth, a little girl with open spine. Lizzy was still childless. Mae had been unsure how to comfort her and be a good neighbor to her, beyond the customary gifts of food and words of solace. Although the Sessoms house was one she passed every day she worked, Mae had stopped there just once in two years, when the last miscarriage occurred and she had taken a bowl of peas and a pan of biscuits to Lizzy and Roscoe after work. Now, Reverend Ethel's message had given her an idea.

Some months before that Sunday, when Mae had just learned she was pregnant again and told the neighbors she was in the family way, Lizzy had offered to take care of Temper while she worked. At that time, Stedman was working on the second shift, and he and Mae alternated caring for Temper between them, with some help from Delphie Carter while Stedman grabbed a few hours of sleep. Mae had thanked Lizzy and promised to consider her offer when their situation changed. Now, Stedman was on the first shift again, and soon she would be returning to work. They could use Lizzy's help then. In light of the message she had just heard, Mae saw Lizzy's offer as an opportunity to share her beautiful child with a woman whose suffering was fully as great as her own, with a friend, a sister in the Lord, who didn't have even one child. This must be what being a good steward of your suffering means, she pondered, as the congregation stood for the closing hymn.

Walking the short distance home from New Faith, Mae heard Miss Ethel's stirring sermon and felt it pumping her steps, the liveliest she had taken in a long time. She resolved to pay Lizzy and Roscoe a Sunday visit that same afternoon and take Temper along to meet their menagerie of cats. There were at least five of them the last time she passed their yard, she had noticed. All of them orange and yellow tabbies with black noses, Temper's favorite kind. She would love them and beg to take one of them home with her. Mae was prepared for her spirited daughter's insistent pleas and would not turn her down. Lizzy would need to watch to see that she didn't squeeze them too hard. It would be Mae's first visit in a neighbor's home since Christmas.

In a day when hospital insurance was unheard of and probably didn't exist, Temperance surmised, in any case not among the poor, her parents had a mammoth hospital bill hanging over them. Not until late in July had Mae been able to pace back and forth, up and down, in front of her long winder eight hours a day with no break to rest her back. For nearly five months, she had been out of work and they had gotten along on Stedman's wages alone, making do frugally with what they had, and managing to pay down the medical debt a few dollars at a time, every two weeks, when Stedman got his pay. (Dr. Dewey forgave his share of the debt owed to him, including charges for the twice or thrice weekly home visits he had made during Mae's long convalescence.) Temper guessed that her mother had slipped a few dollar bills into an envelope she addressed and mailed to Martinville promptly after each payday. Or maybe Stedman had just sold his car and paid the debt off in one, lump sum. Either way, the plan would have fit his character. He hated to be in debt; it was a trait he shared with most of his kin and community. Post-World War Two credit cards and patriotic consumerism still lay in America's looming future. What a peculiar, future world that would be to those who had managed the Great Depression. It never would be Mae's and Stedman's world, although he lived until Americans had walked on the moon with Neil Armstrong and Mae survived until two months shy of the new century and millennium. Someone remarked about what a shame it was that she had not lived to see 2000 come in; Temper responded that Mae had been singularly disinterested in its arrival, as she was in most of the modern day's media-engineered "historic events." It was that to her.

Temper's thoughts stuck on this theme of paying for things as soon as debts were incurred and items were purchased. She had lived through all the decades since the Great Depression, decades which had dismantled frugality and put credit in its place. It was not as if folks back then had done without, although they did, and a good bit of it was voluntary, so much as there had been a lack of covetousness for things superfluous to their needs, which had made that time so different from the present. It is true that most folks preferred to do without, rather than go in debt. Living within one's means was fundamental to the post-Depression perspective. Commerce undid an entire way of life in the second half of the twentieth century, Temperance saw, and it did not happen organically. Clever economic theories and practices and those who promulgated them dismantled a social world, and put in its place, inventively and methodically, an alternative of sanctioned avarice and consumerism.

But in the forties, the old-fashioned simplicity and discipline her parents had learned long before emigrating to the cotton mill hill to find "public work" endured. It got them through the Great Depression and enabled them to do the now nearly obsolete thing, living within one's means, when financial need, like the hospital debt and Mae's months of lost wages, made it a gritty struggle to do so. No creditors knocked at their door. They denied themselves all frivolous purchases. Still, Temper recalled that their little family of three didn't go without anything they truly needed, like food or clothing, or simple toys like jack rocks and coloring books, or simple treats like Pepsi Colas and Hershey bars with almonds. One at a time, not a six-pack of drinks or candy bars; those were not marketed yet, as far as she knew. A solid collusion of greed and surfeit had not yet developed on the parts of industry and consumers in willing fraternity, prompting folks to stock their kitchens with cartons and cases of soft drinks and giant bags and boxes of chips and candy. Not surprisingly, the incidence of obesity was relatively uncommon, though many were "pleasantly plump," Temperance recalled.

For all those reasons, Temperance was sure her father had cut out some things he might otherwise have spent his money on, if he hadn't had that medical debt to pay off, things like gas for his car or, most likely, the car itself. She knew Stedman had owned a gleaming, spanking-new '34 Ford with broad white-walls at the time he and Mae were married. A half-dozen snapshots someone snapped of them beside that car remained in the family's few possessions. Stedman lounged slim as a reed against the side of it, dressed up and handsome, his body language bespeaking his youthful pride in his fine, new automobile. But no matter how much he valued his cars, it is likely Stedman sold whatever car he owned in the summer of 1941. The more she thought about it, the more Temperance believed that was what he had done.

"Thank you, Lizzy. We'll see you Monday morning," Mae called over her shoulder as she followed the girls out the door. It was Hallowe'en, and Penelope, Temperance's cousin, Jacob's youngest daughter, was spending the night with Temper.

"You're welcome. I enjoyed them both. I hope Penelope can come with Temper again another day," Lizzy responded from the porch.

She waved them off and stood a moment to watch the girls skipping up the pathway, practicing their newfound, playground skill, some awkwardness showing it, and touching the soft, affectionate core Temper had claimed in Lizzy's heart. Already, she was missing Temper, and she knew she would all the way to Monday.

From Temper's third birthday until almost her seventh, Lizzy nurtured Temperance out of a stored-up wealth of maternal solicitude and love, protection and delight. And with something else. Constant chatter. Miss Lizzy talked to Temperance about everything in their shared day: the cats (seven of them, not counting the one belonging to Temper now), washing dishes, sweeping floors, Chinaberry trees, four o'clock flowers ("Why are they called that?"), Bible verses, all the songs they knew, like "You Are My Sunshine," which "Miss Lizzy sings to me everyday, Daddy", fried okra (both Lizzy and Temper couldn't get enough), and vanilla ice cream, a treat they went to the company store to get after dinner, the mid-day meal, each Friday. And best of all, "Tell me a story, Miss Lizzy." She told Temper lots, lots and lots of them.

It has been remarked that Mae talked little, but she sang a lot—to herself. Off-key, while she cooked and ironed. She must have done it at work, too, Temperance realized, her hymn drowned by the roar of the winder, giving incidental and welcome privacy, and liberty, to sing without imposition on others or embarrassment to herself. Like her love of trees and birds, Mae's love of hymns got her through monotony and fatigue. Fanny Crosby's hymns were among her favorites. "Blessed Assurance" held the top spot. Always a trifle off-key owing to a mild tone deafness, Mae's quiet soprano supplied the musical accompaniment for their days, hers and Stedman's and Temper's, a familiar, reassuring soundtrack of family life, itself a 'blessed assurance.' When she wasn't singing or humming, Stedman and Temperance experienced something like being put on hold, although that expression was not yet a popular one, and they would not have thought of it that way. They waited, not usually consciously, for her to resume. Until she did, it was too quiet. Things didn't seem right.

"This is my sto-ry, This is my song, Prais-ing my Sav-ior, all the day long . . . ."

No one who knew Mae Lewis Smith doubted that the story of Jesus was, in fact, her story. She sang it and lived it. Not perfectly, but better than anyone else anyone knew. Content with little of this world's material goods, she set her sights on a reality scarcely understood, even in that day when few aspired to conspicuous consumption and fewer, still, could have afforded a life style of pretentiousness. Praising the Lord, caring for her family, doing her work as well as she could, and feeding the hungry of her neighborhood, pretty much summed it up. And gratitude. Gratitude for nature and its beauty and bounties. Gratitude for loved ones. Most of all, gratitude for what God had done for her in Jesus Christ, Mae expressed in song. Though Fanny Crosby died six years after Mae's birth, when Mae was just a child, they were contemporaneous sisters in the Spirit. What Fanny composed and lived, Mae sang and lived. Their faith was one.

If anything, the shattering loss of her baby and her fertility was superseded by a parallel growth in her faith. Fanny Crosby's Christian faith, with that of caravans of believers who preceded her, was also Mae's abiding faith and discipleship story. The suffering Savior was a Redeemer with whom she identified and whose story she now lived, one who had suffered tribulations as bad as hers and worse, who had overcome, and whose love and power were given in sacrifice *for her*, she believed, and for all others. Despised and mistreated, alone in dark Gethsemane while those he trusted most slept around him, the suffering Christ comforted Mae and was her spirit's Companion and Brother. Fanny Crosby's deeply loved hymns brought Him near and nurtured a wish to draw nearer to Him.

The old hymns of the faith did more than comfort Mae in her grief; they made her stronger, more resilient, and somberly hopeful again. They tapped a deep well of quiet joy in Mae's heart, there since her Christian conversion, her singular experience of having been born again. It was that spiritual joy which leapt up and moved her to shouting at New Faith Free Will Baptist. Its wellspring was trust. Trust undergirded her steps and made her sing, everyday. From daylight to dark, Mae hummed and sang.

Chapter Five

She's the youngest, the oldest, the ugliest, the prettiest, the dumbest, and the smartest one I have.

Stedman Smith

Temperance marveled at the fact that Stedman never tried to turn her into a boy. She couldn't recall a single time, she would write in her journal and say to Jeff Singer, that he had made her feel she was less than plenty good enough, either because she was a girl, or because she was his only child and he had no boys. Much to the contrary, she learned early how proud he was of her. He showed her off to his friends and poker buddies by getting her to spell "encyclopedia," or another long word. He knew she couldn't be stumped.

"Shug, come here."

"What is it, Daddy?"

"Spell 'encyclopedia' for us," he responded, his eyes gleaming with anticipation of her performance and their admiration in response to it.

"E-n-c-y-c-l-o-p-e-d-i-a."

Predictably, the men dutifully and honestly exclaimed their impressed surprise and Stedman beamed his satisfaction and pride in her ability and achievement.

At other times, he said with a huge, comical grin, goofy, memorable, to those to whom he introduced her that "she is the youngest, the oldest, the prettiest, the ugliest, the dumbest, and the smartest one I have," not in the least exhibiting a manner expectant of their sympathy, oblivious, it seemed, to the possibility that anyone would ever deem her inferior in any way. Tucking a long lock of wavy, brown hair behind her ear (a gesture she didn't care for but tolerated), he solicited their participation in the serious jest. For his friends' part, they gave the obliging response,

"Well, she shore is a pretty one, Stedman."

Though she had no dimples besides the imaginary one she coaxed with a pencil eraser at the right corner of her mouth (actually, there was a faint one there), some of Stedman's friends and acquaintances went further,

"She looks like Shirley Temple, Stedman."

That response pleased Temper more than it did her father.

It seemed that the loss of her baby brother and any chance of there being more children besides her made Stedman especially grateful to have Temper. In point of fact, Stedman believed he had almost lost her, too. That event had radicalized matters permanently and put to rest any longing he had had for a son. There had been another hospital stay, another serious infection, and another surgery, and it had been Temper who might have died. When she was just four.

Within two years of the stillbirth, a month short of it, Temperance became ill enough to impel Dr. Dewey to order hospitalization for her. She would never know with certainty what her ailment had been, exactly. The most Mae and Stedman could tell her was "an infected gland." Possibly appendicitis, she deduced, since the three-inch incision was on her right side. Or an infected lymph node? In any event, a few days before Valentine's, a special day Temper did not yet know about, Stedman drove her and Mae to the hospital in Martinville, the same one harboring the bad memories of 1941. Fighting a sense of deep dread, Mae went prepared to stay with her child night and day. Stedman had assured Mae he would not let them run her off.

Lastingly, Temperance recalled irrelevant details, like two, tall, green plants on either side of the elevator doors. And relevant ones, like how her daddy walked beside her stretcher after the surgery, holding her small hand tightly, as they got into the elevator and out of it, on the way from the recovery room to her hospital room. She remembered how puffy and red his face had looked when she regained consciousness. She'd seen the faces of people who had been crying for a long time. Though she was probably too young to retrieve the early memory, it was the way her mama's and daddy's faces had looked that evening they returned from the graveyard. Maybe it was the way Stedman's face had looked after he first learned the baby had died. There must have been others. In any case, Temper recognized the look. And she remembered the dialogue.

"Why are you cryin', Daddy?"

"I'm not cryin', Shug, I jus' got somethin' in my eye."

It was the second time that day someone had lied to her, but this, she sensed accurately, was an innocent lie, a humane fib, told to console, rather than conceal. The first lie was the one the operating room nurse who prepared her for surgery had told. Alone with the nurse, Temperance had begged throughout the prep,

"I want my daddy. Go get my daddy. I want my daddy. I want my daddy! Go get my daddy!!"

Did she say 'please'? Maybe not. Probably not.

Working silently and unresponsively, giving no more sign she had heard than a deaf person might have, the nurse gave no answer until she had finished her work. Then, she spoke briefly, disinterestedly, "All right, I'm going to get your daddy."

Temperance relaxed; she believed her. Nothing in her few years had prepared her for a lie. Until then, she had not seen adult deception, or she had not recognized it, if she had. So, whenever she heard a man's footsteps in the long hallway, she looked excitedly over her right shoulder, expecting to see Stedman approaching. Instead, she saw a strange, unfamiliar man, one older than her father and dressed in a long, knee-length, white coat. It wasn't her father.

"Daddy! Daddy! Daddy!" she screamed wildly, jerking at the sheet covering her legs and trying to kick herself into an upright position and off the table, until the mask of ether was mercilessly or mercifully placed over her nose and mouth.

But her daddy had come to her. She had called him, and he had responded, as fully and faithfully as he could do. Although she had not been allowed the comfort of being told he was at the door of her operating room at the very moment the ether mask was pushed over her face, he had, indeed, stood there and cried so long and hard, that his puffy, red, tear-marked face and sad, red eyes were what she saw first, the instant she awoke from the ether coma enforced on her. The person she most trusted, the only one she trusted enough to pull sandspurs out of her bare feet, had not let her down. He had responded to her cries and calls. He was there. No one else would be allowed to hurt her or frighten her. Or deceive her.

"It's all right, Shug," she heard him say. "It's all, all right."

Stedman left the hospital when visiting hours were over, so that he could go back to work in the morning, but Mae stayed with their daughter night and day, out of Temper's sight only long enough to go to the toilet, always beside her, sleeping in the narrow bed with her at night, never absent throughout the hospital stay. And Stedman drove the dozen or so miles to Martinville each afternoon after he got off work, reassuring his baby girl that he would always be back. And that he would take her home when she was well.

After breakfast on the morning of February the fourteenth, the prettiest, kindest nurse on the hospital floor walked into Temper's room and, with a happy, youthful smile, handed her a bright red, heart-shaped Whitman's candy box saved from another year's Valentine's Day. She had filled it to bursting with children's dimestore cards. Such was Temper's eye-popping introduction to St. Valentine.

When she reached her forties, Temperance tracked down the Miss Green who had been a nurse at Shorter Hospital in February of 1943. Hardly a Valentine's Day in all the intervening years had passed that she hadn't recalled Miss Green's marvelous Valentine's gift. Married to a pharmacist named Robert Lawson, Miss Green, she learned, had reared two sons and a daughter of her own and was, by then, a happy grandmother of seven. Temperance wrote a letter to her and told her how much her magical gift of "three hundred Valentines" had meant to her when she was four. At least, she tried to tell her. She hoped Miss Green had always known.

Sandspurs were, hands-down, Temper's arch nemesis. Only Stedman could pull her loose baby teeth without hurting her, and only he was entrusted with the painful extraction of embedded sandspurs, especially the tough, rock-hard, purple-spined ones with cotton lint, everywhere present, tightly matted among the spines. As workers walked home from the mill, the breezes blew cotton lint off their clothing onto the grasses beside the pathway. In a cotton mill village, cotton dust and lint were as ubiquitous as air itself. Sandspurs became laden and entangled with the fiber; this was the kind of sandspur Temper learned to dread the most. A tender-green one she might let Mae pull, but not the old, purple ones. One scorching-hot summer day, Temperance tiptoed around half the day with a purple sandspur deeply embedded in her right heel, the one she stepped down harder on. She squatted several times and inspected it. Undoubtedly, it was the granddaddy of all sandspurs. Bigger than most, older, darker purple, and so matted with cotton lint and dirt, she could hardly tell one spine from the other. It hurt the entire time, gaining in its power to torture, each time she inspected it.

At last, Stedman got home from work, smelling like cotton dust himself, and pulled the demon out as smoothly as he could manage. He had refined a technique of grasping the sharp spines between his calloused, left thumb and index finger, getting a firm hold without piercing his own skin, and, with both gentleness and quickness, jerking the sandspur straight out of the foot, careful not to injure more the tender flesh surrounding the spines. The heel hurt and bled a little, but not so much as it would have if anyone besides her father had extracted the sandspur. Temper knew that. Mae dabbed her foot with iodine, maybe Merthiolate, to kill the germs, and Temper continued to favor the injured foot until bedtime. The next morning, it was sore, but not enough to dissuade her from going barefooted. Children on cotton mill hills had no option of comfortable tennis shoes to wear for play in those days. Even so, it is doubtful athletic footwear would have been the preferred choice over warm, summer sand and unfettered feet, despite the sandspurs, Temperance concluded.

One annoying thing was that other mill village children sometimes asked her daddy to pull their sandspurs, too. Temper felt a little jealous when he did. He was her daddy and nobody else's. She liked it that way. She felt no lasting threat from other children, however. They were not her brothers or sisters, and there was no credible danger they would, or could, take her place with him. Or with Mae. Her mind was easy on that score, a psychological matter perhaps only children alone, for whom sibling rivalry does not exist, resolve fully. Temperance wondered how much that assurance, or the lack of it, affects everything else. In any case, she had had that one in her pocket, she knew.

"Temp'rance, why are you cryin'? What's the matter, Shug?" Stedman flipped his spent Chesterfield stub behind the clump of red and yellow zinnias and stared with a worried frown at his little girl, barefooted and summer-frocked in a yellow and green, seersucker dress with inch-wide shoulder straps criss-crossed over her small, bare back and anchored at the gathered waist of her skirt. The humidity had her hair in ringlets and her attitude popping. Cute as a speckled puppy she was, he liked to say, to hear her giggle. Temper was approaching him from the direction of the company store, which she was permitted to go to now by herself, if she remembered to ask first.

She limped melodramatically toward him, looking down to check the effect. In fact, it had worsened greatly, the limp, when she saw her daddy ahead, sitting on their front porch doorsteps.

"Willie Earl Gordon kicked me!" she wailed operatically, a high, keen note punctuating the lower chords.

It was true; Willie Earl had done that, and there *was* a faint, blue bruise starting to mottle the bony shin of her left leg, the one she was favoring.

"Why'd he do that?!" Stedman demanded to know, blustering, the midsummer humidity making a bad situation worse.

"He wouldn't let me see over the counter!" she announced indignantly, as though her expanded complaint satisfied the requirements of an explanation.

"Did you do anything to him?"

"No, Sir." (a fib)

Now on her best behavior (though not her best morality), Temper had made certain she added "Sir" to "No."

"Well, you jus' wait here beside me on the doorstep 'til he comes back along. He'll be comin' this way soon."

While they sat and waited, Stedman questioned her some more and puffed irritably on another cigarette. Temper answered with polite, but noncommittal, responses and wondered what he intended to do to Willie Earl. Stedman used the teachable moment to give his spirited daughter a lesson in conflict management. Sort of.

"Temper, you're one little girl right by yourself. You don't have any brothers or sisters to take up for you." (This mattered to him, a lot.)

"Don't ever hit anybody else first."

Good instruction and advice she would ever after agree, then and later, whether she followed it or not. He wasn't through.

"But if somebody hits you, you pick up the biggest stick you c'n find and hit 'em as hard as you can. D'you hear me?!"

Stedman puffed furiously on the Chesterfield he was finishing, his face red and his patience gone. Presently, it seemed like hours to both of them, Willie Earl's heedless, overalled form came skipping a rock ahead of him, headed for certain judgment he knew not of, not the Divine Judgment, but something nearly as bad, "hot under the collar" Parental Judgment. It was waiting for him.

"Willie Earl, did you kick Temper?"

"No!"

Two mistakes: a lie and no "Sir" appended to "No."

Without another word and no warning whatsoever, Stedman grabbed the startled boy's right arm and whopped four or five, hearty wallops on his rump with his open palm. While not a belt or a switch, that left hand could get a child's full attention, Temper knew.

"You go on home, now, and don't you touch Temper ag'in, d'you hear me?"

Guilt-stricken, Temperance watched in wide-eyed astonishment as Willie Earl forgot his rock and galloped home. The Lord didn't approve of what she had done, she'd learned that at New Faith, too, and Stedman was going to disapprove just as strongly when he found out; as for Willie Earl, it was unlikely he was ready to put the whole matter behind him either, especially now that Stedman had whopped him like that. The problem was that the truth had been only partly told. The withheld part made things look a lot different from the way she had represented them. She hadn't told her father that she had spat on Willie Earl's clean, blue shirt, before he hauled off and kicked her for doing it. Was that the same as hitting someone first? Temper was afraid so. Her action was sure to come to the light of day when "rest assured, your sins will find you out." The aggressor from the git-go, she had ordered the bigger, older child out of her way, and when he refused to move, she had spat on him. Was a pattern forming? Would Stedman's admonition and its flawed mantra, despite its prudent first article, suffice as guidance and corrective for her explosive spirit? What about Carson? Temperance asked that question now. She had believed she had acted reasonably on Stedman's early advice when Carson had betrayed her. But past and present had merged Willie Earl and Carson.

Now, Temper wondered how much Carson had taken the big stick. She realized her armor might be cracking a little. Only a little.

Temperance pulled her Duke-blue Honda hybrid into Jeff Singer's parking area and before she stepped out, she adjusted the Liz Claiborne, wide-brimmed, straw hat and checked her mascara in the rearview mirror. Confident enough to let her gray hair be gray, she wore eye makeup in excess, perhaps, but it helped somewhat to mask the fatigue in her eyes, noticeable fatigue there from late morning until bedtime, now everyday. She missed it, the grab-your-attention sparkle her dark eyes had held most of her life, according to the words of many. Her wrinkles didn't bother her, but this look of bone-tiredness did. Still, in all, it mattered little, she had decided. She'd lost more important things.

"Jeff, I'm havin' a ball telling this part of my story! These memories are a lot of fun. And safe. I think."

"I'm glad. The fun and safety will help you deal with the part you're dreading to tell. They'll prepare and fortify you. Your remarks show me you've sensed that, and you're responding to it."

"But what does that mean practically? What *will* it mean? I think my subconscious is calling the shots now more than I expected to be the case. Can I trust it—not to hurt me?" she added, a little embarrassed to show her fear of the unknown, her trepidation.

"You absolutely can, Temperance. It may hurt you, but it won't harm you. That's an important distinction, do you agree?"

"Yes," she answered. Jeffrey Singer knew her well.

"Good. Keep going."

"You're sure I'm not just delaying the inevitable, being an ostrich?" That was her other concern. She didn't want to tread water. (Metaphors were flying.) If she could swim, she wanted to do that. Despite her fears, she wanted to face them down.

"We both know you're not an ostrich, Temper. How do you think you got that name?" he smiled. He rarely missed an opportunity to tease her about her name. Or to use it to challenge her. "Don't worry, it'll get sticky again, soon enough. There'll be plenty of battlefield experience in this. Glide as long as you can. It's not just gliding. It's okay to enjoy the ride." (Jeff Singer played fast and loose with metaphors, too.)

"Okay, General. Thanks. See you Tuesday."

In October of the next year, when everyone was celebrating the end of the War then, Stedman and Mae, with Temperance, moved to Martinville for work in the cotton mill there; briefly, it turned out. Just before Christmas, a short two months later, Temperance recorded in her journal, they pulled up their roots again and moved farther from Bladen County, eastward to Lenoirville in Lenoir

County and settled into a cotton mill house much like the two others they'd lived in, in Pineboro and Martinville, this one across the street directly in front of the mill and on the corner next to the town power plant. Between the mill and the power plant, the noise on the cotton mill hill exceeded any they had heard and lived with before, but they were used to industrial noise, and to them, it represented employment and livelihood, as it did to factory workers and their families generally. Temper had known nothing else.

They reached their destination and new home that Saturday evening just as twilight was approaching and, to Temper's exuberant delight, snow and sleet began falling before they could finish unloading their furniture and other belongings. It was her first snow storm. In fact, it was the first time she had seen snow at all, except in pictures. And it was coming down so thick and fast, she could hardly see into the next yard. The nearly impenetrable curtain of snow transformed everything in sight, making it a part of nature's pristine hospitality, it seemed to her, then and ever after. She was thereby programmed, simply and serenely, to love her new home.

Huddled close together around the living room fireplace in which Mae had built a roaring fire from lightwood kindling ("light'ard") and dry firewood they had brought with them from Martinville, the three of them, tired but hopeful and expectant, savored a winter's picnic of sausages canned in oil, fat and salty, fresh slices of Merita bread (Merita would become their favorite brand), and cold Pepsi Colas, ever the *piéce de resistance*. And there had to have been a Hershey bar with almonds in there somewhere for Temper, though she had no recollection of it, she recorded. (Perhaps the inimitable taste of milk chocolate she had not yet discovered, a "new world" adventure awaiting her in Lenoirville, like B westerns at the Carolina Theater.) Temper didn't recall where her parents had picked up the picnic items, the sausages and "light" bread and Pepsi Colas. Maybe they'd brought the sausages and bread along from the company store, but not the drinks, she was certain. She knew they had gotten those on the road, probably at the Esso filling station at the edge of town where they had stopped for gas, just as they entered Lenoirville and a few, promising flakes of snow had begun drifting from the low-hanging sky. Temper's eyes had been on Lenoirville's single skyscraper, ten stories high, Hotel Lenoirville, when she noticed the already large lacework of snowflakes, suspended, nearly motionless, between her and the tallest building she'd ever seen. The snowflakes quickly upstaged the hotel, a greater wonder by far.

Now, like the fantasyland outside their windows, the Pepsi Colas were frosty and cold. Temper resumed her argument for their source in Lenoirville. Pepsi Colas were almost never picked up ahead of time for any event of any kind. They were purchased, opened, and consumed on the spot, and if not that quickly, for some extenuating reason and delaying circumstance, as soon as possible. Case closed.

It was all perfect to her. After the picnic (she wasn't sure anyone had called it that), they snuggled under a heavy pile of handquilted, homemade quilts, most of them a generation old and some of them older than that, cozy and settled on their bed mattresses spread on the bare floor before the glowing, pine resin-fragrant embers. Decades before central heating erased the experience of sleeping in a freezing room under a thick pile of quilts (comforters slide too much), Temper and Mae and Stedman slept "snug as three bugs in a rug," their favorite, funny description of themselves whenever the three of them slept together, their body heat warming the thin envelope of air around and between the spaces where they reposed, and the heavy, layered quilts' weight resting like a comforting hand and holding their sleeping space at a natural, ideal temperature, just as breast milk for a nursing baby is kept by its mother's body at perfect warmth. Years later, deeming it wasteful to heat unoccupied rooms, Temperance would reject central heating in favor of the smaller carbon footprint her use of targeted heating in occupied rooms in daylight hours and heavy bed quilts in cold, winter rooms at night, would imprint. But not before she'd succumbed to the siren's song of profligacy most of her era had embraced. For too long, she had not suitably questioned its extravagance, she at last concluded. The perfection of heavy quilts in a cold room brought her to her senses again, she would tell Fredericka and others. And "thickened" her "thinning" hair, she decided, a benefit and "theory" unsought, but discovered, she believed, and appreciated. Fredericka created a hilarious skit for that notion, too, and used Temper's alliteration, with a lisp.

That first, magical night in Lenoirville, they had decided that tomorrow would be soon enough to set up the iron bedsteads and arrange their few pieces of furniture, the maroon, living room couch and two, matching, overstuffed armchairs, "a real living room suit," Stedman enjoyed pointing out, the hand-carved kitchen table and ladderback chairs, the pine pie safe, also hand-carpentered, its latch set slightly askew, the pine side table, useful and handy for counter space cotton mill kitchens did not provide, and the company bedroom suit, bought at the same store and same time as the living room suit, fine enough for anybody, they believed. And the child's wooden desk and matching chair Stedman had already purchased for Temper's special use, now that she had started to school. It had cost more than he had expected it would when he saw it in the furniture store window, but Stedman intended that she would have what she needed. That and the Bulova wristwatch he later paid half his week's pay for at Johnson's Jewelers were important purchases, he felt. Temper would have what she needed as long as he could afford it.

Outside, the snow and sleet fell until daylight. And continued falling with brief hesitations until suppertime the next day. They had the full day to stay inside and set up their furniture. On Monday, Stedman and Mae would begin their new jobs. But Temperance had only to think of the wonderful reality that she had no school until after Christmas (that was when Stedman intended to register her), the whole world in this new town of Lenoirville was covered in every direction with snow and icicles, they had plentiful snow cream, better than ice cream because harder to get, (and Mae had brought several cans of Carnation evaporated milk, half a five-pound bag of sugar, and most of a bottleful of Sauer's vanilla flavoring, with them from Martinville, all the ingredients needed for snow cream), and Christmas and Santa Claus were coming in less than two weeks.

The snow and ice brought with them fantasy and problems. The backporch pump froze, and the water pipe burst and sprayed the small stoop with a thick sheeting of rock-solid ice, making it impossible for Mae to secure water for cooking and dishwashing. There was nothing to do but heat and melt snow from the porch and icicles broken from the eaves of the house on the stove top. Keeping firewood in the fireplace and cookstove was no problem, however, since they had taken care to bring with them a big turn of it, easily enough for two or three days, maybe four. But Stedman quickly set about finding out where to order a truckload of coal for the heater and their other needs, anyhow. He had decided to switch to soft coal for all their fuel needs, now that they had moved to a town big enough to have a coal company in it. By two o'clock on Monday afternoon, a Lenoirville Coal Company truck had made its cautious way through the slippery streets to their house across the road from the power plant and deposited a heaping load of soft coal in the back yard. To mill hill eyes, most of them workers in houses without coal in their yards and unable to afford that much coal at one time, the new shift overseer and his family were well set. It would be enough to last the winter, folks calculated, impressed by their new neighbors' means.

The snowfall that first evening in Lenoirville may have accounted for Temperance's lifelong love of twilight, the most beautiful and peaceful time of day. Its rival, Shakespeare's "rosy-fingered" dawn, lovely, pink, and fresh, grew quickly busy on hurried weekdays, Temperance had soon learned as a school girl, but twilight softened and slowed on weekdays and every day into refuge and peace. Twilight deftly separated the undifferentiated white light of day and blended a magenta and burnt orange palette of color and glory into the serenity of an indigo night. The early evening snowfall did its part to ensure Temper's love of twilight, to be sure. That, and principally the cozy, fireside communion of parents and child, replete with picnic fun, Pepsi Colas, and trustworthy, protective, and responsive love. The rending incident in 1954, a twilight memory also, would pale beside this earlier, more formative, happy, and restorative one. The dark strip assault's turbulent power, injurious and indisputable, would not efface this bright memory nor vanquish its lasting legacy, its redemptive power to heal. Like twilight's beauty, its beauty, too, would prevail.

Nearly every Saturday in Lenoirville, when the weather was dry, whether cold or not, Mae walked uptown from the cotton mill hill to buy a few groceries, just as she had done in Pineboro and Martinville. If Temper wasn't headed to the Carolina Theater with a friend to see a B western movie with an exotic name like the Durango Kid or an exciting one like Red Ryder and Little Beaver, she went with Mae to the grocery store. Lenoirville had no gargantuan supermarkets in those days. The closest to a Food Lion or a Harris Teeter was a Colonial Store, a mere third their size. Still, Mae and Temper favored the small, local groceries like Cooper's Grocery, tucked inconspicuously between the much bigger Colonial Store and Montgomery Ward. Just four, central lanes wide, in addition to the shelves along the walls, Cooper's stocked all they needed, except fish and oysters, which Stedman sometimes bought at Kennedy's Fish Market on Savage. Mae customarily added to the fresh vegetables and pork chops she especially liked at Cooper's, Temper's twenty-five-cent Hershey bar with almonds and a box of Nabisco butter or black walnut cookies, Temper's favorites. The quarter-sized Hershey was huge, appropriately five times the size of the nickel ones she picked up almost every school day at one of the neighborhood groceries she passed on the way to school, either Calhoun's Grocery or Miss Sadie's.

Neighborhood grocery stores were commonplace in the forties and fifties. Nestled generally on the street corners but situated smack-dab in the middle of the neighborhoods themselves, they were small, intimate, and locally owned and operated. Mae bought her staple items like salt, sugar, flour and lard, at one of those, at West End Grocery, generally, a couple of blocks from their house. But for good pork chops and air-dried sausage and fatback, she went to town and usually to Cooper's. Unless the day was rainy and the cupboard was bare, she did not call a taxi cab. She saved that money. Instead, she and Temperance carried the sacks of groceries home in their arms. Without heavy items like flour and sugar inside them, the bags were easily manageable, because Mae and Temper had not bought unneeded items. Impulse buying was not a temptation for Mae.

Temperance sometimes thought about the "Kilroy was here" phenomenon. For a few months, it caught her attention on her and Mae's grocery-buying trips. First, the white "Kilroy was here" graffiti materialized across the street on the end of the carding room in big letters appearing to have been scrawled in white, school chalk. Next, they saw "Kilroy was here" on the wall of Turner's Esso Station and Garage. When Temper and Mae reached Cooper's, there it was on the side of the Montgomery Ward store next to Cooper's. Other places in Lenoirville bore the mysterious signs, as well. Who was Kilroy? No one seemed to know. What did it matter that he was there? No one seemed to know that either. After awhile, the novelty of the signs wore off, the rain gradually washed them away, and Kilroy apparently no longer was there.

As far as she could tell then or knew now, the Kilroy phenomenon had no threatening implications of violence, either to a person named Roy, or to anyone. Indeed, such a thought never occurred to her, but Temperance had been asked once if the message might have been linked to the activities of the Ku Klux Klan. She doubted it. The Klan chose hooded robes and burning crosses and left subtlety to others.

In Lenoirville, as in Pineboro and Martinville, both concrete and implied boundary lines marked off the cotton mill hill from the richer parts of town. "Lintheads" literally lived on the "other side of the tracks." The Atlantic Coastline Railway's tracks separated the mill village in Lenoirville from all the rest of the town north of the Neuse River. The geographic segregation of White textile workers from wealthier Whites was as impenetrable and absolute as that of "niggertown" from the White part of town. Along with the railroad tracks on the north, other concrete boundaries were the town power plant, noisy and imposing, on the west and the meandering Neuse on the south. Only the east boundary was less clearly designated, and for that reason, less easily observed.

The folks who lived on Cowper Street resisted any association with cotton mill neighbors on their west, just across the street on the same street, including the mill superintendent's family, as they might presume they were from the same place as residents whose houses lined the side of Cowper closest to town and whose workplace was elsewhere than in the cotton mill. On Cowper, the significance of social, political, and residential place had to be established and reinforced by rules of engagement which those who lived north of the railroad tracks felt no need to trouble themselves to maintain. Temperance, despite her sharp intelligence, turned out to be a little slow on the up-take when Sarah Ellen Ivey, who lived on Cowper East, as residents there referred to themselves, showed no interest in walking to school with her and stood her up enough mornings to convey, finally, that she didn't want to walk to school with anyone from the cotton mill hill, not even with Temper who was their class's attendant in May Court that year and who made much more outstanding grades than Sarah Ellen's average ones.

Miss Sadie, a foreign woman with dark skin and a thick accent who told Temper and Rhonda she was Lebanese (they thought she said), operated a neighborhood grocery on Atlantic Avenue just across the railroad tracks directly in front of Rhonda's house. Although her store and home were in the "well-off" part of town, because north of the Atlantic Coastline tracks, though barely, Miss Sadie, unlike the Ivey family and others on Cowper Street, showed no sign of personal awareness of her social advantage. Temper and Rhonda often crossed the tracks and bought Pepsi Colas and twin popsicles from Miss Sadie, who lived in a few rooms in the back of her cinderblock store. When they stood at the drink box, they could see into her living room, that section of it with a couch, a lamp and lamp table, and a rug that looked like an ancient painting spread on the floor before the couch. Occasionally, they glimpsed another older woman there and wondered if Miss Sadie's mother lived with her.

"Miss Sadie, we'd like a Pepsi Cola, please."

"A Bebzi Coa-lah?"

Sometimes, Miss Sadie asked them first if they wanted a "Bebzi Coa-lah," since that was what she expected them to order. They liked to hear her say it. Rhonda and Temper were too polite to giggle to her face about her funny pronunciation, but they let their squeals loose when they left the store, mimicking the way she had said it. It wasn't principally derision or caricature which impelled them to laugh at Miss Sadie's dialect, although Temperance felt guilty about making fun of someone as nice as she was, but it made them feel worldly, cosmopolitan, to go to Miss Sadie's and hear her foreign-sounding speech and then to try to speak the way she did. Temper and Rhonda liked Miss Sadie for a number of reasons.

The old store building yet stood, though unoccupied for many long years, Temperance noticed, one of the last times she took a nostalgic drive through Lenoirville.

———— ∾•α☙◐☙⌀∾•w ————

"My memories are saving me, I think, Freddie," Temperance announced, "despite their mix of good and bad."

"Sounds good, Temp; tell me more," Fredericka applauded.

"Miss Sadie's store across the tracks, snowfall at twilight, Hershey bars and B western movies, Daddy's corny way he introduced me to people, 'the youngest, the oldest, the prettiest, the ugliest, the dumbest, and the smartest one I have,' he might as well have said, 'the princess of the whole world,' because that was what I was to him, and I knew it."

"Man! That was so empowering for you, Temp'rance, I know it was." By contrast, Fredericka's father had been remote and disengaged from his children, generally; she had few memories of the sort Temper had.

"Let's plan a trip to Giorgio's, soon, Fred. I'm getting ready for another of his Greek salads," Temper said by way of signing off.

"Okay. Give me a call when you're ready. Don't forget that the historical society's next meeting is Thursday at two o'clock."

"I'll try my best to make it. Give me another call to remind me, okay? Bye, Fred. See you later."

When the Second World War was over, Miss Pearl and Mister David Amyette's son Roscoe came home, but the Smith family rarely saw him. (Temper's memories of those years often stopped a while there. She recorded them for Jeffrey's consideration. And hers.) All the cotton mill houses in Lenoirville, unlike those in Pineboro and Martinville, sat on yards big enough for backyard vegetable gardens. At least half the families planted a good-sized garden every spring and put up dozens of quarts of canned vegetables each fall. Every penny they could save by growing their own vegetables was a penny they didn't need to spend at the grocery store, folks said. The Amyette backyard, however, was completely filled with rosebushes. It was a rose garden. Miss Pearl grew roses of all kinds and colors, and Temperance struggled mightily to resist the urge to pick one of her saucer-sized blooms. The Amyette backyard intersected theirs at right angles, and when Temper walked past it on her way to school on warm May mornings, the sweet smell of roses (the smell would linger in her memory and make Oil of Olay her favorite lotion) was hanging in the air already. Miss Pearl's roses were some of the biggest, most exquisite roses she would ever see, and hot house, no-fragrance hybrids, imported or homegrown, beautiful though they were, would never compare to the flowers in the Amyette rose garden, then or in all the years ahead.

But after Roscoe came home from the big War, Temperance seldom noticed Miss Pearl working there anymore. And she rarely saw him at all. She faintly remembered a gangly, freckled-faced, high school boy who used to live there and who helped Billy Whitley make an impressive soap box racer which competed in Lenoirville's annual soap box derby and won, the only cotton mill hill boy and soap box ever to win the town derby. All the menfolk who knew about such things credited Roscoe's design and crafting, and allowed as to how that had most accounted for Billy's victory, although the boy himself was a good little driver, they acknowledged. Temper had heard them talking about it with Stedman, and the story itself had become a mill hill legend.

Temperance hardly recognized the boy in the story, in the man who came back from the War. Once or twice, she glimpsed him walking with his head down near the kitchen steps. If he'd been out to the roses, she'd missed that. He was tall and skinny (people didn't call it thin), hunched over in his overalls, and walked with his head bowed, like he was studying over something, or worrying about something, Temper thought then. She would later remember him as a Boo Radley-like figure.

Stedman said Roscoe had been shell-shocked and wasn't quite right anymore. Folks remembered the soap box racer he'd helped Billy make and the promise he'd shown as a cracker-jack mechanic before he quit high school and went off to the big War, and he was a pretty smart boy, they said. That was about all the discussion they ever had about Roscoe Amyette, but Temperance noticed that Stedman and Mae got quieter and more thoughtful after they'd said that much.

———— ·w·o·e·o·o·e·o·w· ————

"Jeff, the nightmare's back. I woke up about midnight, sweaty and agitated. The water was dark, hip-deep, and the dress was heavier than I remember, fuller and longer and super-saturated. Try as I might, I could not pull myself out of the water and the mud sucking at my feet. This time, I could see it, the dress, I mean, was made of some kind of organza material and adorned with small, pink rosebuds, at some time lovely, maybe, but it was making my progress more difficult, like a long, heavy bag I was dragging wearily behind me."

Here, she stopped and sighed. Jeff could read the fatigue on her face, but he pushed her past it,

"Keep going, Temperance. Was anyone else in the dream?"

"Only in the distance. There seemed to be a celebration, a party maybe, of some kind, at a restaurant, or a house, I don't know which, on the banks of the river I was trudging through, or on the beach. I don't know whether I'm walking along the shoreline of the ocean or what kind of water I'm in; I just can't get out of it."

"You're going to make it, Temper. When your mind gets you where it wants you to be, I believe you will step out of whatever is signified by the dark water." He added, "And the nightmare will end."

"Oh, God, I hope so, Jeff."

Temperance rose and gave her friend a slight hug. She left without further comment.

—⁓•◦◖❦◗◦•⁓—

Temperance wrote:

At school in 1946 and '47, Temper's days were packed with patriotic fervor. They sang "Onward, Christian Soldiers" a lot, at least two or three times every week. The Marine's fight song was especially favored by the children, although most of the teachers preferred the former, more stately hymn.

"From the halls of Montezuma, to the hills of Tripoli," or was it "From the hills of Montezuma to the halls of Tripoli?" the fight song went. Temperance couldn't remember, and one was about as coherent as the other, then and now, to her. No matter, the children really liked it, so spirited it was, "We will fight our country's bat-tle . . . ."

Seven- and eight-year-olds belted it out with gusto, ready to kick butt, in their turn. The "Star-Spangled Banner," "America, the Beautiful" (Temper's favorite), and "My Country, 'Tis of Thee," were other, more beautiful and subdued, and rather less favored, regulars, not quite bellicose enough. One would have imagined the

War was still on, considering the amount of energy and attention given to battle.

It was all entirely natural, it seemed to her then. And, to be sure, it was rather exciting and got the blood stirring, though children seldom require such excitation. Although Temperance didn't recall thinking her teachers were pumped, to use a contemporary expression, she was later convinced they were and had conveyed that frenetic energy to their pupils. Perhaps in part to energize their academic performance, or maybe they just couldn't turn loose of the War just yet, she postulated. And it seemed evident they didn't have any Boo Radley's or Roscoe Amyette's at their homes or in their neighborhoods. Upon reflection, those teachers' quasi-religious patriotism and fervor seemed to Temperance to have been a disturbing contrast to the listless inactivity and sad quiet at the Amyette house next door. The juxtaposed memories of that solemn contradiction between patriotic enthusiasm and lost promise, on the one hand, and the aromatic splendor of Miss Pearl's fragrant and beautiful roses, on the other, commingled, rather in the manner of daffodils and bruised arms a generation earlier in her family's story. War by any name was War, she couldn't help thinking. She had been given a lot to work on for a long time. It was part of what made growing up hard, and necessary.

The nightmare held off. But its return was a dreaded certainty, Temper felt. She pushed onward and gave her mind to her parents' always-crucial attention to money matters.

For someone like Stedman with good sense and reasonable priorities, frugal money management did not mean deprivation and want. It did mean restraint and sensible choices, putting away money for a rainy day, and gratitude for enough money to do that. The same perspective was growing in Temper. A half dollar, heavy in her palm and big enough to cover most of it, was enough for a Johnny Mack Brown or a Lash LaRue picture show, a box of movie popcorn and a drink at the show, and then paper dolls or jack rocks at McLelland's after the movie. The rest of Saturday until bedtime she spent cutting out her new paper dolls, as much fun as playing with them, and dressing them and "playing like" she was one of them, or all of them. Or sharpening her eye-hand coordination at jack rocks with Rhonda or Kathy Jordan who lived behind her on Dawkins, or Polly Wills who scratched her nose with her second knuckle and had to bring her little brother Buddy with her, and was her third choice on that account.

Paper money was a lot of money, and no child Temper knew expected to be given that much. Nonetheless, on rare special occasions, Stedman handed Temperance a wad of paper bills, like the memorable time he told her to go uptown to Montgomery Ward's and buy that Victrola she wanted for her birthday. Of course, he went along with her and carried the record player back home in his arms.

"The nightmare took me by surprise this time, Fred. More than it usually does. Much of my writing has been about pleasant things, I thought. So why is it back now?!" she nearly shouted into the phone, her intensity building with each sentence. Temper's dream just as she was waking up had her again in black, cold water, pulling the heavy weight of her sodden dress and struggling to free her feet from the mud encasing them.

Fredericka sensed that her contribution as the Listener was what Temperance most needed right now, and she waited, with no audible response, for her to continue.

"I need to talk to Jeff. There was a difference this time. A shadowy figure either sat, or lay, on the bank between me and the place where there are people and lights in the dream. So far as I could tell, it did not move, and that terrifies me when I think about it," Temperance said. "I can't even tell you whether it was animal or human, or whether it was alive. It was just a form, or maybe only a mound. I can't say which. Or what."

"How are you doing with the headaches, the jagged line?"

"They're okay. No trouble with that. But who knows, after this?"

"Do you want me to come over? Or do you want to get out? Maybe Giorgio's?"

"Maybe for dinner. Today is my day for Story Hour at Miriam Lamb Library, remember? I have to read to the kids at ten, and after that, I'll just need a good nap, I think. Call me about four?"

"Okay. Maybe seven for dinner? Is that too late for you?"

"No, seven's fine. See you then. Bye."

The infantile paralysis epidemic of the late forties and early fifties had a direct connection, it turned out, to outhouses and their use, Temperance believed, and to similar, poor sanitary conventions and practices of mid-twentieth-century culture. However, on the other hand, wherever hygiene was adequate, however marginally so, a measure of protection was afforded which a later, over-sanitized, anti-bacterial-obsessed citizenry forfeited, perhaps.

The polio epidemic left its mark on Temper's sleepy, cotton mill town. Every afternoon, the *Lenoirville Daily Free Press* printed front page the number of new cases reported across the country the day before, with an updated tally of infantile paralysis cases nationwide. Each day, the Smith family and their neighbors looked to see in the box above the fold how high the dreaded number had risen. Too often, a picture of someone in an iron lung appeared in the newspaper alongside the article reporting new incidences of illness. The iron lung, with just a head sticking out, looked ominous, a cylindrical prison, killing movement and freedom, Temper felt. She despised seeing it and feared its meaning, but she always looked whenever Stedman showed her the picture and felt sorry for the person entombed in the breathing apparatus. Meant to preserve life, the iron lung looked like a prison and a coffin to her.

The number of new cases climbed steadily, day after day, leveling off only when the cooler, less humid weather of autumn returned. Then, at last, new cases tapered off and, by winter, mercifully subsided altogether, or nearly. But each summer, when the hot weather and high humidity returned, so did the polio fever, in pandemic proportions.

When Temperance later read about the annual recurrences of yellow fever in the hot summer months of the years of the Revolutionary era, she had strong memories of the summers of her childhood and early adolescence when Americans experienced something much akin to that earlier scourge.

Temper hated the quarantines prohibiting the re-opening of the single, town swimming pool in Lenoirville and canceling children's passage on public transportation vehicles like the Trailways and Greyhound Buses they rode a few years to Bladen County to visit her grandparents. The polio bus quarantine meant they didn't go to White Lake, either. Temper and Dorcas enjoyed Crystal Beach more than any other two children have ever done, both of them were certain and contended aloud to all who would listen, adamant, Temper more so than Dorcas, that this was true. Dorcas was the first cousin who would remain Temper's White Lake friend for a lifetime, but the summers the virus kept her quarantined in Lenoirville were lost to them. They could not retrieve them. They also would not lose the ones they had.

Movie theaters, while not officially quarantined, as was the swimming pool, were listed with ball parks and restaurants as places parents were advised not to take their children during the summer months of high contagion. A few children, including Temper and Rhonda, went to the B westerns as frequently as before the epidemic, however. Still, the Carolina Theater was noticeably less crowded than in the winter and spring. Of the smaller audiences, there were substantially more adults than children, and in the cooler months, it had been the other way.

An air of worry hung over much of Lenoirville, and occasionally a bit of hysteria, mainly in the richer parts of town, and sometimes that, too, filtered across the railroad tracks onto the mill hill, but for the most part, mill village parents didn't let their minds dwell on the infantile paralysis epidemic, despite their concerned interest in the news reported in the paper and on the radio about it. Perhaps for them the more immediate and year-round threat of hunger and poverty relativized the genuine, but less likely, risk of infectious disease. While better off than many of their millworker friends, Mae and Stedman were among those people and shared their perspective. They did not generally discuss the infantile paralysis scourge, either between themselves or in Temper's presence and among others. No doubt, they were sensitive to the fear it would instill. While it was true they allowed Temper to go to the movies, they were glad they didn't have a way to go to the lake and, thereby, expose her to added risk, though it is unlikely they associated the warm water with the virus. No one quite knew what caused the fever, except that it was advisable to avoid big crowds, they were told. Without a car and with both Trailways and Greyhound under quarantine, they didn't have to keep explaining to their headstrong daughter why they were staying in Lenoirville all summer long. Besides, with Stedman's kidney trouble, he didn't feel much like getting about, the way he had, until then, been used to doing.

Callie Sanderson made the infantile paralysis epidemic a part of their community's experience. Like so many other towns big and small around the country, Lenoirville had its number of cases of the dread disease. Callie lived on Glenwood Avenue, not in the richest part of town, but in what would come to be called a lower middle class section, neither poor nor rich. She wasn't placed in an iron lung at any point, but Callie was seriously stricken. She got it in her right arm. Having fallen ill in July, in 1947, the month Lenoir County reported three cases, Callie didn't enter fourth grade until after New Year's. The fever was gone, but she looked wan and sickly. Without sufficient medical attention and proper exercise therapy of the kind she needed, Callie's withered right arm, atrophied from disease and disuse, forced her to have to learn to write with her left hand, and she did pretty well with it. Because it was wintertime, she was able to keep her arm hidden inside her sleeve, but the sleeve hung loose and limp, and her shoulders looked smaller and narrower. Her inert, shriveled arm, held tucked in next to her side like a little puppy, sort of, drew only modest curiosity at school or elsewhere. Even at the beginning, when she returned to school, it was noticed much less than Callie realized. Except when she asked someone to open something for her. Or when she asked someone to sharpen her pencil for her.

Callie appeared to those who were unacquainted with her merely to be chilly and holding her arm close to her body to stay warm, in the manner people commonly do when not dressed quite warmly enough. And she rearranged it with her good arm when she needed to do so. On summer days, as well, when Callie wore short sleeves (she wore long sleeves until school got out for summer vacation), her body language suggested a normal state, appearing quiet and composed, with a kind of stillness which composure exhibits. But she was timid about participating in any games or any other activities which attracted attention to her arm. It was not composure, but timidity, folks saw in Callie's stillness.

Callie's afflicted arm seemed not to grow anymore after she contracted the disease. It just hung by her side, small and inert and a little blue-looking, evidently on account of the poor circulation, especially in her hand. The fingers grew surprisingly long and healthy-looking nails, and Callie took good care of them and painted them with fingernail polish sometimes, when she grew old enough, but always it was clear polish.

When Callie grew into her teens, she had a pretty face and shapely legs Temper envied and enough confidence to show them off in short shorts, which she wore all summer long. Temper's face was as pretty as Callie's, but her own legs were skinny by fifties standards, and she was a little jealous of Callie's heavier, shapelier legs and their olive tone, almost like a light tan without any suntanning at all. Suntanned skin was coveted in the fifties. Nearly everyone worked on a good tan, the darker, the better.

The confidence Callie gained from her pretty legs had little carry-over in school, however. Although she was intelligent and made average grades, she showed little interest in school and exerted no effort to excel in academics. She got into some trouble with boys, and her reputation became tarnished. Temperance thought Callie was just looking for someone to love her. Or maybe, like Grandma Addie had said, "someone to believe in her." Maybe she doubted they would, love her or believe in her, either one, on account of her arm.

———— ⟶•⟨⟩⟨⟩⟨⟩•⟵ ————

"Well, at least, I half expected the nightmare's return this time," Temperance sighed. "Remembering the summers of polio contagion and quarantine, and Callie Sanderson's withered arm, was enough to kick up some bad vibes, I guess," she remarked to Jeff Singer.

"I imagine so," Jeff commiserated, "I've always thought those years must have been scary for everyone, with no vaccine available and no antibiotic, either, to prevent lasting impairment, or death, in some cases."

"I am most troubled by the frequency with which the nightmare is returning, now, Jeff. Are we doing the right thing? Do you still think that?"

"I still think so, Temp'rance. I think your subconscious is working hard on it. Keep on with your narrative. Okay?"

"All right. I do have something important to tell next," she smiled in agreement, though tentatively. She paused at the door and looked back, "Why is there no Gabriel Laughinghouse in the nightmare, or is there, and I just haven't recognized him?"

"I think we'll know the answer to your question later, Temperance."

When Temperance was in the fifth grade, Stedman's chronic kidney trouble took a turn for the worse. When his urine became dark and bloody, the color of strong tea, and made the house stink when he urinated, Stedman's long procession of visits to the doctors of Lenoirville, almost all of those practicing there, in hope that one would be able to help him, ended in Dr. Oliver Hardy's office. Dr. Robert Winslow, diagnosing a condition more advanced than he could handle, had sent him to the surgeon. Stedman had felt punier than usual for several months, and a surviving snapshot showed him looking tired and ill. When he returned home after the visit to Dr.

Hardy that Thursday afternoon, Stedman talked more about his condition than Temper had heard him do before that time.

"Dr. Hardy thinks I need a' operation," he got out between ragged cigarette puffs and deep drafts of nicotine.

Mae's troubled eyes widened as she turned from the dishpan and wiped her hands on her apron, "What for?" she asked.

"He thinks I've got a stone that's too big to pass—and it's cuttin' my kidney up, he thinks. If a' infection gets hold—or it blocks the tube to my bladder—it could kill me, he says." Dr. Hardy had been measured but forthright in his diagnosis, concerned that his patient not underestimate the seriousness of his condition.

The litany had been a lengthy one for Stedman and would have been for Mae, if she had been telling it. She had no further questions. For them now, as when the baby had died, the doctor's opinion was considered the final word. With their limited education and his medical degree and experience, there was no doubt who knew best. All that remained for them to consider were questions of when, and how they would pay for it.

"He wants to do it a week from tomorrow, that fast," Stedman added, swiping his hair front to back with his fingers, a mannerism of stress they saw when he was worried or aggravated. "I guess I can work that out with Bill Foster. If not, we'll just have to put it off a little longer."

By the time the week had passed, Stedman's pain and weakness had become so bad that everybody, family, mill workers, and neighbors, could see that he wouldn't have been able to go on much longer without having something done. With Bill Foster's blessing and encouragement, "we'll hold down the job while you're out," Stedman admitted himself to Lenoirville Memorial Hospital and Dr. Hardy operated that same day.

Nothing went the way Dr. Hardy, or Stedman, had expected and hoped. The diseased kidney was more damaged than the surgeon had reckoned and, according to his later report to Stedman, he had determined that there was no way to repair and save it. With Mae's reluctant but resigned permission for it, Dr. Hardy removed the kidney, and worst of all, Stedman began hemorrhaging severely. In an emergency effort to stanch the profuse bleeding, Dr. Hardy packed Stedman's body cavity with absorbent material and closed the incision as rapidly as possible. (The storytelling afterward would say that Dr. Hardy packed Stedman's side with bath towels.) All the hospital's blood on hand, type A positive, was transfused into Stedman's vessels and Mae was alerted to call in relatives who might also be A positive who would agree to hurry to Lenoirville to donate their blood. Stedman's brothers and three or four cousins arrived in force, eight or ten of them. Several women and children rode to Lenoirville with the men that Friday evening and, throughout the weekend, gave Mae and Temper some comfort and diversion, more to Temper than to Mae, though about half of them left after donating their blood. The women joined Mae in the kitchen and cooked and talked, performing the healing, homely ministrations of feeding and care, while the children played hopscotch and jump rope, cowboys and cap pistols outside, and paper dolls and checkers inside, when it got too dark to play longer outdoors.

For the weekend, Mae's fears were held to manageable levels by the comfort of kinfolk and the necessary, humane ritual of cooking and eating and the bonding it supplied. On Sunday night, when everyone had left Lenoirville to return to work and school, it was then that Mae realized how close to death Stedman had come and still lay.

"Hello." It was Fredericka, asking how she was coming with the writing.

"Fred, I've remembered something. Stedman's hemorrhaging during the kidney surgery evidently made me remember it. I've just been writing about that—you know, I've told you the story, of my father's hemorrhaging, I mean—and the imagined sight of all that blood jogged my memory of Rhonda's period. Her menstrual period! I had forgotten that. *That* was the reason we waited later to go to the movie that Saturday, that and the heat. She was having bad cramps and flowing, it was her second day, her heaviest day, and she felt nauseated and didn't want to walk to town in the heat. Not that early in the day. The heat made it worse, the cramps and the nausea. So we didn't go to the five o'clock movie—or the three o'clock movie, we might have done that any other Saturday—for that reason."

Rhonda had said, "I know we've been plannin' this all week, Temper, but I don't feel like walkin'; it's so hot, I can't stand it. Maybe if it's cooled down enough, we can go to the seven o'clock movie, okay?"

"I even objected, Freddie, mildly, I'll admit, but I really was a little uncertain about going that late—I had forgotten my misgivings and the fact that I had wanted to cancel the trip, instead of going so late. At least, I remember now that I didn't talk Rhonda into it. You know how tortured I have been by that thought."

"I'm glad you've retrieved that piece of it all, Temperance. You've blamed yourself irrationally. I've wanted to shake you, sometimes. That was part of it."

Though Fredericka's last statement was unclear, Temper let it go, inferring that she meant to say that her new clarity on the events of the movie afternoon was a valuable part of the resolution she sought and needed.

"Bye, Fred. Thanks for calling and listening again. I'm in the middle of the kidney surgery story, and I want to finish it before noon. See ya'."

—·ᵛᵛᵛ·oᴼᴼᴼᴼᴼᴼᴼo·ᵛᵛᵛ·—

Bill Foster had visited Stedman on Saturday morning while all the kinfolk were there donating their A positive blood (all but three of them shared Stedman's blood type), and proved, like them, the extent of his compassion. He talked with hospital staff persons and employed, with their assistance, three private nurses to sit in Stedman's room and give to him undivided attention and care, one on each eight-hour nursing shift, around the clock. It was Bill who had pulled Stedman away from the Martinville mill and promoted him to the shift overseer's job. Now, he told Mae not to worry about how the medical debt would be paid. He would see to it. She never learned just how Bill Foster did that. Everybody prayed.

The kinfolks'gift of blood, Bill Foster's generosity, and the nurses' inimitable, watchful care, Mae's and Temper's love and singular presence, and much solicitous concern and prayer from others, gradually pulled Stedman over the hump. Temper's school, Sabiston Elementary, sat directly across the street from the hospital on its west side, and each day after school, she went there instead of home. Because Mae had six blocks to walk when her work shift ended at three, Temper generally was sitting in the waiting room doing her homework and sometimes finished with it when Mae walked through the big front doors. The hospital had a strict rule that children were not allowed to visit the ill in their rooms. Only with express permission from the head nurse could a child under twelve visit a patient in the hospital rooms. Mae and Temperance had no trouble getting that permission.

"Hey, Daddy, how do you feel today?"

"Pretty good, Shug. How're you?"

A hand reached out and tucked a lock of hair behind her ear. On the first day Temper met the second shift nurse, Mrs. Brewer, Stedman introduced his child in the old way,

"Miz Brewer, this is Temp'rance, my little girl. She's the oldest, the youngest, the prettiest, the ugliest, the dumbest, and the smartest one I've got."

Private duty nurses were typically older nurses, retired from staff nursing. With many years of experience and well-honed compassion, they were the elite corps of nurses in the late years of the forties. Only momentarily confused by Stedman's unusual introduction of his comely, little daughter, Mrs. Brewer responded to the clarity of Stedman's and Temper's non-verbal language and the obvious affection and pride it communicated silently, unambiguously.

"She's a very pretty little girl," Mrs. Brewer obliged, mentally registering the improved color in her patient's face and the energy his wife and daughter infused in him, her own smile meeting theirs.

"Thank you, Ma'am."

Finally, after a week of anxiety and uncertainty, and later, mounting days of gradual improvement in Stedman's vital signs, Dr. Hardy removed the packing from his side and closed his incision permanently. Everyone, Dr. Hardy not least, was relieved that the hemorrhaging did not begin again. A few days later, Stedman went home. Mercifully, his temperature never rose above normal. He nearly bled to death, but he didn't get an infection.

Some funny anecdotes came out of it all. Stedman regaled his friends, his brothers and overseer colleagues and poker buddies, and Bill Foster, with the story about the day he started breaking wind and fanning the window curtains. Mrs. Carroll, his first shift, private duty nurse, was sitting quietly beside the window, knitting a yellow and blue baby sweater for her expected grandchild, when she heard a rolling fart start slowly and rumble toward a crescendo. Stedman, helpless to stop it, sheepishly apologized, but the fart kept rolling. Mrs. Carroll, like Mrs. Brewer and Mrs. Kinton, their third shift counterpart, was professional and kind. She calmly moved her chair away from the window and down to the end of the bed, out of firing range, and encouraged Stedman,

"Don't try to hold it back. Let it all out. You'll feel a lot better when you get it all out."

Not surprisingly, Stedman could hear an old echo in her words, their syntax and their meaning, and the spirit in which they were spoken to him. "It's all right. You'll see. It's all, all right."

He did. Let it all out. Still embarrassed to have a woman in the room and to fart in front of her, Stedman nonetheless relaxed his muscles and with them his whole self and let it blow.

"I pulled up the corner of the sheet and let 'er out. It went so hard and so long," he chuckled, still a little sheepishly, "it fanned the curtains at the window."

The story was too good not to tell. Each time he told it, he laughed at the memory and they, his listeners, howled. Was that true? The fanning the curtain? Even if not, it made the story funnier. The fanning part sounded like an exaggeration; the farting part everyone believed.

———✶————

"Jeff, I loved writing this part about my early years. There are so many good memories there, mixed in as they are with some hellacious ones—and despite the spate of nightmares," she added.

Jeffrey Singer smiled and nodded and adjusted the athletic shoe perched atop the toe of his other one.

Then, more brightly, "The blood might have catalyzed a breakthrough—at least, a small one. Instead of dredging up the nightmare yet again, I mean."

The question she thought she saw in Jeff's eyes prompted a reminder, "Rhonda's menstrual period and its being the reason we waited to go to the later movie that day. My call to you about that?"

"Oh, yes! Yes, I think you're right about that. Your subconscious has been knocking on that door a long time, I imagine, Temper. You opened the door in response to another threatening and related image and the two images conflated, it appears. That was a breakthrough, I think; you can feel good about that," Jeff applauded.

"I think I can turn loose of blaming myself for our going too late in the day, now," Temperance ventured, softly and tentatively, still tender on that score, but freer now.

"Good job. I hope so." Then, "What comes next, do you think? In the story, I mean. Perhaps I should ask, 'Who comes next?'" Jeffrey prodded.

"Pa Gabriel. It's time for Pa Gabriel now."

Both Jeff and Temper herself were glad to hear the confidence with which she said it. Temperance was ready, it signified, or nearly so, to tell the story behind the nightmare.

Chapter Six

That best part of a good man's life, his little, nameless, unremembered acts of kindness and of love.

William Wordsworth

Pa Gabriel moved in with Mae and Stedman and Temperance a week after Hannah died of a massive stroke on one of the hottest days in August of 1952, Temper wrote. It had already been decided, his moving in with them, well before Hannah died. It took her right out, right across Gobbler's Knob, that stroke, fast as lightning; at least she didn't have to lie there and suffer a long time or lie there unable to know or do anything much, they all said. It left Pa Gabriel alone with no one to cook for him. Worst of all, it robbed him, that was how he felt, of his conversation partner and life's companion.

Gabriel and Hannah had learned early, no doubt because they were already bent that way, that loving and living with each other meant talking to each other—about everything. Everything. Little, unimportant, on the scale of cosmology, matters, and big, we'd-better-talk-about-this matters, with a wide variety of subjects in-between; they talked about it all. It had kept their marriage strong, not to mention interesting. Perhaps strong because interesting, communicative. Bonded.

To be sure, Gabriel was unusual. Most men, and husbands especially, were tight-lipped and shut-mouthed, in comparison to Gabriel Lewis. Mae's talkative father and almost equally talkative mother were so different from their quiet daughter that Temper wondered all the more, on account of the difference, how her own mother had become the exceptionally quiet person she was. Temper had early noticed the difference, on the occasional visits they had made to her maternal grandparents' home.

Hannah's sisters and other relatives said they'd never known a man who talked to his own wife as much as Gabe did to Hannah. He even discussed business matters with her, they said, a virtually unheard-of practice, in their experience. He told her about his worries and his dreams. He asked her to think matters over with him and give him her opinion. He confided his regrets and his fears, and confessed his shame, and he gave voice to his aspirations and hopes—to her.

Gabriel talked constantly. He talked while he worked and ate, when he rested and played, and when he made love. Gabriel made love with words, words of fire and hunger, naughty-but-sweet bedtalk, words of tenderness and joy, passion and satiety. Words spoken and meant only for her, Hannah, his lover, helpmate, companion, friend, and partner in talk. His wife. Hannah, mother of his children, grandmother of his grandchildren.

When age began to cool the body's fires, Gabe sometimes joked, "There may be snow on the roof, but there's still fire in the furnace—or at least an ember or two," with a self-deprecating, but raucous laugh.

In truth, the cooling furnace had no effect on his and Hannah's smoldering love. It had only partly been fueled by hormones and chemicals. Years of day in, day out, living and loving, talking and planning, talking and struggling and bearing up under trouble and hardship, talking and thinking, talking and relating, had made their love bigger, stronger, more lasting and resilient, than physical desire and sexual pleasure had power to do. Not that they had denied any of that to themselves either. Physical love was important, you bet, but it was not the "be all and end all" some folks made it out to be, they agreed. Some of their funniest and naughtiest, private jokes were about the lessening importance of their diminished, libidinal fervor,

"The ole, grey mare ain't what she used to be."

They laughed about being "too old to cut the mustard," a corny, country music lyric quickly absorbed into the community's vernacular and theirs. Hugs and kisses and cuddling sufficed when "the flagpole fell."

"Besides," Hannah laughed, with a girlish squeal she still had and Gabriel still loved, "I'm dry as a powder house. This ole lady's dryin' up all over."

And sometimes, when Hannah was feeling especially playful and mischievous, "Gabriel, I believe it's jus' dried up and stuck together!"

This with squeals of mirth you'd think a sixteen-year-old had laughed, not a sixty-six-year-old. That was her age when they'd married. Sixteen. He was twenty-one. Sixty-six and seventy-one, they were still light, gamboling youngsters in their spirits and memories, their joy and outlook. As long as they could talk things out.

Their joints had stiffened and some health problems had emerged over time. And then the stroke. Now, Hannah was gone. Since Gabriel was Mae's father, it was assumed by everyone that he would go to live with her and her family, all of his other children being either dead or boys. Cotton mill houses and the folks who lived in them typically had room for one more, either relative or friend, and acquaintances and strangers were not ruled out, but commonly accepted as boarders, despite the fact that most of the small, wooden, frame houses had no more than three or four rooms, no closets, and no plumbing or running water. Resources of food and shelter were shared with whoever needed them. That was established.

The overseers' houses, situated on a block to themselves at the east end of the mill and closest to town, had five, fairly large rooms, some with wallpaper, and were the first to get a bathroom with a tub at the turn of the decade. Others' houses lagged behind, however, and the Smith family was still living in the house near the power plant, a house with four rooms and an extra, smaller room enclosed at the end of the backporch, when Pa Gabriel moved his few belongings into the front bedroom, the company bedroom furnished with the best furniture in the house, a matching, carved, wooden bedroom suit with flower stencils on the head and foot boards of the double bed and on the chest and dresser drawers, as on the door and drawers of the also matching, tall wardrobe, their only "closet." Mae kept their winter coats and a few other special articles of clothing in the wardrobe.

Temper had slept in the company bedroom before Pa Gabriel moved in, and she had enjoyed gazing at the gleaming wood. She especially liked the small dresser and its center mirror flanked by stenciled drawers on both sides, and the chair, too dainty for Pa Gabriel, she argued mentally, with its small frame and seat and its floral, upholstered cushion. And she had liked to dress herself before the full-length wardrobe mirror. Temper hated to give up the room, but she would relinquish it to her grandfather without a fuss. It's doubtful she would willingly have done so to anyone else. Besides, the backporch room had attractive features of its own, privacy especially, and Pa would give her the dresser chair for her own use out there, she knew. No doubt, the whole set, the dresser, too. There would be no argument about that.

It wouldn't have mattered to Gabriel which room he slept in; he wasn't hard to please about things like that. The small, backporch room would have been fine for him, plenty good enough, he told them. Families which had one of those add-on rooms used it for a variety of purposes, sometimes for storage, sometimes as an extra bedroom, as they were now doing, and occasionally, as noted, as a room rented out to a boarder, or an entire boarder's family, until other housing could be obtained by the cramped, but grateful, family. When families shared a house that way, they typically shared household chores and childcare and care for the feeble, too. They were schooled in how to be helpful to one another.

One end of the backporch, farthest from the pump and kitchen, was given two windows and a door and enclosed on the three open sides to improvise an extra room. With permission from the cotton mill, since all mill village property was owned by the mill. Neighbors gave a hand in the construction, and in less than a day, a room was ready for use. Temper had claimed that special room as her playhouse when they first moved to Lenoirville. Since then, it had been used for that and several other purposes. Now, they had converted it to her bedroom and she and Mae had bought a new, chenille bedspread with pink roses sculpted into the fabric, one which Temper had seen in Belk-Tyler's store window. At fourteen, it made her feel grown-up and private to think of being out there all by herself. And she was growing up fast. Mae had some worry about her daughter's isolation, with a door opening directly from the outside into her bedroom, but she did her best to put those thoughts out of her mind. Still, "Blessed Assurance" kept the nagging thoughts only momentarily at bay.

Temper's preference for the backporch hideaway made Gabriel feel better about taking her room, but he had no expectation of being "put up" in the company bedroom, he repeated. Still, despite Mae's anxiety, she and Stedman insisted that he make himself at home in their best room. He deserved the respect his ripe years had earned for him, they thought. Gabriel's daughter and her husband took seriously the commandment to "honor your father and mother." The pay-off, long days upon the earth, didn't matter to them. He mattered. That was the point. They would provide him their best, they agreed.

Pa Gabriel was an easy fit. He knew how to get along and make do, whatever the circumstances called for in terms of adjustments and accommodations. And he knew how to make himself useful. Just seventy-one and descended from many generations of octogenarians and two grandparents who lived until their early nineties, he could do a full day's work still, though the odds of his finding a job in public work, he thought, were slim. The coal bucket stayed full, however, and Mae never had to clean the ashes out of the heater or fireplace, or yet the stove, after her father joined the household. Nor did she have anymore fish to scale and clean, whether they came from the Neuse or Ned Potter's fish pond. Furthermore, Pa could shell peas and butterbeans as fast as any woman and, best of all, he did all of the vegetable picking in the stifling humidity, thereby saving Mae a lot of back-breaking work. Mae's back had not been strong since she lost the baby, and the hot temperatures and high humidity washed her out and made her feel faint and queasy. Besides, she took after Hannah in almost every way except her mama's talkativeness, and that caused them all to worry about the prevalence of strokes on her side of the family. Gabriel's line, on the other hand, suffered few strokes, although nearly all of them died of heart disease, eventually, usually of congestive heart failure at an advanced age, and he could take the hot sun, morning, midday, or afternoon, with little trouble.

When Pa helped Mae in the kitchen, he fried up the best cornbread on the cotton mill hill. Crisp and light, mouth-watering, his own recipe mixed in enough buttermilk to moisten the meal, no more, and blended more water than buttermilk with Moss's white cornmeal and self-rising flour, and a heaping dash of salt, no sugar, thank you, (sweet cornbread was 'northern' cornbread), for the perfect consistency and flavor his cornbread patties had. All who ate Pa's cornbread suspected he had a secret ingredient he kept to himself, that, or a peculiar way of apportioning amounts which made the singular difference between his cornbread and everyone else's. He insisted not and gave away the recipe liberally. Theirs was good; his was better; that was simply true.

Mae took the honors with the buttermilk biscuits. Gabriel did that with his cornbread. Both, father and daughter, knocked their socks off with their home cooking specialties.

Despite Gabriel's notion that a paying job would not come up for him, within two months after his move to Lenoirville, he was offered three hours of work a day, on weekdays, and all of Saturday, at Holloway's West End Grocery, the biggest of the three neighborhood groceries in, or near, the cotton mill village.

"Ed Holloway offered me work at his grocery store today, helping out from two 'til five in the afternoons, and all day Saturdays. I took it. It won't pay a whole lot, but he said we can get a discount on all the groceries we buy from him. That'll help, too," Gabriel announced to the family at suppertime.

"That's good, Pa," Mae responded, "but you don't have to work, you know."

Stedman picked up the baton, "You know you don't have to work, Gabe, not as long as I'm able to work. You don't eat that much," he reminded his father-in-law.

"Yeah, I know, Stedman, an' I really 'preciate it. But I wanta' do my part around here. Besides, it'll give me somethin' t' do," Gabriel explained.

"I think that's great, Grandpa!" Temper interrupted them, "Does that mean I can get ice cream sandwiches at West End for a nickel?"

"I don't know, Honey, maybe so. Anyway, we'll get you all the ice cream you want," Pa responded. Her delight in his news he reciprocated with a grateful smile.

The pie safe change yielded generous amounts of money for ice cream, they all knew. Still, everybody, including Stedman, felt glad about Gabriel's part-time job, and Pa especially so. With no Medicare yet in existence, and only a small, social security check to help out, Gabriel had little to fall back on; with the extra, few dollars he would make a week at Holloway's and the discount his employment would afford on staple groceries like coffee and lard for their household, including cornmeal and flour for his cornbread, he could more nearly pull his own weight in Lenoirville. That was important to him.

Those who knew Gabriel George Lewis allowed as to how he had been given the most suitable name he could've gotten. Gabriel. Messenger of God. Things he said reliably made good sense. As often as not, they seemed to be divinely inspired. His innate love of language—'language pleases me most,' he'd said—made Gabriel a natural as a proclaimer, a messenger. Thoughts he expressed and the language he used were seldom randomly chosen, never recklessly so. His natural, genetic gift of linguistic capability had been honed and grown by his fifty years of life with Hannah and their invigorating conversations and discussion of ideas and values. His insights had been shaped, as well, by his considerable, though slightly idiosyncratic, faith. Gabriel was proud of his biblical name, so much so that sometimes he felt convicted over it and prayed to be delivered from his unseemly pride. Like Augustine and other venerable forebears of the faith, Baptist Christians believed pride headed the roster of sins of a humanity rebellious against God. Little in Gabriel's life experience had given him sufficient cause to reject that basic datum of his religious heritage. Unless it was hate. In fact, pride itself in its most virulent embodiment was hate under another name, he had decided. Hatred against God and humanity, and hatred against the creation itself. Finally, all sin boiled down to hate disguised by euphemisms less obviously that, he believed. Maybe pride needed to be revealed as the euphemism for hate, which it also was, he had concluded. That was the reason his pride worried him and made him pray for deliverance from it. The Bible, he knew, said that the love of money was the root of all evil. What was greed but pride, when all was said and done? And what was exclusion but pride? And what were they but hatred? You couldn't tell a nickel's worth of difference between them, he liked to say and often did. He thought he had it worked out. Gabriel Lewis was a notable theologian in his own right, Augustine notwithstanding, with all due respect to the revered churchman and scholar, but Gabriel was confident in his understanding of what it meant to love God and love his neighbor.

When Harley Pate told Pa Gabriel he was going to start visiting Miss Jessie, his mama, every week in the old folks' home, because he felt so guilty about how he hadn't been going to see her enough, Pa Gabriel replied,

"Things we do out of guilty feelings don't generally last, Harley. Guilt grows shallow, knotty roots, and too often, guilty feelings are just another form of self-absorption, anyhow. They don't suck up enough water, those roots, Harley, not enough to keep us faithful to what we said we were going to do."

Whether Harley recognized it or not, a homily was coming.

"Love and what goes with it are all that sink deep, porous roots and suck up lots of life-giving water. They're the only roots that have nurturing power, and staying power, Harley."

Gabriel paused to let that sink in and then he asked, "What roots does Miss Jessie have, Harley? What kind did she have when you were growing up? How did she treat people? How about the love she gave to you?"

Pa Gabriel wouldn't slow down enough to give Harley a chance to speak up. If Gabriel had a fault, and of course he did, that was it. He forged onward, "How much do you love her? Let's not think about guilt. As a motivator, it won't stand. It's weak as cat pee. Let's think about love."

Pa's love of talking carried him away, often, but not always, on wings of soaring rhetoric; "weak as cat pee" was an example, but reliably he got his point across. Sure enough, Harley started visiting Miss Jessie every Sunday afternoon, and it lasted, right up until she died about eight months after he began his regular visits. Studying on what Pa Gabriel had said to him, Harley felt compelled to recall those boyhood times Miss Jessie had taken him neighboring with her, carrying food to the ailing and comfort to the grieving. He remembered, most, the times his mama had sat up with him long after midnight when he had a hot fever, placing cool, damp washrags on his forehead and worrying over him, and the way she put aside a drumstick and a biscuit for him, no matter who the company at table was or how scarce the food. Not even the preacher got fed better than he did, and Miss Jessie had plenteous hospitality at all times; when the table groaned with its weight of food and when the food was short, Miss Jessie dispensed heartfelt hospitality at all times. Finally, the love won out over the guilt in Harley's thinking.

By usual standards, Gabriel Lewis was not an educated man, though his intelligence was undisputed, to be sure. Still, though he was the first in his family's known history to have completed the fourth level, and was in many respects, a self-taught man, his formal education was meager. His intellectual curiosity and mental agility were not. He had distinguished himself by earning a high school certificate in his forties, and after that, he had qualified for and taken a number of correspondence courses in English and American literature and one or two courses in world history from the University of North Carolina at Chapel Hill. He had excelled in all of them.

Folk were surprised to see the thirty or more volumes of literature and history he kept in a bookcase he had built for himself, volumes including Milton's *Paradise Lost,* John Bunyan's *Pilgrim's Progress,* and Shakespeare's tragedies, which he had studied with a noted Shakespearean scholar at the University of North Carolina through the correspondence program, as he had the sonnets, as well. And Thomas Hardy's *Return of the Native.* On occasion, he added a new book, like a thin volume of Wordsworth's poetry and another of Robert Frost's, and a copy of Thoreau's *Walden* he kept with the Bible beside his bed, once he had acquired it. He had set up the bookcase in the corner of the company bedroom Mae had insisted he make his own. The space between the wardrobe and the door opening onto the front porch was exactly right for it.

When he had been settled in Lenoirville just two weeks, Gabriel applied for and received a library card at the Lenoirville Public Library situated across the street from the courthouse and housed in an ancient Victorian mansion which stood on the imaginary boundary separating, and linking, the White and Colored sections of town. Gabriel and Temper never knew whether to attach any importance to that fact or not; whether the location of the town library, bastion of implied commitment to enlightenment, signified anything or not, whether it was an auspicious sign or not, they couldn't say and never discussed between themselves. Temperance hoped it was, and she knew Pa did, too. Not everything had to be said between kindred spirits. Certain things were a given, and they had pretty much covered the important subjects, anyhow.

Permitted to borrow three books at a time for three weeks, Gabriel made regular trips to the library, a brisk five-block walk, no more than that, and maintained full use of his borrowing privileges. Gabriel enjoyed holding forth on the unparalleled wisdom of those who conceived the idea and implemented the vision of the lending library and its rich benefits to the populace. Like the freedom to vote, the liberty to borrow books was one Gabriel Lewis did not treat with disdain.

"Temp'rance, three books every three weeks suits me just fine. Perfectly, in fact. I read about a book a week. By the time I've finished them all, I can borrow three more. Suits my readin' habits just right, I'd say, wouldn't you?"

The Lenoirville library offered other reasons Gabriel was pleased with it. Its collection was more than twice as big as the small one in Water Oak where he had lived most of his adult life. And it was within easy walking distance from the cotton mill hill. That made a big difference. Accessibility had been a problem in Water Oak.

"Since your grandma died, I'm spendin' more time readin' than ever before—since she's not here to talk to," he finished.

With access to the *Lenoirville Daily Free Press*, (Stedman had subscribed to it soon after moving to Lenoir County), Gabriel was well supplied with reading material, counting his library books, his own volumes, and the daily newspaper. His informed and imaginative language was an individualistic mix of "proper" English, meaning grammatically and syntactically correct usages, and community and familial colloquialisms, including incorrect constructions used by the local folk. Though he did not capitulate to tense and number errors, except for occasional emphasis, he slid easily from standard usage to sub-standard and back again, depending on his subject of discussion, his mood, or the neighbor with whom he was talking. Gabriel's father had explained once, long years ago, to kinfolk they were visiting, "Gabe talks proper."

His kinfolk had noticed already and accepted his difference; something like that had been apparent from his second year. He had picked up his ABC's when he was barely three, just by overhearing his older sister practicing hers. He recognized the letters in print, too, in the Bible, both upper and lower case. Gabriel surprised everybody by figuring out how to tie his brown, lace-up brogans, all shoes were lace-up then, before anyone thought to teach him. What stood out most about Gabriel, though, was his peculiar and avid interest in the grown-ups' topics of conversation and his own precocious ability to converse on an age level beyond his years. Often, he would sit and listen to the grown-ups talk whenever company had called and filled the house, rather than playing with the other children, particularly if the others were girls or younger.

Gabriel's happiest discovery in Lenoirville, surpassing that of the unusually good collection of classical and modern literature at the public library and the pleasant staff he fraternized with there, and exceeding that of the friendly, personal relations he had found so easily with mill hill neighbors, was the exemplary way he and Temperance hit it off. Like him, and like Hannah, his granddaughter was a reflective, spirited thinker and conversationalist, as eager and animated as he in discussion and debate. Like him, too, she gravitated toward justice and fair play. They drew her like a magnet, a moral compass, pointing her to a wider moral universe. He would rather have seen that in her mettle than anything else he could name. She would not squander herself on lesser things, he wagered.

———————

It was natural then, in truth inevitable, that Gabriel would tell his granddaughter about Seth Laughinghouse. Seth, friend of his boyhood. The story he would tell concerned incidents, and particularly one, which had occurred the year they were boys of twelve, just three months apart in age, self-defining in import for him, likely for both of them.

Like many other children of the rural South at the close of the nineteenth century and the birth of the twentieth, Gabe had played with Colored children as often as with White cousins and other White, neighbor children, during his growing-up years. Of them all, his hands-down, best friend was Seth Laughinghouse. Ever since they had been big enough to walk across the road and their mamas would let them. Seth was an autumn-hued, golden-skinned boy of mixed Negro, Native American, and Caucasian heritage. In him, his rich ancestry was uniquely wrought; he would be an artist, a splendid, spiritual scion of the Abraham Laughinghouse family who lived in a ramshackle house engulfed by wildflowers and some planted by Seth's mama, Essie, across the road from the Lewis homestead. Like others ill-suited to this world, Seth would be star-crossed, and it would begin to show early. Even his name made some people mad.

A settlement of Laughinghouse folk had emigrated into Bladen County sometime in the late eighteenth or early nineteenth century, no one was quite sure just when, but at about the same time another one settled in Pitt County north and east of Bladen and not so far from Lenoirville, it turned out. Gabriel now considered trying to look up some of the Laughinghouse descendants in Pitt, when he could find someone with a car to take him there. Maybe Stedman, he thought.

The distinctive Laughinghouse family name was conspicuously Native American. That made some people mad. Its joy made others mad; they heard derision and arrogance, not joy, in its imagery and cadence, and how dare half-breeds stick up their noses at anyone? They had best drop their heads and avert their eyes in the presence of their superiors, the mad ones thought.

To the boy Gabe, the meaning of the Laughinghouse name was both self-evident and wonderful. Its origin was unknown to him, as also to Seth and the Laughinghouses themselves. It didn't matter. If he hadn't liked Seth as the best friend possible, Gabe still would have been drawn like a bumblebee to a flower to the Laughinghouse surname, he believed. It brightened his spirit and, in fact, made him laugh; the image of a house filled with laughter and made for that purpose evoked another image of a house itself laughing, and Gabe broke into giddy laughter in response. More times than he had counted.

Seth's given name was at once Negro and Caucasian, or most correctly, that of his Negro and Caucasian forebears. His mother Essie had a Negro mother and a White father, and there were Seths on both sides. Essie herself had entered into a common law union of love at twenty, with a hardworking, honest, and sharp-as-a-shoetack Native American boy two years younger than she, but ten years older in life experience and wisdom. Abraham Laughinghouse was as good a husband as a woman could want, Essie believed. As for Abe, his thoughts about Essie were that "if the Lord made any prettier than her, He kept them for Himself." Abe intended no blasphemy by that at all. Wasn't it funny that the Lord liked pretty women, too? Abe meant to say. The Laughinghouses laughed heartily and often out of the bottoms of their bellies about all things wonderful with an energy and humor contagious and surprising.

To Gabe, Seth reminded him of a kerosene lantern, ready to shine and light up whatever was around him. His white, wide smile did half of that, and his belly laugh topped off the other half.

"Shucks, Seth! You got the loudest laugh I ever heard! You 'bout busted my eardrums!"

It was an excuse to punch and kick, tumble and wrestle, male-bonding stuff. Gabe knew it was easy for him to turn Seth's lantern on, their camaraderie being so tight. And Seth lit a light in him, too. No doubt about it, they brought out good stuff in each other. In school, they carried on a friendly, but fiercely competitive, rivalry to see who could best the other. Not uncommonly, it came to blows, or rather, 'rasslin' matches. Gabriel and Seth waged a physical and psychological joust to prove their comparative worth. In different schools.

"McLean's Crossroads," Pa Gabriel told Temperance, "had two, one-room schoolhouses, one for the White children and one for the Colored children, Colored children of any and all mixes of race and color."

Gabriel's language took on an instructive, academic tone natural to someone who was, by inclination and design, a teacher, though not by training or profession.

"Both schools were roughhewn, unpainted, single-room structures," he described, "with oil lanterns mounted on wooden, pedestal supports hammered into the walls on two sides of the room, and heated with a pot-belly heater standing in front of the teacher's desk."

Pa Gabriel reached into his shirt pocket and brought out a peach kernel and began working on one of his hobbies, his favorite one. Reading didn't count as a hobby; reading was more than a hobby. Peachseed monkeys. Carving peachseed monkeys out of peach kernels, that was his favorite and most relaxing hobby. And the one which earned him the most acclaim. Temperance had known this engaging, endearing part of her grandfather's identity all her life, though her opportunities to visit him had been limited throughout her childhood. Already, she had amassed a good-sized jungle, replete with real grass and twig-trees regularly freshened and replaced, populated in impressive numbers by the custom-made simians carved to perfection by her grandfather. The one he was carving now would make thirty-three, she tallied silently, that many for her; he had promised this one to her. Pa Gabriel carved more than a hundred a year. All the children who knew him owned at least one, most of them several, but not so many as Temperance. Her Lewis cousins didn't have as many as she had.

Pa Gabriel resumed his narrative.

"Wooden pegs beside the door held our coats and toboggans in cold weather, and about a third of one wall was blackened with something, soot, I think, so that Miss Newkirk and Miss Caviness could write lessons on it in white chalk."

Gabriel related how the children's ages ranged from five to fourteen. There were only one or two fourteen-year-olds, a pair of girls, he thought. Most school-age children, however, had been taken out of school and put to work, either in the fields or in the house, by the time they reached that age. Only a fortunate, or sickly, few were allowed to continue with their schooling past their twelfth year.

Gabriel continued, relishing the chance to talk and tell so much to an avid listener,

"The White school was about half again the size of the Colored one, though neither one was very big, and stood nearer the unpaved state road passing through McLean's Crossroads and running to Elizabethtown, in the southern direction, and Clinton, in the northern. The Colored school stood about a fifth of a mile back from the highway," and here Pa Gabriel pointed to the left, as though he could see it there and had no reason to think she couldn't, "and about the same distance in the direction of Clinton."

The two schoolhouses, the Colored and the White, sat well within sight of each other, though segregated by an abandoned cotton field Edmond K. Long had surrendered to nutgrass invasion not long after the end of the War Against Northern Aggression, as Southerners were wont to call it. This story Gabriel related to Temper, while looking yet in the imagined direction of the Colored schoolhouse and the vacant field twice-abandoned now and forgotten by most, by all, perhaps, but him. His mind had jumped ahead, or back, to long-ago incidents which had happened there, especially to one.

"It would've been a miracle if anyone could've gotten a plow through that ground then," he reflected, "so knotted with nutgrass it had been since the War," Pa recalled. "It was better just to give it up and not risk spreadin' seeds to another field."

That had been Edmond K. Long's wise decision. Besides, the cotton field was no more than a good-sized patch, barely big enough for a cotton field, anyhow. Might as well let the scholars (a general term for schoolchildren then) use it to play on, he reckoned.

In that circumstantial and unintended way, McLean's Crossroads acquired what might have been North Carolina's first racially integrated playground. But no one was thinking in those terms, not Gabriel nor anyone else. And Edmond K. Long might've changed his mind, if he'd realized what lay ahead. It's not as though he wanted to be a catalyst for social change, or anything like that.

Both schools used the vacant field as their playground, too small for a cotton field, but nearly ideal as a playground, or close enough, with the tacit but strong agreement among the McLean's Crossroads community that joint use of the field was permissible so long as the two schools observed separate recess periods and the Whites and Coloreds played there at different times of the day. That was the assumption. Over time, folks lost track of the assumed consensus, since it was nowhere written down, and gradually, depending mainly on the perspective of the schoolmasters or schoolmistresses, and their respective levels of bigotry, the agreement, still theoretically strong and unchallenged, was, nonetheless, all but forgotten. By the time Gabe and Seth attended those schools, the children were, more often than otherwise, turned out for games and fresh air and noontime dinner (which lunch was commonly called, the evening meal being commonly called supper), at the same time of day. The children ate fast and played on the nutgrass field a good twenty minutes, White and Colored together.

Pa Gabriel's story revealed that Miss Rachel Newkirk, a red-haired beauty of nineteen years of age, engaged to be married to the young minister of the Piney Grove Methodist Church, and Miss Flora Caviness, an equally winsome young woman of mixed Colored and White ancestry, just eighteen and a half years of age, had taken things a step farther than that. Some said two or three steps and threatened to take their children out of school and teach them at home in the old way. But those who said so kept their complaints pretty much to themselves, because pretty Miss Rachel was Judge Davidson Newkirk's headstrong, independent daughter, reputed, indeed widely known, to be Judge Newkirk's favorite among four daughters, three sons, and two step-daughters, his beloved Mary having died in childbirth when God gave him Rachel Rosemary and took her.

Because the White children's schoolhouse was larger and had a couple of church pews at the back of the classroom providing extra seating for visitors to the school, on infrequent days when one or the other of the teachers, Miss Newkirk or Miss Caviness, was sick in bed, but only then, the Colored children were marched single file, in orderly fashion, from their smaller schoolhouse over to the White schoolhouse for their day's lessons. There, they sat on the Baptist church pews, the only time they were used except when parents, grandparents, and visitors and dignitaries attended on Examination Day, when the scholars held their annual Recitation. If it was Miss Caviness who was sick, Miss Newkirk fetched the Colored students and walked them over to her schoolhouse. If it was Miss Newkirk who felt poorly, Miss Caviness walked her pupils over to the White school and taught her nine there with Miss Rachel's thirteen.

As surprising as that all seemed from a historical perspective, in point of fact, for that day and time, McLean's Crossroads was a progressive community surpassing ordinary practice for the singular reason that it had a Colored school at all, Temperance thought. Both the Newkirk and the Caviness families had been instrumental in that unique development, something which had transpired when Miss Flora and Miss Rachel had not yet been born, Temperance had learned. Visionary forebears in both families had seen that the whole community would benefit from giving as many children as possible as much education as possible. It was as simple as that. As profound as that.

But Rachel and Flora, themselves visionary granddaughters of pioneering ancestors, now had brought the two schools together in unimagined ways. When they had first talked over the possibility (though vast improbability) of such a cooperative undertaking, Flora hesitated, skirting, avoiding, the tough issue at stake,

"It might be too much for you to have all those rowdy children at one time, Rachel," she worried, objecting in cautious words to what her heart also coveted.

The children were, in fact, very well-behaved. Skipper Boykin being the one exception, but he had a puzzling and unfortunate condition which made him blurt out anything and everything, without any degree of editing at all, which came into his head, with no discernible regard for relevancy to any subject under consideration.

"Oh, I don't mind!" Rachel had persisted, "I'm glad to do it. Thirteen's an unlucky number, anyhow," she joked, tongue-in-cheek. Superstition was not one of Miss Newkirk's frailties, and Miss Caviness knew it.

It had, in fact, been Rachel's idea, that was true. So far-fetched and dangerous, it could be, it might be, Flora would not have imagined putting Miss Rachel, or herself, or the children, in harm's way like that. Maybe only someone accustomed to safety and feeling safe would have, or could have, conceived it, despite its inherent and attractive validity. At that time in history. The proposal made Flora at once deeply uneasy and strangely hopeful, and even after she hesitantly agreed to it, her heart hammering with hope and anxiety and keeping her awake until well past midnight the day it was made, a shadow of dread clouded each day they dared act on it. Flora Caviness paid a substantial, personal price for their courageous venture, one which Rachel Newkirk was never charged. Every day the two schools met together under one roof, Flora looked anxiously out the window many times and slept fitfully that night. But by and large, the community looked the other way. Perhaps if it had happened every week, they wouldn't have, but Rachel and Flora were both strong and healthy, young women, and they missed their classes rarely.

Each teacher had a primary motivation to stay healthy and present to do her work. These children got no more than three good months of schooling a year. Fall harvesting lasted until nearly Thanksgiving and spring plowing began in March. The months intervening were all the rural community endorsed as an official school term. Miss Caviness and Miss Newkirk meant to do all they could in the short time they had.

The White children never went over to the Colored schoolhouse for lessons, and the Colored children sat in the back of the room whenever they went to the White school for instruction. Those observed requirements counted toward keeping the community from kicking up a fuss over how things were on Edmund K. Long's abandoned cotton field and in the schoolhouses bordering it, but the likeliest reason harmony prevailed was Miss Rachel's close relation to Judge Newkirk, indisputably the most respected and most powerful judge in the county. And among the Presbyterian faithful, Judge Newkirk was accounted the spiritual patriarch of the Cape Fear presbytery, despite his not being himself a member of the ordained clergy. Everyone knew Rachel Rosemary was the apple of his eye. What she did was pretty much all right with her father. Not many people wanted to touch that. Not even the Klan.

Pa Gabriel's story fascinated and claimed Temperance. She could not let it go. He had started it, but she kept the battery charged. She had immediately identified with both the young teachers, especially with fiery Miss Newkirk. Hurrying home from school to hear the next installment of her grandfather's narrative, she looked him up, following him to West End Grocery and traipsing around behind him as he stocked shelves and filled the drink box with ice. Mr. Holloway didn't mind, maybe because she pitched in and helped her grandfather as they talked. Besides, Mr Holloway enjoyed hearing them talk, so long as it didn't get in the way of Gabriel's waiting on customers, and it seldom did.

Miss Rachel and Miss Flora inspired and excited her. Their derring-do and their intention to teach their students without obstruction from narrowmindedness and bigotry claimed her heart. Flesh-and-blood role models they had become, who had acted to change their community in a way which made a difference. Perhaps teaching would be her profession, too, she was thinking. Already considering it since first she discovered how much she loved writing on blackboards, especially clean, just-washed ones, Temper found these outstanding women to be persuasive influences on her to make that commitment, and for better reasons than the fun of writing on blackboards.

Rachel Newkirk had been ahead of her time. What she effactually created with Flora Caviness, whose own creativity was a happy match for Rachel's, was a proto-team teaching program and course of study. The two of them together, though never in the same classroom, nonetheless planned their lessons cooperatively, and not just for those occasional days when one or the other was out sick. Both schools studied fractions at the same time and both attacked phonics by the same method. Both read *The Adventures of Tom Sawyer* during the same weeks in February and March, and both classes celebrated President Washington's and President Lincoln's birthdays with cherry pies baked by Miss Flora and Miss Rachel in Miss Rachel's kitchen and sliced and eaten outdoors communally and festively. Red cherry stains went home on White and Colored children's homespun bodices and shirtfronts after those annual, gleeful observances.

Whenever the two schools convened lessons jointly, Miss Caviness or Miss Newkirk, whichever one was teaching that day, enjoyed calling the children to the front of the room, from whence they then lined up along the two sides of the room for spelling bees.

And now and then, history and geography bees. Too good at what they did and who they were to pit White and Colored children against one another adversarily, they mixed them alphabetically, instead. In one group, the Red Birds, they lined up all the children whose first names started with A-J, (first, rather than last names, because Miss Rachel and Miss Flora didn't want kin folk all on the same team), and all whose given names began with K-Z, they lined up on the other side of the room in the other group, the Blue Birds. That arrangement worked out well. Nothing about its happy outcome materialized without effort, however. Flora and Rachel had meticulously calculated every possibly relevant detail, even breaking their own rules by using second names instead of first ones for Olivia and Lonny, in order to allot equal numbers of children to both teams. Aaron, Arthur, Beatrice, Billy Joe (it was pronounced as one name), Constance, David, Effie, Fanny, Gabriel, H. Y. (or Junior), and Katie, were the eleven Red Birds. Lonny, Mattie, Noah, Nathaniel, Olivia, Patsy Ann (also pronounced together), Seth, Sarah, Thomas Earl (one name), Van, and Zellie, were the opposing eleven Blue Birds.

The one thing noticeably unfair about the composition of the teams was the irresolvable fact that the youngest children, and particularly those who still had most of their milk teeth, were outmatched by the older ones, several of whom were beginning to sprout armpit hair. But that inequity was a given, and everybody pretty much accepted it. Even the littlest and most disadvantaged ones preferred inclusion and being outmatched to sitting and listening and being left out of contention. Especially in light of the guarantee that all losing contestants were extended a consolation prize of one peppermint stick (Miss Newkirk regularly ordered a fresh batch at McLean's Grocery and Mercantile) when they fell out of contention. Most of these children got peppermint sticks only at Christmas. "Bee" prizes were their one other chance for peppermint year-round. The lucky winner got two. And they were permitted to eat it right then. That meant those who lost first ate first. Less academically capable children figured that one out right away.

Now and then, a particularly ambitious and competitive, younger child shed a tear over life's unfairness, but for the most part, everybody got excited over "bee-time." Spelling expertise soared above the ordinary and mundane, and the competition generated energy and resolve, setting academic hearts to beating fast and the hearts of the ill-prepared faster. And saliva to flowing. The standard bearer of the little children was Zellie Margaret Matthews who, though not yet past her eighth birthday, typically beat out most of the nine-, ten-, and eleven-year-olds. That kept the little children hopeful.

Miss Flora began.

"Lonny, spell 'gratitude'. Here is a sentence: 'We should feel and express gratitude whenever someone has helped us.' Gratitude."

"G-r-a-t-i-t-u-d-e," Lonny spelled loudly and proudly.

"Very good. Beatrice, spell 'compassion.' Here is a sentence: 'Words and deeds of compassion are hallmarks of noble character.' Compassion."

"C-o-m-p-a-s-s-i-o-n."

"Excellent, Beatrice. Patsy Ann, 'perseverance,' please."

Without waiting for a sentence containing the spelling word, Patsy Ann jumped in, "P-e-r-s-e-v-e-r-a-n-s-e."

"I'm sorry, Patsy Ann, incorrect. Persevere, dear, and you'll remember that final 'c'."

Miss Caviness's weak joke and attempt to encourage didn't help a lot, at least, not immediately. With a long face, Patsy Ann took her peppermint stick and her seat, unhappy but salivating, and determined to get it right the next time. The word itself exerted power and influence, Miss Caviness knew, with a child like Patsy Ann Franklin.

"David (one of the little ones with all his milk teeth), spell 'true'. Here is a sentence: 'I trust that what you say is reliably true.'"

"T-r-u-e."

"Very good, David. Zellie Margaret, 'courageous,' please."

Brimming with courage, Zellie lit out, "C-o-u-r-a-g-e-o-u-s!"

The little ones cheered. They knew she had it right. They had faith in her. Miss Flora smiled and excused the outburst, "Superb,

Zellie. H. Y., spell 'fortitude,' please. Here's a sentence with it: 'A person with fortitude overcomes disappointment and unfair treatment.'"

H. Y. needed this one, she reasoned, the word and its virtue and concept.

"F-o-r-t-i-t-u-d-e."

"Excellent, H. Y., well done. Billy, spell 'sacrificial,' please."

"S-a-c-r-i-f-i-c-i-a-l."

"Seth, 'magnanimous,' please. Here's a sentence: 'The magnanimous person cultivates a spirit of generosity toward all others.' By the way, do you agree with that assertion?"

"Yes, Ma'am," Seth responded, "Magnanimous, m-a-g-n-a-n-i-m-o-u-s."

"Well done," Miss Caviness smiled.

Like Billy Pridgen and Zellie Margaret Matthews, Seth Laughinghouse rarely missed a word in these spelling bees. Oftentimes, the three of them stood victorious in a three-way tie at the end of the match. When that occurred, everyone felt vindicated and enjoyed a measure of triumph and reward, owing to the fact that both sides, Blue Birds and Red Birds, had garnered a win, and Zellie, the little ones' champion, had not let them down.

It was no secret that Miss Caviness and Miss Newkirk selected words for the spelling bee like "gratitude, magnanimous, and compassion" with character formation in mind. Lots of ordinary words made it onto the spelling lessons and assignments, but the bees were heavily salted with words related to character building. Miss Rachel and Miss Flora gave careful thought to the sentences they composed, as well, and sprinkled their reading and history lessons, too, with injunctions like, "Don't work to make great sums of money for just a few people, not even your family." What notable person of wisdom and largesse had said that? No matter, it needed to be heard. And this: "Enough is as good as a feast."

A values distinction they especially strove to impress upon their young charges was the difference between "nice" and "good." Some nice people were also good people; a great many were. Some good people were not always nice. For example, some with nobility would fart and kick at it, Rachel's Uncle Ernest liked to say, (he was one of them, most agreed), but Miss Rachel found another way to express the useful concept. The nice ones who were not good were the hardest to spot. They were the ones Miss Caviness and Miss Newkirk intended to make their pupils aware of, if they could. Ku Klux Klan members supplied them copious examples, but only theoretically, since names were not generally known. What *was* known was that Sunday morning church pews were occupied by Saturday night cross-burners. Judge Davidson Newkirk's fearless daughter and her courageous colleague and friend made the children of McLean's Crossroads knowledgeable about the moral contradiction inherent in that fact.

Believers in Christ themselves, they deplored the hatred embodied in cross-burning and the blasphemous practice of using Christianity's holiest symbol for hate and murder. Making known the difference between nice and good was an important part of the Newkirk-Caviness curriculum.

A favorite contribution to Miss Rachel's lesson plans, included also in Miss Flora's, was a nugget Miss Rachel had gleaned from her Grandmother Newkirk's storehouse of wisdom: "Mankind got into trouble when we started sewing pockets into our clothing." It was like Grandmother Newkirk to employ a sewing metaphor, natural for her to do that. There was in this fact a delicious, a superb, irony. A uniquely talented dressmaker, Grandmother Newkirk designed her own elegant frocks, exquisitely handworked and regal with short, elegant trains, and possessing one distinctively peculiar feature, withal. Most of her dresses had long pockets, more like long pouches, extending down both sides of the garment nearly from hip to hem. Grandmother Newkirk kept all her sewing accoutrements in those highly functional, unusual pockets: threads, buttons, needles, scissors (a small, lightweight pair), ric-rac trim, decorative laces carefully wrapped (two or three designs), a measuring tape, and a favorite, silver thimble her mother had given her when she made her first dress. With those implements of her art, she generally also squirreled in one corner of her left pocket a few dainties like gumdrops and a licorice stick or two, folded in a white napkin and separated from the sewing supplies. With dresses of her signature design, Grandmother Newkirk had no need to cover her beautiful handiwork with utilitarian, pocketed aprons, and her talent enabled her to disguise the pouch-pockets in the lovely folds of her long skirt. There was that touch of vanity in this gracious woman. No one who knew Grace Newkirk begrudged her that earthen attribute and its benign indulgence. Despite her family's ample wealth, material possessions held little allure; her values, personal and eternal, lay elsewhere than in ostentation and pretension. She wore no jewelry except her wedding band and an heirloom cameo bequeathed to her at her grandmother's death.

There was no contradiction in Grandmother Newkirk's perspective on pockets, that is, with the size of her own, and humanity's game-changing folly. Specifically, the relation between those. Wondrously talented and as sensible and generous as talented, Grace Newkirk embodied the meaning of her given name as fully as one could reasonably have expected of a saint, which she, indeed, was. She was celebrated far and wide for the pastel, "flowerdy" dresses and Scottish, brilliantly-plaid ones, with lace-edged collars and sleeves, or multi-colored ric-rac borders, which she sewed for the poor girl-children of McLean's Crossroads, White and Colored, two per child, twice a year, two summer dresses and two winter ones. Every summer and every winter, spring and autumn, too, for more years than anyone remembered, Grace Newkirk had worked steadily, designing and crafting spring and summer dresses in the cold, winter months and fall and winter dresses during the hot, sticky ones. (In the interest of fairness and charity for boy-children, too, she donated bolt cloth of high quality to poor families whose boys needed new shirts. However, a dressmaker herself, she left the sewing of those to others.) Because she couldn't hurt a child in any way, the well-off children of McLean's Crossroads (there weren't many) got one of her special frocks, as well. And her children's dresses did have pockets, pretty, decorative, patch pockets, on the bodice, rather than on the skirt, not too big. And, now and then, skirt pockets of modest size. She was no literalist and growing girls needed pocket space for handkerchiefs and occasional, cherished items, Grace Newkirk acknowledged.

McLean's Crossroads children learned other values in Miss Newkirk's and Miss Caviness's schools, Pa Gabriel related to Temperance. Values like forgiveness, fairmindedness, honesty, truth-telling, and mercy. Mostly, they learned by example from folks like their teachers, but in Miss Rachel's and Miss Flora's estimation, if it was worth learning, it was worth inclusion in the curriculum, and pointedly so, not just obliquely, as with the spelling bee words, the illustrative sentences, and the concepts the words and sentences symbolized.

"Today, we're going to talk about kindness. What it is and why it's important to be kind."

Something as central to human community as kindness could not be treated as coincidental or ancillary or left to chance, they believed. On days of values discussion and character formation, the entire day's work they carefully planned to rotate around reflection on, discussion of, and practice in, acts of kindness, or whatever the value of the day was. Rachel Newkirk and Flora Caviness bent over their lamplight together, usually at Rachel's small house, many an evening, working out how they would instill crucial life lessons in the minds and hearts of their young scholars. Far more valuable than random bits and pieces of information those formative values were, they knew. Their carefully planned efforts would pay dividends; they were convinced of it. Dividends of strong character.

Gabriel Lewis and Seth Laughinghouse would be signature products of their teachers' creative wisdom and effort. Their competitive friendship flourished on the schoolyard and in the schoolhouse. And prophetically so on Edmond K. Long's nutgrass play lot. Seth was as fast as greased lightning, and his long, sinewy legs, almost too long in proportion to his maturing body, could jump the proverbial ten-rail fence at a bound. Once, in a game of "Keep Away," he leapt straight over Rob Emory's head, not even mussing his hair, it looked like, those who saw it reported. Rob was about a foot shorter than Seth, but even so, for Seth to elevate that high, at least four and a half feet, or higher, with no extra speed and yardage to catapult him over, took everyone by surprise. They knew he could jump and they knew he could run, but not like that. Gabe was a better-than-good athlete himself, but on the field, in nearly every game, Seth was better.

One sub-freezing night in December, a fortnight after Seth's athletic vault over Rob Emory's head, Gabriel's pa, Horace Lewis, a well-meaning, hard-working man who farmed a few acres of tobacco and corn, and some years cotton, and who cut railroad crossties in the winter months, called Gabe into the kitchen for a serious talk before going off to bed. Gabriel knew something was awry, because Horace Lewis seldom had direct talks with his seven children, anything more than brief instructions and guidance. Instead, he passed his sparse communication to them through his wife, their mother, Lucy Ann. Like many other parents of that time, such was their custom. Women talked with children first. If the father needed to talk to them, it generally meant there was trouble in the camp, or at least, trouble had to be headed off, and that was a man's job, most times. Such was the case, now.

"You wanted to talk to me, Pa?"

Lucy Ann had prepared Gabe for the talk.

"Yeah," Horace mumbled, in a nearly inaudible tone ambiguously hesitant, or distracted.

Horace turned from the stove with a lit splinter at the bowl of his pipe and motioned Gabe to sit at the kitchen table. Positioning himself across the rectangular, pine table from his son, Horace smoothed the worn, checkered oilcloth with his free hand and fidgeted with his pipe with the other. At length, he spoke,

"Clarence Emory came by here today. He was a mite upset, Clarence was, had been for awhile, it seems, about sump'n that happened at the school lot. He says his boy Rob was shamed by a Colored boy there. That friend of yer'n, Gabe, the one that comes over here so often."

Horace's reference sounded strangely impersonal and peculiar to Gabriel. His father knew well that Seth was Abraham Laughinghouse's son and they lived right across the road from them. And had for a long time, longer than Gabe knew.

"Seth—is that his name?"

The question surprised Gabriel further. Seth had been coming over there since he could walk across the road. But, what shaming? For a moment, he had difficulty remembering what might have constituted a "shaming." It was true that Rob had blushed fire red and wilted visibly when Seth jumped clear over him, and did the same every time someone mentioned the incident at school. Sensitive to Rob's discomfort, Gabe had felt some of his embarrassment. Rob had been thrust into the spotlight along with Seth, but he had been made to seem small and weak, to himself and perhaps to others, while Seth's prowess and agility cast him as strong and dominant. Gabe could understand how the unfavorable attention might have deflated him. Especially in light of the fact that Seth had become for a few days a play lot hero at Rob's expense, though Seth himself had never intended it to be that way.

Still, the whole incident had happened two weeks ago, and both schools had moved on. At least Gabe had, and as far as he could tell, everyone else had, too, including Seth and Rob. Though Rob hung back a little on the play lot, that had generally been pretty much his way, anyhow. He was a quieter boy and noticeably smaller than most of the others. If he had been harmed or changed at all by the incident with Seth, others around him had not been aware of it, though Gabriel, in time, would grow to wonder if he should have been.

When his father had called him into the kitchen, Gabe hadn't realized how bad things had gotten. He was, until then, unaware that Rob Emory's father had even heard about the incident, and he was taken aback to learn that it mattered so much. It seemed too much, in Gabe's view, to call what had happened a "shaming." To his way of understanding, a "shaming" was a deliberate act, at times coldly calculated, at other times, hot and off the cuff, but deliberate and malicious, either way. Nothing like that had happened on the nutgrass lot. Seth had been carrying the ball, and Rob had attempted to block him. Not even Seth knew he was going to launch himself clear over the top of Rob's head, Gabe was sure. It had been a spontaneous, reflexive act, with no element of malice in it. The surprise in Gabe's eyes met Horace's worried look.

"I don't see what happened as a shaming, Pa, if you mean Seth jumpin' over Rob's head."

Gabe offered his witness with a nervous smile twitching at the corners of his wide mouth, his smile an unconscious plea for understanding of boyish rambunction. Then, Gabe told his father the story his way. The right way, he figured. Though he was just over twelve years old, it mattered to him that things be told in a way that was fair to all concerned. But Horace's mind was made up, and he had little patience for his son's nuanced analysis. In a turn-of-the-century climate of Reconstruction, rife with suspicion, hostility, and insecurity broadly, Horace Lewis's ears were unreceptive to Gabriel's forward-thinking perspective.

"I cain't have that Colored boy makin' trouble for us with our neighbors, Gabe!" Horace interrupted, heat rising at the edge of his homespun collar, not at this intelligent son of whom he was mightily proud, but at the whole hornets' nest of problems he foresaw on account of this mess.

"It ain't right for a Colored boy to outdo a White boy, you know that," Horace blurted, more loudly than he intended.

His father's words shocked Gabe with their elemental injustice. By what decree?! Not God's, surely! Gabriel was, in early adolescence, a better theologian than many thinkers older than he. But Horace seemed oblivious to the absurdity of his moralism and its inherent bigotry.

"We all need to stay in our rightful place. What he did was gittin' out'a his place, an' that kind'a behavior makes trouble for a lot'a steady folks like us," he alleged, in a flustered tone betraying his consternation and what Gabe wanted to believe was some degree of doubt about the justice of what he had said.

Gabriel's heart slid into his stomach. He saw now why he had been summoned to this kitchen table talk. Horace was still talking, puffing energetically on his pipe, and he was saying,

"Clarence Emory has standin' in this community, Gabriel, bein' a county commissioner an' all, an' we cain't let any uppity Coloreds give him call to fall out with us."

A sick knot cramped Gabe's intestines, making him afraid he'd have to head for the outhouse before his father dismissed him; it was a feeling of deep dread, more for Seth than for himself, but for himself, as well, and by extension, for their whole community.

Horace tugged at the ragged corner of the faded oilcloth, as though getting it straight would straighten out this calamity, too.

"I'm stoppin' you from bringin' 'im over here anymore, Gabriel. I want you to start bringin' White boys like yerself over here more than you do. I've allowed it 'til now 'cause you boys were little younguns, too little to know any differ'nt, but now yer full growed, taller than yer ma. It's time to make friends with yer own kind."

"Yes, Sir," Gabe heard himself intone. The sound seemed to him far off, like someone on the other side of the house was talking and using his voice. He knew full well not to contradict his father. At this point in their talk, any further comment from him would be accounted disobedience. It wouldn't be countenanced. In the Lewis household, as in those of other families they knew, children didn't sass or contradict their elders. They accepted their parents' instruction without protest or comment of any kind.

Besides, already, Gabe had internalized and committed to memory his father's words, what he had said and what he had not said. He knew his father was more complex than his simple words and superficially unambiguous decisions tended to indicate. What he had not said was as important as what he had said, Gabriel knew. Horace Lewis had not told his son that he was forbidden to associate with Seth at all. He had not said that he couldn't play with him at school, or across the road at Seth's house, or anywhere else, except at their home. He hadn't told Gabe he was forbidden to plan fishing excursions to the Cape Fear. Gabriel knew he could infer that they were still allowed, as long as they began and ended elsewhere than the Lewis homestead. Or at least they were not noticed and prohibited. Most important, his father had not ordered him to terminate his friendship with Seth Laughinghouse. That meant something, and

Gabe would find a way to continue it. To strengthen it. Did his father know that? Did it matter?

In the weeks following, Gabe spent more time than before with Seth at school, on the play lot. The two were inseparable whenever joint school events were scheduled. And he observed the letter of his father's law, if not its spirit entirely, and invited H. Y. Ash and Billy Pridgen to his house, something he had done only once or twice before, and by and large, they had a pretty good time. By nature fair-minded, Gabe had in the past called sometimes another boy's name first, when sides were chosen up, Billy's or H. Y.'s, or occasionally Aaron's, rather than Seth's. Now, he called Seth's name first without fail. Years later, Temperance learned that her grandfather was then developing what liberation theologians would call the concept of God's "preferential option for the poor." Gabe Lewis knew and practiced its meaning decades before Christian theologians honed the concept and gave it its descriptive slogan. He had lived into it.

More and more afternoons and Saturdays, as soon as the weather was warm enough, Gabe and Seth launched a fishing trip over at Seth's house and lit out for the Cape Fear River, little more than a mile away, due south toward Elizabethtown which had been founded on the major river's highest bank in 1773, before the country got its liberty. Barges with stores of flour, coffee, sugar, nails, and other precious necessities, made their way up the river from Wilmington and docked at the town's eastern slip. On occasion, the boys watched as men unloaded the staples from the barges onto mule carts and the barges set their courses again downstream for the port city, which Seth and Gabe dreamed someday of seeing. Whole afternoons were spent imagining outloud that quickening scenario. They imagined stowing away on one of the returning barges, city-bound inside the empty barrels headed coastward for more goods. Like Tom and Huck, their alter egos, Gabe and Seth were drawn to the river, the Cape Fear being as mighty to them as the Mississippi was to Huck and Tom. Besides, their river, the Cape Fear, had a better name, more foreboding and suggestive of danger and adventure ahead, they thought, and made much of it. And hadn't Blackbeard captured and ransacked vessels off the Carolina coast? Cape Fear and Blackbeard went together, they concluded, and the hair bristled on their ears and at their necks when they spoke it aloud. Heck, that was probably how the river got its name, they allowed. Those ideas made their way into their recitations on Twain's novels. The other boys agreed with them outright. And their teachers applauded their fruitful imagination.

It would be their last year of school together. And their last year of boyhood freedom. In April, Horace Lewis came down with severe kidney colic and spent the summer trying to piss stones too big to pass, bleeding his tea-colored water daily into a wide-mouthed, canning jar, hoping to see a gray, jagged rock through the bloody, foul-smelling discharge. From then on, Gabe, first son, second offspring in his family, was needed at home for heavy plowing and field work Horace was no longer physically able to do. Before Stedman, the son-in-law he would someday have, Gabriel experienced the same loss. His formal schooling had ended for the same reasons. Most of his boyhood was over, as well, although he and Seth managed to get away to the Cape Fear for fishing, now and then, and to watch the barges unload and load again at Elizabethtown. Their fantasy of stowing away to Wilmington subsided, however, as hard work and premature family obligations pressed them into a world drained of thoughts of Blackbeard and a Cape named Fear.

Seth, also, was needed at home, too big to send to school any longer, no matter how smart he was at book learning. With a head for numbers like Gabe's, already on broad shoulders, though thin, and a long-legged stride capable of any work he might be assigned requiring strength, stamina, and speed, Seth would be hired out to White folks who needed another hand for farm labor, a "plow boy," or for blacksmith's work, the latter a skill which Abraham Laughinghouse had taken care to teach his son, meaning to give his boy a useful trade for feeding himself and a family. Abraham, like Horace Lewis and many other men, though still healthy and strong himself, needed his son to pitch in to help feed the ten hungry mouths in the Laughinghouse family. It broke Abraham's heart to remove his boy from his opportunity to educate himself, and to hire him out as a day laborer instead, but he felt there was little else he could do, times being hard as they were, and he hoped the blacksmith training was sufficient education to get him through what he knew would be a tough life for his son, as it had been for him.

So, the school time at Miss Newkirk's and Miss Caviness's schools ended. The friendship did not. Their memories would subsist and, when they could no longer be together, those thoughts would be the recollections of boy-men, following a mule and plow and traveling above the dust and heat to a transcendent plane of fun and laughter, a realm above time and space, where they could be carefree schoolboys again, with only mischief and frivolity on their minds. But Seth decided, with Abraham's reluctant permission, to try his luck up North, two years later. The summer he turned fifteen, Seth rode a train to Detroit with his Uncle Rafe, Essie's younger brother, the flashy one, who had persuaded and promised he would help Seth find a good-paying job in the big city.

"A strappin' boy like you can make a good livin' up there, Seth. Jobs are easy to find. You'll make it big, I know you will!"

To Rafe, everything was big, and he knew it to be so.

Abraham Laughinghouse hoped Rafe wasn't just blowin' hot air. He was known to do a lot of that. In any event, Abraham couldn't, and wouldn't, deny Seth's chance at a better life. And he and Essie wouldn't be losing his help; whatever good fortune he found he would share with his family. Abraham knew that, too.

Gabriel heard many years after that, that Seth had, by then, landed a good-paying job at the Ford automobile plant and was making enough money to send regular help to Abraham and Essie. Abraham had figured that right.

Before Seth headed off to his future up North, he and Gabe had made an implied promise, if no more than that, vowing they would remain close, best friends, despite the distance in miles separating them. How they would do that neither attempted to say. Gabe would come to wish that they had.

Gabe's kitchen talk with his father, that signal night after Clarence Emory's visit, had set in motion a train of thought he would ride, off and on, for years. For the rest of his life, in point of fact. Again and again, Gabriel replayed the verbatim, something he was a natural at, just as spelling a new word seldom required more than a steady looking at for him to know it. After that, it was pretty much implanted in his mind. The same held true for dialogue. He just had no trouble remembering exactly how it went. Once he'd heard it, it was there.

His father had said, "It ain't right for a Colored boy to outdo a White boy, you know that." He didn't. He didn't know that. In fact, he saw nothing wrong with it. Seth Laughinghouse had outdone him a lot of times. There was nothing wrong with that. Gabe felt ashamed and angry that his father had let Clarence Emory dictate his view and attitude. But it went deeper than that. What agitated Gabriel most was the certain realization that the views his father expressed were not just a lazy agreement with Clarence Emory and a political expediency, bad enough. They were Horace's views, too, he sensed, and those of most of the neighbors living around them.

His father had said, "We all need to stay in our rightful place."

Gabriel could not accept that a "rightful place" had already been assigned to anyone, whether divinely or humanly, eternally or temporally, no matter what his racial heritage and identity were. Later, Gabriel's conviction would expand to distinctions (a euphemism, he knew, for exclusions) made according to social and economic class. Still later, exclusions made according to gender. And about the same time as that movement into a larger moral awareness, exclusions made according to sexual orientation. By then, sometime in Gabriel Lewis's thirties or forties, he had seen what too few see at all. Exclusion is hate. Discrimination is hate. He would be adamant on that point.

First and most, while still in his adolescence, Gabriel rejected the virulent pseudo-theorem and rank ignorance of White supremacy, the preposterous claim that White was inherently superior to

Colored. He had seen sufficient evidence to the contrary. Seth had shown it convincingly, day after day, one way. Rob Emory had displayed it just as often, another. Not to mention a long list of others who had shown their own evidence, some one way, some the other. Rob's sniveling, tattle-tale habits had marked, and disfigured, his personality, Gabe recognized, since the first year they had started to school, or as long as he had known him. Right off the bat, Rob had set out to ingratiate himself with his teacher, hoping to be the teacher's pet. Every child in the room saw it. At that time, the schoolmaster was Master Curtis Nelson, who tended to bend to the perceived wishes of those who held observable status in the McLean's Crossroads community, those like Clarence Emory, and Rob made some headway with him. But when Rachel Newkirk took Curtis Nelson's position, she was impervious to Rob's fawning manipulations.

Gabe could have stomached Rob's ambition, if it hadn't been for how he went about it. It was his ways that stunk like a dead polecat. Rob looked for opportunities to tell on his classmates for any and all rules infractions, however piddling. Worst of all, unable to make impressive grades himself, both untalented and too lazy, willing victim of an enervating, double jeopardy, Rob jiggled the desk of Beatrice Autry, his deskmate, whenever writing assignments were given, making poor Beatrice's life miserable. Good penmanship mattered a lot to her, and Rob's mean-spirited action made it impossible for her to write neatly. Only a suck-egg dog would do that to someone like Beatrice Autry, Gabriel fumed. Meek and quiet, but generous and helpful to everyone, Beatrice deserved better, he knew. Rob's abuse of her had not escaped Gabe's discerning notice; he'd seen the daily pattern and, on occasion, the tears on Beatrice's cheeks. Her wooden desktop was attached to Rob's seat, and without fail, Rob set it to rocking whenever she had writing to do. He did it to get back at her for being a qualified teacher's favorite. The "genuwine" thing.

If Gabe could've gotten away with it, he'd've kicked Rob Emory's butt. What he did do was to report Rob to Miss Newkirk. Beatrice was too timid to speak up for herself, but he spoke up for her; he wasn't bashful. It set his teeth on edge ("It makes me mad enough to chew wire nails!") to see anybody treated the way Rob treated her. But Rob didn't act that way anymore after Gabe reported him. Miss Newkirk moved him away from Beatrice and whacked his open palm with four or five, smart licks of her wooden ruler. Gabe saw the red, ruler imprints after she finished and thought the punishment justified, though puny, but the main thing was getting him away from Beatrice's desk, and Miss Rachel had done that. Furthermore, nobody's desk was attached to Rob's anymore. Justice was served. Hell is separation from God and the godly, Preacher Goodfriend had preached. Gabe thought he knew what that meant.

If hair and skin color had anything on God's green earth to do with character, White people were shit out of luck, Gabe reasoned. Rob Emory's skin was corpse white. His eyes were watered-down blue. His hair was faded-out orange (why did they call it red?). And his teeth were dingy yellow. Rob was in no wise superior to autumn-golden, black-eyed Seth Laughinghouse. Gabe knew it. All his senses and rational faculties told him so. And his informed experience confirmed it.

Reminiscing from a vantage point of a lifetime of memories and experiences of her own, Temperance was proud of her grandfather's loyalty to his boyhood friend. More than that, Pa Gabriel's keen passion for fairness and social justice had shaped her own moral development. Her years of college had bequeathed to her language like "social justice" to name his values. On both sides of her family, Temperance was molded by strong, male role models. Pa Gabriel on her mother's side. Stedman himself, her father, on his side. What Gabriel had done a generation earlier by standing up for Seth Laughinghouse and Beatrice Autry, Stedman had done for the textile workers who trusted his good sense and good will. Both men had engaged in a kind of promise-making and promise-keeping not typically evident to most others around them, but vividly so to Temperance. In and over time.

Pa Gabriel had not finished with Seth's story. He had more to tell his granddaughter, and she was eager to hear it. Seth, he told her, had owned, nay, he himself had embodied and irradiated, one, prodigious talent he had to be careful not to brandish. It was not his considerable, athletic prowess. Rather, this talent had greater power to bring him down, to stir up the jealous rancor of the White community against him, than anything he did on the nutgrass play lot. Since he was ten, Seth had made some White folks, the White supremacist ones, nervous and uncomfortable with his poetry. Miss Newkirk and Miss Caviness had featured him and his poems at funerals and weddings, at the annual county fair, and once, when the governor made a brief stop in Elizabethtown to campaign for local politicians of his party, at that austere event. Seth could compose poetry suitable for any occasion. Easy as taking a drink of water, it seemed to those around him. Especially for weddings. His love poetry could charm the angels in glory with its lyricism and beauty, folks allowed, the ones who appreciated a gift like that, no matter to whom it was given by the Giver.

Other boys began asking Seth to compose love poems for them to give to their sweethearts, or to the young ladies they hoped to win with his pretty rhymes. At first, Seth accommodated their requests free of charge. Gradually, he realized he could earn a few pennies by selling his compositions to eager suitors. By the time he rode to Detroit with Rafe, he had built a small business for himself selling his love poetry for a few cents a poem.

———

Temperance reprised aspects of her grandfather's story, seeing in them hints of things to come, of events which had come later. She wrote:

Within two miles of McLean's Crossroads, the Cape Fear River is banded by a half dozen sandy beaches, each about the size of a small, elongated room, surprising and inviting in their gleaming smoothness, sprinkled down the southern bank of the river. All of those pristine strips except one can be readily seen and approached from either the woods or the river itself, but a singular, thin beach cannot be observed from the river until one is directly at its perimeter, owing to four, magnificent cypress trees, ancient and thick as redwoods, standing in zigzag formation, a leafy, wooden curtain in the water's edge. As if hiding behind those trees, the sliver of beach, a mere ten feet wide or less, drops back on its south side to a natural, tunnel-like, but shallow, cavern concealed by the overhanging bank, on the one hand, and the mammoth, cypress partition, on the other. The dense, woodsland acres fringing this beach and the Cape Fear itself, have belonged for several decades to a commercial paper company which periodically harvests the pine trees for its product and protects its interests with a formidable, chainlink, border fence and iron gate denying fishermen, boaters, and other trespassers, access to the river through their property. Hence, the beach cannot be approached easily now either from the woods or the river.

But when Gabe and Seth were boys, they could follow a mile-long, winding, turpentine trail through the woodsland acres, not yet the paper company's, directly to the beach. More often than not, and in warm weather always, they chose to wade along the river's edge from the beach nearest to it, a mere hundred feet upstream on its west side. They had named the tight, shallow cavern their "fishing cave" and kept their fishing line and hooks and other, assorted paraphernalia stored inside it. Squeezing and squirming their way into it, a warm alcove of tangled tree roots and pungent river dirt just big enough to hold them both, they could huddle unobserved, dry and warm, on blustery and rainy days. Because it was surprisingly dry, though on the river's edge, the boys had had little trouble keeping water moccasins and turtles out of it. While Gabe and Seth dreamed of a cave like Tom Sawyer's and Huck Finn's where those exemplars had organized Tom Sawyer's Gang, a cavern opening far back inside the earth into numerous, mysterious passages and rooms, the Cape Fear afforded no deep caverns of the nature of those along the Mississippi, as far as they had any knowledge of; hence, they had accepted that reality and were tolerably glad to make do with their cozy, cramped hideaway. They had repaired to it as often, that last spring and summer, as they could find excuses plausible enough to have them accepted.

Their sublimest hours had been spent there, in the fishing cave and on the narrow, alabaster beach, and they had pledged to keep it their secret refuge forever. In the manner of Huck and Tom, Seth and Gabe had vowed eternal allegiance to each other and their special retreat. They intended an unbroken pact. For them, a promise made guaranteed a promise kept.

———————

One of the first things Gabe did after he went to stay with Mae and her family was to explore the Neuse River running less than two hundred yards below the Lenoirville mill village's southern boundary. Intuitively, he searched its banks for a retreat like the beach cave he and Seth had claimed. No gleaming, sandy beaches rimmed the Neuse like those unique few dotting the Cape Fear, however. He was now in a different, geological area of the Atlantic's coastal plain, and the white sand lay south, closer to the South Carolina border. He did discover, though, a concealed nook very like his and Seth's fishing cave and enough bigger than it to accommodate his larger, adult size, should he have reason to crawl inside, something he hardly expected to need or want. Although its proximity to the river afforded no gleaming shore upon which to sun himself, or to search for minnows or yellow-bellied turtles like the ones he and Seth had hunted and found, as the patch of white beach on the Cape Fear had done, it offered an alternative equally as pleasant in its own way, and more suitable to his mature years and changed interests. This was an expansive, wooded shelf above the cave opening, supported and buttressed by a woven sieve of pine, poplar, and dogwood roots, and blanketed with a thick bed of pine needles and soft moss upon which to sit or recline. Conveniently bounded by a small grove of pink and white dogwood trees interspersed with pines and one, sturdy tulip poplar positioned nearly ideally for leaning against, whenever he fished or napped or carved or read, the shelf could have been created and customized for him, Gabriel thought, so well-suited it was to him and his needs. Or to Seth's and his, if they had been able to enjoy their friendship into their "old fogey" years. He sometimes dreamed of their propping against opposite sides of the tree at conversationally amenable angles from each other and talking and fishing, reminiscing about the Cape Fear, and growing old together.

Gabriel spent some part of nearly every morning beside the Neuse before going to work at West End Grocery at two o'clock. After his three hours at the store and Mae's hearty supper, he often returned to the river shelf to wet a hook, or read another few chapters of a novel or a book of poetry, or simply to absorb a quiet, twilight communion wih the Neuse and the life in and around it. Mae and Stedman encouraged his going there. They knew it was good for him. He was not over Hannah's death. Loneliness was his great antagonist now. It was a curious thing to those who had not experienced it, but the river's solitude helped keep the deep loneliness away. It was all about love.

Several times a week, Temperance joined her grandfather at the river to hear his stories of Seth and his boyhood. On a number of those occasions, she got him to talking about his love of rivers. Or did she? His grandmother had teased him when they crossed the Cape Fear on the Elway ferry, "Look at the river, Gabe. It may be a sin to cross a river without looking at it." He had understood her meaning perfectly then and now.

"Rivers remind me of the good times Seth and I had on the Cape Fear. But it's more than that," he mused thoughtfully, "the flow of the current makes me peaceful." From a man who knew about peace. Also about conflict, and about peace in the midst of conflict.

"And grateful."

Her grandfather had paused and studied awhile, and Temperance had wondered if that was all, but hearing his assertion of gratitude, she was confident there would be more.

"God made that river, Temp'rance, just like He made us, you and me, and it's always goin' in the direction He set it movin' in.

There's a meanin' there for us," he declaimed, not in the manner of one who thinks he knows what it is, but in the manner of one who hopes to discover it, or be granted it.

Temper nodded quietly. And waited.

"It's beautiful."

He said it reverently, so quietly she scarcely heard it. Her grandfather was talking as much to himself as to her. That was often when she learned the most from him.

"That's enough, Temp'rance. Keats was right. Or was it Shelley? 'A thing of beauty is a joy forever.'" And then, "'Beauty is its own reason for being.' One of 'em said it. Maybe Byron," he laughed, poking fun at his literary amnesia.

Gabriel was just getting started, now. Temperance registered the signs. He had shifted his position against the tulip poplar and absently rearranged his books beside him. He predictably touched his books when he was winding up, gathering steam. Or, he reached for the peachseed monkey he was carving that day.

Gabriel resumed, "But I don't have to have a river to sit beside and look at, much as I love them, there's no doubt about that," he smiled nostalgically, the Cape Fear filling his mind's eye again. "Every patch of sky, especially with a tree in it, whether leafed out or winter bare, is a scene of beauty to me."

Temper had seen the greeting card quotation, clipped and stuck in the crack between the glass and the wood of the wardrobe mirror, not a vapid, commercial nostrum, but John Ruskin's simple acclamation, "Nature is painting for us, day after day, pictures of infinite beauty." The poet's words were Gabriel's.

Pa Gabriel's deep appreciation of nature's beauty, "infinite beauty," had taproots in his unconventional, but rock-solid faith. A homily was forming. Temper was again a receptive congregation of one. Perhaps Gabriel had taken to sermonizing in his latter years, in part because he had stopped listening to others' sermons. He seldom went to services anymore, preferring instead to listen to the cadenced march of the wind sweeping the tall pines down the river's edge. He could follow the wise sound a full quarter of a mile when the wind was strong; almost prophetic, it sounded to him, when he listened intently and reverently. On those occasional Sundays when he did go to church, he invariably sifted as much chaff as wheat from what he heard, he felt. It tired him. It disappointed him. The Christian Gospel was mind-boggling in its power to transform, he well knew, but he rarely heard anything like a transformative proclamation of truth. It had ever been that way. And beauty was hardly mentioned at all. He could hold forth on that topic, if anyone would stand still to listen.

"The river is beautiful," Pa said again, "but I don't have to see the river to see more beauty than I can ever be thankful enough for, Temp'rance, so, when I'm too feeble to make it down here to the riverside, jus' find me a spot beneath a window and set me a book an' a cup o' coffee on the windowsill, maybe a peach kernel or two," Gabe chuckled, recognizing he'd pontificated, but he wasn't finished yet. "Any window will do."

Pa reached out, soliciting the patience he knew she'd already granted, and patted Temper's shoulder affectionately. Knowing he had her forebearance and her unfeigned eagerness to hear what he had to say, he thought of Charlie:

"Temper, beauty is available to ev'rybody who has a window to look out of; Uncle Charlie doesn't have a house by the river or the sea or on the lake, but he doesn't have to see those to enjoy immense beauty."

The relevance of his statement had to do with Charlie's poverty-burdened circumstances. They were poor; he was poorer.

"As long as I can still see (both his and Charlie's eyes were still good,), I can count on that sky. It'll be up there ev'ry day, blue and clear, or storm cloud gray, either will do, and that pine tree, it'll be green all year."

Temperance thought of Mae's passionate love of trees and sky and windows. She'd gotten it honest. Like father, like daughter.

"The richest and smartest people on the planet, workin' all together, couldn't give me one patch of sky and trees one day of my life," Gabe concluded, with a staccato burst of laughter. The sound startled a brilliant cardinal and his mate pecking nearby; the naturally retiring birds flitted, retreated.

Pa Gabriel had waxed spiritual, Temperance reflected. She had expected it. It was his customary way. When not waxing, he did not wane. His hungry, grateful eyes conducted a reverent search for beauty, habitually.

Many years after that time, Temperance read something which fit Gabriel Lewis to a tee. The quotation was, "We see the world not as it is, but as we are." Of all the people she had known whom that fit, and it fit them all, she recognized the singular fit on her grandfather and experienced it as a uniquely spiritual lesson in itself. Seeing the world, he changed it, making it like the person he was, though he would have been surprised to hear anyone say that and to know that anyone thought it. He didn't merely occupy his place in the world; he shaped and formed it. Whether he knew it or not.

———ⱳⱳⱪⱪ◦◦ⱪ◦◦ⱳⱳ———

About a week after Pa Gabriel located his bower by the Neuse, an elderly Colored woman, bent nearly double with years and burdens, accompanied to the river by her great-granddaughter for what might reasonably have been a final fishing trip, encountered Gabriel there. They talked amiably for a spell, about the weather, the fishing, each hooking a red species of earthworms onto the lines of their cane fishing poles, and, out of the blue, she said to him, with a new, mournful note in her quavery, aged voice,

"There was a time when the river was full o' Colored boys' bodies."

He couldn't get it out of his mind.

———ⱳⱳⱪⱪ◦◦ⱪ◦◦ⱳⱳ———

"Jeff, I think I'm ready to write about Gabe again. Gabe Laughinghouse. It's time. This is where he enters the story," Temperance said.

"You've written enough of your story?—the early years which remind you who you are? Who you were—before Gabe—and before the events you're sorting out," Jeff said, both as question and confirmation. Not waiting for her response, he agreed, "All right. Let's see how you do with it. What you learn from it. I expect that you'll discover some things you haven't before this time." Then, in his most compassionate, pastoral tone, Jeff finished, "You'll be all right."

It wasn't what Stedman had said to her and Addie to him, but it was good enough, close enough. Besides, the nightmare held a clue to something she needed to know, she was now convinced.

"Yes, I'm ready," she responded, if not so confidently as she tried to sound. "It's still going to be hard, I know that, perhaps harder than I can imagine. The nightmare will probably hang on, but I can accept and believe the possible usefulness of its reappearance now, I think. You've helped me with that, Jeff. Thank you. Besides, maybe the nightmare has changed, or will change, as it has somewhat already, and that can tell me something, too."

PART TWO

Through the Dark Strip

Chapter Seven

I believe that unarmed truth and unconditional love will have the final word in reality . . . . I have the audacity to believe that peoples everywhere can have three meals a day, education and culture for their minds, and dignity, equality, and freedom for their spirits. I believe that what self-centered men have torn down, men other-centered can build up . . . . I still believe that we shall overcome.

Martin Luther King, Jr.

In the late spring of 1954, Seth Laughinghouse's grandson traveled to Lenoirville from Atlanta on the Greyhound Bus. Pa Gabriel had heard news about Seth from time to time, and less frequently than that, he had received from him a line or two, but for a number of years, there had been no word. And he had sent none to Seth. Gabriel had lost track of his friend and knew nothing about the family he had raised. Now, Gabriel Lewis Laughinghouse had come to North Carolina to look up his grandfather's childhood friend for whom he was named. Almost as if submitting a claim of authenticity and belonging, Gabe Laughinghouse informed the elder Gabriel:

"My grandfather's umbilical cord was buried in North Carolina earth."

Pa Gabriel reacted visibly to this startling revelation. Seth had never told him this about himself, about his heritage and story. The sudden realization that a part of Seth remained in North Carolina soil mattered to him; it seemed to bring him home, in some way to restore a portion of all Gabe had lost when Seth had moved away.

When he—they—the both of them, let the lines of communication drop. His namesake continued,

"The Laughinghouse side of our family followed the old customs and ways pretty much. Our ancestors believed burying the umbilical cord would keep us bonded to the earth we'd come from," he explained. "Perhaps they were right; it seems to have brought me back here," he quipped.

Gabriel, Sr. wondered why Seth had not told him the old story. He had told him a lot of other narratives about his Native American forebears. Why not this one?

Gabriel the Second brought his thought back into the moment.

"That's one reason I came," he announced, with a searching look into the older man's eyes, a mannerism strikingly like a familiar one of Seth's which Gabe now recalled.

It was then that Gabriel Lewis recognized that his first and best friend had kept his promise. And the way he had kept it. Seth had returned. Their pact was unbroken. At least, it was on Seth's side. This child of Seth's child, given Gabriel's name, both his first and last names, was Seth's very flesh come back, standing now before him. That was why the umbilical cord story was, at last, now told.

Initially, Gabriel had extended his hand to this younger Seth named Gabe, but now he grabbed, clutched, him spontaneously, roughly, to his heart. Without meaning to, but with no embarrassment or apology, he wept loud, copious tears of joy and loss commingled, pounding young Gabe's back and dampening his shoulder.

"I'm mighty glad to see you, to meet you, Son," he finally composed himself enough to say. "You're home here. Come on in."

Pa Gabriel studied Seth's grandson while the young man talked. The youth was mighty like his grandfather, tall and rangy like Seth, and he had the same wide, quick smile, full of broad, gleaming teeth, with a booming, hearty laugh worthy of the Laughinghouse name. This one's skin was darker. Young Gabriel told them that his mother, Mariana, was Nigerian, second generation. The Native American honey tones in his father's Laughinghouse blood line had been deepened, thus, and enriched with the darker, stronger pigment of his mother's venerable African ancestry. More Negro than Native American in physical appearance than Seth had been, Gabriel Laughinghouse was among the first of an emerging, pioneer generation of Black Americans who would claim and celebrate their African roots with fierce, true pride, willing and determined to struggle for a just place in American culture and society. A graduate student at Morehouse College in Atlanta, Gabe had emigrated back to the Southland, home of his American ancestors, both to study sociology and to get to know, and reconnect his family to, his kinfolk. His research study was devoted to an investigative project intended to examine and, with others similarly devoted, to expose the social system which soon would be widely spotlighted and broadly known as *segregation*.

Young Gabe explained to the Smith family and to Pa Gabriel that he was pursuing a master's degree in sociology at Morehouse, and the specific, academic reason he had come to Lenoirville was to research the opportunities, or the lack of them, for Negro workers in the textile industry in the South. He had expected to find that only a marginal opportunity of employment, at best, was afforded people of color in the cotton mills of the Carolinas. That expectation had been, in fact, thus far confirmed. What Stedman told him further confirmed his data.

Here is what Stedman told Gabriel Laughinghouse: A few Negro men, like Levy Butler, to name one, gained employment in the textile industry by signing on to drive the big trucks which hauled raw cotton to the mills, (and later, synthetic fibers like nylon), and transported processed thread away from them to other factories elsewhere. And a few, like Pete Davis, an impressive goliath of a Colored man, stoked factory boilers with coal, solitarily usually, and kept the boiler room hot as Torment winter and summer. The huge boiler supplied steam to keep everything else moving.

But as for working inside the environs of the mill alongside White folks, that wasn't done, Stedman told him, looking embarrassed to have to say it. Despite the well-known fact that mill work was considered unskilled labor, and poor, uneducated or minimally educated men and women filled the jobs, mill work was off limits to anybody but Whites. The skewed logic of segregation, the American apartheid, prohibited the mixing of Coloreds with Whites in the workplace, including cotton mills, as also in the schools. Stedman, though not with the same language, pulled no punches with that admission.

Among segregation's defenders, no effort had been made to argue that workplace conditions and arrangements were "separate but equal" where job opportunities and economic realities were concerned. What had been claimed about education had not been attempted in economics. Gabriel Laughinghouse had a hypothesis to test and a part of his research would tackle that incongruity. The Supreme Court had more work to do, Gabriel and those of like mind could see.

It wasn't just in the mills and factories that bigotry held sway, but in every corner of the economy, Temperance would write. She was warming to her subject, and a new reason to write was gaining momentum. In the nineteen fifties, no Negroes worked as clerks in department stores or as receptionists in doctors' offices. No Colored librarians checked out books for borrowers in public libraries. No Negro women or men waited tables in White restaurants, or ate there, although they were incongruously hired to cook and wash dishes alongside poor White folks in those establishments, on occasion. No people of Color exchanged money at the cash registers of hotels or grocery stores. No Colored nurses attended the sick in hospitals.

All Temper could make of it was that certain jobs were considered so menial as to permit a provisional bending of the rules of engagement and employment. Hence, Colored women cleaned hotel rooms and cooked soul food in school cafeterias and college dining halls, incidentally working alongside poor Whites who also qualified, if qualify was what it was, for those jobs. Here, at least, conditions were equal but not separate. Colored men collected garbage and worked on the grounds of public buildings. Inside those buildings, they performed janitorial services of scrubbing and sweeping floors, washing toilets, and emptying ash trays, and they not uncommonly did it alongside poor White men. Nonetheless, neither Colored men nor women of Color could hold down a job inside the walls, within the premises, of a cotton mill. It all made little sense. Figuring out the meaning of place required more intelligence than humankind had been granted, or so it sometimes appeared, Temperance felt, but she knew the fault lay elsewhere.

Gabriel the Elder and the Younger, with Stedman and Temperance (Mae went off to bed about nine o'clock that first evening), sat at the kitchen table until nearly midnight, talking and eating leftovers of biscuits and fatback and drinking iced tea, catching up as best they could on decades of news wanting to be told.

—◦◦◦◦◦◦—

Here, Temperance reviewed the account she had first written about Gabe's applying for a job in the cotton mill. That incident had taken the Smith family and Pa Gabriel by surprise, coming so soon on the heels of Gabe's arrival in town. He hadn't let on that he intended to do that. For all that the Smith's and Pa knew, Gabriel Laughinghouse intended to interview some people and ask a lot of questions, both of management and of workers, but they didn't suspect that he would actually apply for a job, especially in light of what Stedman had told him.

The run-in with Butch Morris and Craven Herbert troubled Stedman most. He dreaded the calamitous potential of that fracas and the insinuations he had picked up from the two men outside the mill that day. There was no doubt about it; there could be "trouble in the camp" ahead. Stedman felt it as strongly as he had felt anything in a very long time.

Temperance wrote:

Stedman puffed nervously, thoughtfully, on his cigarette, the nearly empty Chesterfield pack close at hand atop the porch railing. Somberly, he gazed outward in the direction of the mill, toward the spot where he'd talked to his help that day. They'd been ready to fight.

He knew what could happen to a Colored man for a foolhardy act like that. Gabriel Laughinghouse could call it research or whatever he wanted to, but it could hurt him, and he'd better know that. The Klan, secret and cowardly, had ears and eyes everywhere. No telling where or when he might walk right into their trap.

He was staying with a college friend's kin on the Colored side of town; that much was smart. But he was sticking his nose into mighty dangerous places. White places. Where most folks thought he had no business. A part of Stedman applauded Gabe's resolve and vision. His courage. Another part was scared as hell. For him. Something was going to blow because of this mess. He knew it. The dread he felt was more than intuition. He'd detected the undercurrent in Butch Morris's voice. And he'd suspected Morris and Herbert of being Klan sympathizers, maybe members themselves. No telling where all this would lead. He raked his fingers through his hair, front to back, and inhaled his Chesterfield deeply, smoking it down to a glowing stub and almost burning his fingers lighting another.

"I'm worried about you, young man," Stedman cut to the chase, as Gabriel Laughinghouse climbed the porch steps. "You didn't tell us you were goin' t' ask for a job."

The greeting sounded more accusing than he intended. He continued less gruffly, "That was a dang'rous thing to do. You know that, don't you?"

Gabriel managed a weak smile and settled into the ladder-back chair next to Stedman's. "I'm sorry if I caused you trouble over there," he said and nodded toward the mill a stone's throw away. "You folks have been awfully hospitable to me. All of you," he said, as he looked up at Temper who had joined them on the porch to say that supper was almost ready.

With a solicitous glance toward them both, he appealed to his new friends, "It's something I had to do, Sir. Temperance."

He was drawn especially to her, and that, perhaps, was what was most dangerous in this situation, if Stedman was of a mind to point out danger.

"Nothing's going to change, unless we make it change. Some of us, Colored and White, are beginning to see that."

Now, *he* sounded accusatory, and he hadn't meant to; he dropped his eyes and shifted his posture heavily, more like a man double his age and weight.

A dense dread had gathered and hung in the clammy, evening air stifling them. More than, and different from, midsummer heat and humidity, it was heavy, ponderous, with a palpable foreboding on it, a visible burden stirring it and troubling each of them.

"It's okay, Son," Stedman said at last, "I've got some idee what it's like for you," meaning him and all people of Color. "Seems any person with a grain of sense and fairness about 'em could see it ain't right what you folks have to go through."

He composed his thoughts another moment and continued, forgetting, for a spell, his craving for a cigarette,

"Everybody's got to eat. I don't see how Colored folks make it. Too many jobs are closed off from 'em. Shucks, a Colored man can't even sell me a Pepsi Cola, unless I go into a Colored store (which he did occasionally). They for sure couldn't get a job in any of the clothing stores uptown and sell me a new suit o' clothes."

He studied awhile longer.

"Mae's got supper 'bout done. Let's go wash up."

It was a couple of weeks before Seth Laughinghouse's grandson recounted the specific circumstances of his grandfather's death. He had first said only that Seth had passed away. Pa Gabriel knew before the young man got underway what he was going to tell them, the insane event he had hesitated to speak. Gabriel had sensed it, because he had already dreaded its possibility, its awful probability.

Seth had been stabbed one night and then dragged to death by a man whose unfaithful wife had received a love poem written by him. But it had been given to her by the man's own brother, his only one, Gabe told them. She had hysterically confessed her real guilt, better his brother than a Colored man, she herself thought and believed he would, and named Morton as her actual lover. Morton had given her the love poem, she insisted. Her cuckolded husband, already crazed by the searing image of his wife's giving herself in sexual union to a Colored man, could not and would not hear her explanation. He could not absorb it. Deaf and stunned, and further overwhelmed by the fraternal betrayal his silly wife had revealed, the husband could not admit that image and excise the one of her and Seth already filling his brain. His wife, mounted by a black man, and now this she had told him, all of it together tabulated to more than he could handle or decipher. The stark humiliation, and vertigo, of his wife's opening wide her slim thighs to a man with Black skin and mythically superior sexual prowess rocked his foundation catastrophically more than did the notion that a younger, less intelligent brother of his own might have trespassed on his conjugal property. Hell, he'd thought of sharing her with him, anyhow. And watching. They'd even joked about it.

But the thought of Christine hungering for a Black-skinned man had already driven him stark, raving crazy. The racist stereotype in his brain had dismantled all possibility of a measured response to anything. What did that picture say about him? he couldn't stop thinking. Desperate with humiliation and rage, he grabbed like a drowning man a straw his brother's denial of guilt. Revenge against the archetypal enemy, the Black devil alone, would effect his restitution, he believed.

For Morton's despicable part, he had twice betrayed, first, his mother's son (no matter their drunken jokes about Christine), and next, his distraught lover, with a lie he had calculated his older brother would latch onto, once he had realized its possibility. Maybe he wasn't the dumb one, after all. Morton was fiendishly on target. It was the blood brother's word against the adulterous wife's. Who would've bet against the brother?

Desperate to reduce the crescendo of torment in his brain, the dishonored husband tracked Seth down and waylaid him in darkness. Waylaid and stabbed him, without uttering a word of accusation or warning, without mentioning the incriminating poem, without looking into his open face. Then, he dragged his dying body face down behind his truck until Seth's noble visage was obliterated, erased, a gaping, ragged crater where a singular, human lantern had shone.

Gabriel mourned.

When the case went to trial, a seated jury of eight White men, two White women, one Colored woman, and one Colored man, heard the evidence. The defence quickly established that the amorous poem was not written in the husband's childish, unlettered, and hesitant handwriting. No other love poems composed in Seth's elegant script and sold to others were produced and submitted as matching, circumstantial evidence. No witnesses were subpoenaed who testified to the common knowledge that Seth Laughinghouse had operated a modestly successful cottage industry, composing and offering for sale love poetry for sweethearts, as also greeting cards handwritten on inexpensive, unlined paper, handfolded, for celebrants of marriages, births, high school graduations, and fiftieth anniversaries. Nor had anyone submitted as evidence the cards of condolence he had written and offered, simple in their beauty and compassion, to suffering and grieving parents of children who had died too young and children of parents heavy with age, gone to be with the Lord.

Seth's poems had provided him and his family welcome, supplementary income to the basic living he had made with Ford Motor Company. They gave to Seth artistic expression, and opportunity to connect his creative gift and life with the lives of those who chose his thoughts and words as theirs, expressed in a way they could not. All of it in Seth's beautiful handwriting, poetry and poetic prose, important evidence easy to obtain, but ignored and concealed in the court of law.

In point of fact, neither the state's attorney nor the defence lawyer labored to prove Seth's culpability, the implied allegation against the dead man of adultery and the more heinous crime against nature. Most of all, the capital offense of getting out of his place. Both lawyers assumed it, implied it, insinuated it, but never went there directly. To have done so would have required producing witnesses and artifacts of evidence which would have contradictorily weighted the case toward Seth's innocence and the White defendant's greater, more reckless, guilt. Still, and worse yet, the state prosecutor did less to prove the murderer's guilt than the defence attorney did to invoke Seth's. A more obvious travesty of justice could hardly have been imagined, Gabe Laughinghouse told them, and his somber listeners agreed. Gabe had sat with his father in the courtroom and listened helplessly while his grandfather's life had been dishonored and violated, taken, anew. It had shattered them, but young Gabe had recovered with resolve snatched from that crucible. His father had not faired so well. It had broken him.

Both Gabriels, and Stedman, were convinced that the court entire, prosecution, defence, and bench, the judge included, intended from the outset to exonerate the White defendant and conducted the trial accordingly. How else could they have ignored such troubling, available evidence as lay at hand? The whoremongering brother (their name for him) who bought and used Seth's poem was never put on the stand. Nor was the discredited wife. A man's wife could not be required to testify against him, the assumed eleventh commandment. Where did that law come from? Temperance wondered.

A guilty Black man, a man out of his place, had violated a trusted wife and injured a good man who had done him no harm, the defence had intoned. Some in the courtroom had actually looked around for the defendant, for Seth. The plaintiff-defendant, this injured husband, had taken a life, the defending attorney conceded, but a Colored man had gazed with lust at a White woman and subsequently violated her; thereby, he had violated her White husband, as well, the lawyer hammered. Expressions of horror and disgust on faces throughout the courtroom showed his words had hit home. Seth had become, in all their minds, the guilty defendant; the murderer, the innocent plaintiff.

Left ambiguously unclear and implicitly denied was the matter of the wife's compliance, nay, willing complicity, in the dead man's alleged crime. To have put her on the witness stand would have, in Stedman's characteristically forthright words, "flung dung against the shit house wall," and the prosecutor knew it. So did the defence and the judge. The poor jury hadn't a clue. On the one hand, the prosecutor irrationally suggested the guilt was Seth's alone, virtually exonerating the defendant himself in a bizarre reversal of roles with his competing, defending attorney, though to have stated it outright would have strained the bounds of credulity, even for the unsuspecting jurists, and would have made it difficult to maneuver the process of the trial toward any coherent conclusion at all. He had sense enough not to do that. At other contradictory points, (contradictions abounded, Gabe reported), both defence and prosecution stoked the hot fires of opinion and condemnation against Seth, and in favor of the murderer, by illogically intimating, in relay formation, a sordid cohabitation which wantonly violated and robbed the husband intentionally, on the one hand, and a violent, explosive act of which the wife was innocent, on the other, either of which sufficiently explained his taking the law into his own hands, the defending attorney suggested. Any prosecutor worth his salt, Stedman thought and said so, could have exposed the defence attorney's long string of *non sequitors* (Stedman said "lies"); the prosecutor's own list was as confusedly long and indecipherable for the boondoggled jurors.

The damning subtext of the lawyers' arguments and the virtual, indistinguishable identity of prosecution and defence, unrecognized, unanalyzed, hung ominously in the courtroom: a Black-skinned man had touched the hem of a White woman's skirt, reached his rough, dark hand underneath and lifted it, exposing, and stroking, the White thigh flesh beneath the flimsy skirt, and he had drawn her warm, woman fragrance, her sweet and secret, inviolable self, to meet his own taut flesh. Black Othello had ravished fair Desdemona. For that ancient insurrection, he had paid with his life. The beast with two backs, the bard's most shocking image, would not further torment the superior, White psyche. It must not.

Such was the troubling archetype: the beast with two backs, one Black, the other White, the inferior, threatening, Black-skinned man mounting the superior, dominating, White-skinned man's claimed human property, his very wife, and thrusting repeatedly his Luciferian, animal member into that part of her to which the self-appointed, White master had established inviolate, absolute, property rights. For such there must be a final solution.

But wait. Gabriel saw it. Both of them did, older and younger. Farther down in the psyche than that, farther down than its mere fact alone, and farther down than conscious reflection and deliberation can fully plumb, crouching to spring, lurking in the deepest depths of the mind and refusing to be dislodged, lies the irresistible, ineffaceable image of the mixed-hued beast, its two backs, its rebellious organic mount and orgasmic lock, at once revolting and compelling, at once disgusting and enticing, at once frightening and tempting, primordial, driving, impossible to eradicate finally. The unconscious mind insists, screams,

"You might enjoy watching! You might enjoy doing! Check your physical responses. How are your juices and blood vessels, your heart rate, doing?!"

The White consciousness struggles to hate it and subdue it. The fated struggle lies at the substratum of both fear and hate. Because of that struggle, the archetypal injury must be repeatedly, vigilantly, and eternally satisfied, resolved. They saw it. The Gabriels. Both of them. And the both of them saw something as equally fundamental.

The both of them, the Gabriels, and Stedman in his way and on his own journey, all of them journeying on the edge, had seen an elemental datum. They had pushed through to a new level of understanding. It came in the form of a question and a challenge. Now that we can identify it, at least partially, what will we do with our unconscious fear and hatred? What *must* we do with it?

Pa Gabriel's profound grief and suffering threatened to overwhelm him. But his analytical proclivity snatched him back, upward, into thought. He would think. He *must* think. He had a dark place to travel through ahead of him, that he well knew. He would have to contend with his grief and depression. And *think*. Already, he could see it; language and reflection must be his course. As they had ever been.

Few had been surprised by the outcome of the trial. Community revulsion and social mores, and the primal compulsion driving them, had levied an absolute judgment: the Colored man's crime was more heinous than the White man's revenge. The skewed, familiar logic was the community's own, not merely the court's, a tradition anciently and widely accepted and spuriously validated. The murderer was exonerated.

———~w·σ¢σ¢σ¢°~w———

Gabriel spent every moment he could find beside the river. He escaped to his refuge, his sanctuary, at dawn in the morning, and hurried there after work in the evening. With no supper, he stayed until well past bedtime, sometimes all night, falling into fitful sleep, never long, on the shelf over the fishing cave whenever exhaustion overtook him.

Mae worried about him, "Ain't you afraid you'll get on a snake down there in the dark?"

Gabriel wasn't. He hardly cared. That worried her most.

Hour after hour, by day, he slumped and stared across the dark water to the bank beyond, as though, if he looked hard enough, he would see Seth there. Reciting mute lines and bits of poetry, in other troubled days, had helped moderately. The literary word had soothed him when Hannah died and when Mae nearly died. Longfellow's familiar lines, "Into each life some rain must fall/ Some days must be dark and drear," had afforded him then a measure of comfort and enabled acceptance of his circumstances. He tried it now. Now, no comfort came. Because no acceptance was possible or decent. Still, he must think.

When the burden was too heavy, he crawled headfirst inside the fishing hole become an earthen, embracing womb, and willed himself into fetal unconsciousness. Gabriel *couldn't* think about Seth all the time.

———~w·σ¢σ¢σ¢°~w———

As bad as the visceral pain of all his tortured thoughts about Seth's violent murder was the guilt Gabriel endured because he had not been there to help him. Or at least to insure that the trial was a just one by attesting to Seth's practice of selling his love poems to suitors. He would have found a way to do that. By witnessing to the fact that it was vastly unlikely and ridiculously unconvincing that a love poem in Seth's handwriting had been given *by him* to anyone at all.

But Gabriel had not been there. That was the rub. He had not been there. Any of the time. Not there to help Seth fight off the crazy, White man. Not there to expose the lying bastard who caused it all. Not there to see it through with Seth's folks, with this strapping, brilliant grandson of his, so much like Seth it hurt to look at him. That was the part he couldn't forgive himself for, no matter that hundreds of miles prevented his being there or even his knowledge of what had happened. What about letters? What about telephones? Telegrams? He could have written to Seth now and then. He could have called him on the telephone, if he had cared about getting in touch. The recriminations were stripping him down; he saw that, but he had to endure that darkness; he had to go there. Not there where and when it mattered, he at least had to go where a reasonable penance lay now, a penance sufficient to his restitution. He had still to find it. Or not.

He could fail.

In the evenings, Temperance took him the supper Mae had cooked and wrapped inside a paper, grocery bag, aromatic and warm, as soon as they figured Pa Gabriel was back at the river, but he had no appetite. He ate little of it. He couldn't. Most days, he managed to wash down two or three crackers with a Pepsi Cola at the store, but that was about all he felt he could choke down. He had no stomach for food or anything else. He was getting skinny as a rail on a frame with no fat to draw on, and that was what worried Mae about his refusal to eat the food she sent him. Worse, his granddaughter's presence and care failed to move or comfort him. Gabriel had no energy remaining for anything except guilty grief. He had let Seth down. He had broken the fishing cave promise.

Still, he would think. He had to think.

Temperance suffered again those hard days as she wrote the story. For the moment putting aside the narrative of Pa Gabriel's depression and struggle with grief and remorse, she returned to the chronicle of Gabe's application for the cotton mill job. She knew the end of the story. It would be extremely hard from here on out. She wrote:

On the day after he had applied for a job, Gabe Laughinghouse had returned to the mill office to request a second interview with Mr. Foster for the purpose of gathering data for his thesis research. He had forgotten to make that request in the nervous intensity of his foray into social activism, for that was what his job application had been. While not his first, public challenge to racial discrimination, his action had been, as on those few other such occasions, heady, rather frightening, and momentarily disorienting.

Nora Winters received him courteously and curiously, again, wondering that he had returned so soon, and Bill Foster agreed amiably to talk with him about his master's research, happy to anticipate a talk of that kind, missing, as he did, opportunities to engage in such discussions. Bill Foster had enjoyed his academic experiences and would have liked to revisit them more regularly. Like Nora, too, he was curious about Gabe's specific purposes beyond the academic one of research. Gabe made his request known, received Mr. Foster's courteous agreement, they set a date and hour, and he thanked him and left.

Déjà vu. The first shift had let out, and the second was coming on, when Gabriel stopped at the dope stand just inside the mill door to pick up a soft drink, though he wasn't sure a Colored person would be permitted to buy anything there. Was he pushing the envelope? Maybe so. And maybe he had to. Craven Herbert and Butch Morris were that moment getting cigarettes before heading upstairs to their second-shift work. They had observed him coming out of the small, red-brick mill office adjacent to the mill.

"Hey, little black Sambo, wha' cha doin' back hyer? Don' cha know they ain't no niggers workin' hyer? We don't eb'n let you people sweep de floors," Butch sneered loudly, thrusting his chest forward and moving into Gabriel's social space.

He was drinking again, in broad daylight and on the job. You could smell it on him, Gabriel noticed. It was true about the job. Stedman himself had started out on his first mill job sweeping the floors, he had told him. Only Whites were hired for the least skilled work. It was not about skill or ability, Gabe knew. It was about exclusion. Hate is. About exclusion. Both Gabriels, Lewis and Laughinghouse, were clear on that one.

Temperance was feeling acutely the pain of writing her words. She had to take a break. The zigzagging lines shuffling her vision confirmed it. No talking to Jeff or Fredericka or anyone. Damnation! she hadn't talked to Fredericka in days, so absorbed she had become in her narrative. What a dreadful narrative it was; she both despised and resisted it and loved and desired it. How could that be? She couldn't think about that now. She had to rest. To nap, if possible.

Temperance snuffed out her cigarette and began again. The nap had helped, the cigarette, too. She resumed:

Gabe turned and looked at Herbert and Morris.

"Yeah, that's what I've learned," he spoke, quietly, hardly a note of inflection in his somber tone. His eyes said more.

Butch threatened, "You jus' need to git yersef on over to niggertown whur you b'long. Or might jus' be someb'dy needs t' teach you sump'n 'bout whur yer place is," he slurred.

"Aw, c'mon," urged Craven, pulling on his arm, "he's leavin'. We don't haf t' worry 'bout him."

Butch was enjoying himself too much to stop just yet.

"I think I need t' beat 'is black ass," he persisted drunkenly, thinking the slight Gabriel would be easy to beat.

"I c'n whip 'im!" he blustered, "wiv' one han' tied behin' my back."

"Aw, c'mon, c'mon! Smith's gonna' dock our pay! Fire us! The shif's been started ten minutes already!" warned Craven, pulling out his pocket watch and checking it agitatedly.

Gabriel turned lightly, fluidly, on a pivot graceful as a fencer's and acquired in just that way. He headed out the door and in the direction of the Smith house. Simultaneously, Temper skipped down the porch steps, black curls flying, and crossed the street toward him, calling out,

"Gabe, Mama said to tell you supper will soon be ready. Come on over and eat with us."

Following him outside the mill, Butch had made one, last, drunken lurch after Gabe before Craven yanked his buddy back, fairly jerking him off his unsteady feet and pulling him inside the mill again. In that brief moment, Temper had recognized them and saw that Butch Morris had grabbed for Gabe.

"What's wrong, Gabe?!" she asked, the alarm ringing in her voice.

Thinking it judicious to ignore her question, he pretended not to have heard it and said instead, "Well, if it isn't the comely 'dinner bell girl' telling me it's time to eat again!" he teased. "Thanks, Temper, I was headed that way," he smiled, the admiration in his eyes genuine.

She wouldn't be put off, "Gabe! What happened?!"

"Oh, it's okay. Fella's liquored up. How's your day been, fair lady?" he sidestepped.

Temperance pressed, "I know who those men are, Gabriel. They're troublemakers! You need to be careful around them!"

Temper rarely hesitated to offer passionate advice when she deemed it needful. This was one of those times. She remembered Herbert and Morris from a neighborhood fish stew the Smith family had attended on a Saturday night in October. It had been held three houses down from theirs in Leslie and Helen Furr's backyard. The autumn social had drawn a sizable number of millhands who lived off the mill village in an equally poor, poorer, section across town, so near to the Colored section they were ashamed for people to know where they lived. Most were people whom she had regularly seen, all of them employees of Stedman's. Some were not familiar to her. Craven Herbert and Butch Morris were two who stood out that evening, mainly because they were noticeably high and paid unseemly attention to her and Rhonda, staring without averting their eyes and grinning foolishly and lewdly at them. Barely fifteen and thirteen, respectively, Temper and Rhonda looked older, and both were uncommonly pretty, most people thought. Still, they were much too young for adult, male attention, and the men had no business paying them any mind at all. It had made Temperance uneasy to be looked at in the way they had stared at her. She had been discomfited by their behavior all-round, and it had ruined the get-together for her, but fortunately, it had served a useful purpose, because it had sensitized her to the bizarre and potential hazard it represented. The lesson would serve a timely role, and it would not be long in coming, it turned out. Like all else she experienced, Temper had mentally registered the episode, storing and filing it for further reflection and analysis. She had pointed the men out to Stedman and asked him their names. They were soon instructed to leave. Alcohol was not allowed.

Now, that autumn evening's experience and Temper's premonition had popped up for deferred analysis. She had identified the men, and while Gabe deflected her probing questions, she had read the hostile body language and she had seen Craven Herbert pull Butch Morris away from him. Gabe would not tell her what had happened at the dope stand, but she knew something was amiss, askew, and it was not inconsequential, despite his efforts to pretend it was; she felt certain of that. She knew their intentions could not be trusted. Or dismissed. The fish stew episode had raised a number of red flags, and they were waving again. She would not ignore them.

When Gabe left around six-thirty, Temperance couldn't put it off any longer. She filled a plate with Mae's fresh butterbeans and cabbage, a big helping of yellow squash, a tender pork chop, and a bigger helping of rice and gravy, and stuck it inside a brown grocery bag which she wrapped securely under the plate. Inside a smaller, brown paper sack, she tucked a saucer with two of Mae's biscuits on it. Temper dipped her head and smelled the mingled, familiar smell of warm, homecooked food and brown, grocery paper, a unique aroma she loved and had grown up smelling with delight. Then, she picked up Mae's frosted Mason jar of sweet, iced tea and turned toward the door. Pa Gabriel needed to know what was going on, and she needed him to know what was on her mind.

When she entered his riverside refuge, he was propped against the tulip poplar, rubbing the moist residue off two, freestone peach kernels he had extracted from a couple of the half dozen, overripe peaches he'd brought back from the grocery store. Mr. Holloway had given them to him because they had begun to rot and would not sell. Beside Pa, golden against the green river grass, lay an exquisite peachseed monkey. Temperance's heart quickened when she saw it. Pa Gabriel was carving his monkeys again. That was a reliable sign he was feeling better, interested again in his beloved hobby, his family craft, taught him by his father as early as he had been big enough to learn it.

Great-grandpa Lewis, Temper'd been told by Pa Gabriel, had been taught the craft by his father, and he by his father, and so on, back for more generations than anyone recalled any longer. Lewis homesteads grew peach trees, all of them, those home places, as much to supply kernels for carving as fruit for eating and canning. In those years when the peaches were wormy, the kernels were still "fittin' for carvin'," the Lewis men allowed and took consolation in that fact. No other fruit, apples, cherries, or pears, they had those on the property, too, offered kernels like the peaches, good as those fruits were to eat, and as much as the whole family loved them and thanked the Lord for the jams, jellies, and pies they yielded when the Lewis women got hold of them. Still in all, something was missing in all but the peaches. Kernels for carving.

The simple, lovely craft, ordinary and homely, like Mae's pillow case and pocket handkerchief embroidery, gave to the Lewis men who practiced it a creative outlet which soothed and relaxed, lowered the heart rate and blood pressure, healthful, though minor, benefits accounting in part for their longevity, perhaps, and helped them through troubled times, a major benefit of unquestioned duration. Mae sometimes said her embroidery rested her. This was spoken by a woman who spoke little and who most often ate standing at the kitchen sink while she simultaneously cleaned up the mess she'd made cooking supper. All to leave time for ironing before bedtime. But on the evenings she didn't need to iron, or another chore wasn't pressing, she sometimes sat and embroidered and hummed or sang her hymns, resting before going to bed. Her work in the mill and the hours of housework afterward had her "too tired to sleep," if she didn't rest that way first, some nights, she allowed, strange as that seemed to Temper's mind.

Gabriel, too, rested when he carved, he commented regularly. Indeed, he often said his "passel o' monkeys" rested him like nothing else, even better than a good night's sleep, a rarity for him now. Old people, he'd learned, didn't sleep like they used to when they were young. Temperance guessed her mother and grandfather rested when they plied their crafts of embroidery and carving because they were off their feet and sitting still for a change, both of them inclined to working without cessation throughout their daylight hours.

There was something else. When, after gleaning the joy of creation, Pa Gabriel gave a peachseed monkey away to a child, or to anyone at all, a magical thing happened, something in the rarefied stratum of valentines and handsewn dresses, mustard biscuits and daffodils. Something mutually transformative.

The day Gabriel extrapolated that seminal insight to his thoughts about Seth Laughinghouse, he realized that Seth must have felt exactly that way about his poetry and the love poems and cards of celebration and condolence he had sold for much less than their true worth to others. It hadn't been the modest boost to his income which his cards provided that had motivated Seth to compose. Gabe had never thought that it was. The inimitable joy and daily surprise of his creative gift itself—that—and the pleasure and comfort it gave to those who also enjoyed it had motivated Seth to write. This insight was what Gabriel now had firm hold of, and the realization was a breakthrough for him. It helped him escape the irrational madness of his grief, the anger he had felt toward Seth for writing and selling love poems, in the first place, for God's sake. Gabe had believed that, if Seth hadn't done that, he would still be alive.

He saw clearly that he had succumbed to the ubiquitous temptation to blame the victim. In doing so, he had repudiated Seth's creative core, the divine spark which had made him who he was most truly. Gabriel's peachseed monkeys had revealed his error and given him back that important part of Seth. Now, he wondered, was that the reason Ed Holloway had put those rotten peaches off on him? To get him to carve again?

He wouldn't put it past Ed.

Gabriel had had time to think about all of this before Temper arrived with Mae's supper that breakthrough evening. He aimed, now, to collect and preserve all of Seth's poetry he could find. A trip to Michigan would be required for that effort, and he was sure he could find a friend to help him get there. Probably Stedman. He couldn't remember the name of the little crossroads community outside Detroit where Seth had lived, and died, but he would ask young Gabe again. There was another reason he meant to go to that place, to visit that county. The justice system was in mighty bad shape there, it appeared to him. Somebody needed to see about getting that fixed. Some things were worth whatever they cost, he reckoned.

With his salvific reclamation of Seth's art, Gabriel had begun to feel more gratitude than anger and depression. At least, the anger toward Seth for dying was gone. The anger at the man who had murdered him, and the social cancer which infected everyone and everything, spawning and spewing hate which killed, blazed hotter than ever. Paradoxically, white-hot anger and fierce gratitude grew side by side in Gabriel Lewis's heart. Grateful for his climb out of the pit of depression and malaise, grateful for all he'd had, and still had, in Seth, his eternal best friend, and grateful for a second chance to make something happen, Gabriel Lewis was a happy man again. Happy because angry. Righteous anger did that for a person, he had concluded. It had done it for Jesus of Nazareth, Gabriel believed, when he drove the moneychangers from the house of grace, and it had done it for him.

Art had conferred grace, and grace had conferred righteous anger. Such were Gabriel's thoughts when Temperance found him beside the Neuse, when she handed to him Mae's food gift, loving creation and expression of her simple, culinary art.

Instantaneously, Gabriel's appetite returned. He smelled the warm food through the grocery paper and his mouth watered such that the saliva spilled out the corners of his parched mouth. Wiping his chin with his handkerchief, he drew from the smaller bag Mae's delectable specialty, her buttermilk biscuits. The taste and texture of them were ambrosia to him, very food of the gods, Olympus fare, better than that, country cooking at its best, he thought. There weren't enough superlatives to describe them. They were Art. They were grace, human and divine.

Temperance sat and watched with glee as he devoured the meal, ravenously consuming, relishing, every bite and morsel, and within seconds, it seemed to her, he had poked the empty plate and saucer back inside their paper sacks. One would have imagined him a worthy contender for an eating contest at the county fair, so fast he had eaten it all, she thought to herself. Wait until she told Mae. How relieved her mother would be, she knew.

"Thank you, Sweetheart. I don't know when I've enjoyed a meal so much." To be sure, Temperance thought, as she smiled back at him and nodded her response.

Temper picked up the just-carved peachseed monkey,

"This is beautiful, Pa, I really don't see how you do it. I mean," she continued, "the peach kernel itself is so ugly and wrinkled before you carve it. But this monkey is cute and adorable," she added quickly. "The transformation is remarkable."

Mercifully, her mind was briefly off her worry over Gabe's scuffle with Butch Morris and on her grandfather's restored spirits and appealing craft.

"Thank you, Sugar. That one's for Ed Holloway's little grandbaby," said he.

She repeated, "I don't see how you do it."

"It's easy, Sweetheart. I just carve away the ugly."

Was he the first to think it or say it that way? Probably not. Maybe Michelangelo. In any case, before Temper could form her response, Pa continued,

"I think that's what the good Lord does with us, if we let 'im."

Temperance laughed out loud. Now, she knew he was better! No doubt about it. A sermonette was coming, sure sign the old Pa Gabriel was back.

"Oh, Pa! I love you so much, and I, we all, all of us, have been so worried about you! These last several days. Forgive me for laughing. I wasn't laughing at what you said. It was a laugh of gratitude at having my Pa back!" she explained, and grabbed him around his scrawny shoulders for a tight hug.

Pa laughed, too, and promised to tell her what he had been thinking about Seth's art and the breakthrough she was witnessing in his experience. But first, he had more to say about the subject at hand and begged her patience to let him finish his homily.

"Problem is, we don't hold still like that peach kernel did, for the beautifyin' process," mused Pa, spinning out his thoughts and looking at the monkey she was holding in her hand. "On the other hand, there's a lot more to us than there is to a peach seed. That makes the carvin' harder, I imagine, even for the good Lord . . . for us, too."

With Pa Gabriel, one thought always led to another one. He studied an extra moment, "Maybe more worthwhile, too. For Him an' us."

Pa Gabe was carving, thinking, talking, preaching, and eating: those were five good signs. Good signs and good news, Temper thought, relieved. But instantaneously, the relief and its balm gave way to remembered anxiety about Gabe Laughinghouse.

"Pa, I'm worried to death," she announced, ready to say it all. "Do you recollect what I told you about those two men, Butch Morris and Craven Herbert, after the neighborhood fish stew at the Furr's last fall?"

"Uh huh," he mumbled and nodded, his hushed reply an alert one, no less. He was listening; in part, because those two had already been on his mind. He had made it his business then to ask around about them after Temperance confided her worries. What he had learned was not good. He had warned her then about them; he hoped she remembered that. They were on his mind again.

"They were talking to Gabe Laughinghouse outside the mill this afternoon. I don't know what they said to him. Gabe wouldn't tell me, but he was mighty quiet-acting at supper this evening, and I saw Butch grab at 'im before Craven Herbert pulled 'im back away from him," she finished, feeling drained by what she had been forced to articulate.

Pa Gabriel had observed the men's behavior at West End Grocery when they came into the store to buy Lucky Strikes and brag. Rough, loud, obscene, more bark than bite, Pa had guessed, but with a reckless, insecure edge he wouldn't trust, the kind most people like that have, they had seemed to him then, and that initial impression had held. They were not the sort of people he would want around his granddaughter. Or around Gabe.

"That Butch Morris was staggerin' around like he'd been drinkin', Pa. I think Craven Herbert had to pull 'im away from Gabe," she repeated, her voice rising with the threat's repetition and the fear pushing her to say it again. In point of fact, she continued her repetition, she'd seen Craven yank Butch, almost jerking him down, before he had listened and turned away from Gabe. That image was what alarmed her most. She was talking herself toward identifying just what it was about the confrontation that had frightened her most. There was more than innuendo and verbal bullying going on there, she now identified clearly. What she saw was more than ignorant bravado. It had turned to physical threat. She said so.

"You didn't see them pass any licks, did you?"

"No, but it came close, I b'lieve." She felt mighty close to tears, herself, and he could see it.

"Temp'rance, those two characters are rough customers. I've watched them at the store, and I don't like what I've seen. I want you to stay away from them, you hear? Gabe needs to keep his distance, too."

Pa picked up another uncarved kernel and turned it over between his gnarled, skilled fingers, "I'll talk to Gabe about it."

His promise gave Temper some measure of reassurance, but her agitation would not subside yet. Still, he was the right one to address the situation, if anyone was. Stedman was a good one to call on, too, except that he sometimes fired up too easily and got ready to kick ass too fast. His volatility made him unpredictable, and she couldn't feel calm about how he might choose to handle things. Pa Gabriel's more measured approach was no less effective, and sometimes, it was a sight better than Stedman's, for those reasons.

Pa continued, "Those boys might not do anybody any harm as long as they're not high, but I'm afraid they take a bottle with 'em about everywhere they go."

He was again quiet, quieter, than usual. He began to etch the kernel with the sharp point of his knife. Then he said,

"Temper, they're ignorant, badly raised boys, dragged from pillar to post, snatched up by the hair of the head, you might say. I've learned some things about 'em. They didn't have the raisin' you've had, Temp, neither one of 'em." He smiled then, "Love carves you a different way," he said, with full knowledge of the bounteous love which had carved her.

Temperance returned the smile, thinking his metaphor a suitably natural one for him to employ, and knowing the truth in his words.

Sounding mournful more than anything else, Gabriel continued, "Butch doesn't know his daddy's first or last names, and Craven's not much better off. Look what they named 'im. The sad thing is, I'm afraid it fits. He's grown into it. I'm not makin' excuses for those men, but there're sensible, logical reasons people turn out the way they do."

Temperance knew she could count on a balanced, thoughtful analysis from Pa Gabe. If she had been privy to his ruminations about anger, his own and the subject of righteous anger, she might have engaged him on that topic and asked how it related to the matter at hand. That would have been a worthwhile exchange. And it could have turned their thoughts in another direction. Still, Pa Gabriel's anger over Seth Laughinghouse's brutal murder and the justice system which failed him, and whatever anger over any new outrage which lay ahead and he could not yet see, though stormclouds loomed, even that, she might well have reasoned, he would express in a suitably characteristic way. A way his own. It was a prophecy of which she was capable, and she had good warrant for it.

Young as she was, but in substantial ways cut from the same pattern, the same cloth as Pa, in other ways, more like Stedman, both of those ways good, she thought, she knew Pa Gabriel's balance and sound analysis were what she and everybody else needed now. His innate good sense. His clear head and calm heart.

"Thanks, Pa Gabriel. I'm glad you're going to talk to Gabe. He needs your help," she said, as she hugged his thin shoulders again.

"Don't forget what I said, Temp'rance. Stay away from those men. They're not well-carved," he repeated, trying to finish on a lighter note, but jumping the track even as he said it. "If you run across Gabe before I do, tell 'im I want to talk to 'im, either at the store or here, okay?" he finished, his attempt at levity abandoned and a heavy expression on his face.

"I will. See you at home," Temperance waved. It was preferable, in her opinion, to get away from the river and the water moccasins before nighttime. Pa needed to do that, too.

Pa Gabriel joined his family at home for supper the next evening. He hoped to see Gabe there and have the talk he'd promised Temperance he would have with him. But Gabe didn't show up. That evening or the next day. On the third day, however, he stopped by the grocery store a little after three, and Pa Gabriel pulled him aside.

"Gabe, Temp'rance told me about Morris and Herbert sayin' somethin' to you outside the mill. I know you applied for a job there several days ago. What's goin' on, Son? Temper's worried about you, an' I'm wonderin' if she hasn't good reason to be."

"Pa," Gabe responded almost reverentially, "you before the others must know what I'm up against. You saw it with my grandpa. I chose sociology as my field of work because I have to know all that I can about the social realities people of color are up against."

The "up against" language named the psychological and social universe in which Gabe Laughinghouse moved, had moved, all his life. His acknowledgement that Pa Gabriel had walked there with

Seth was appropriate and showed that he had heard stories from his grandfather like those Temperance had been told. He knew the Rob Emory story, too.

"This Morehouse research project of mine isolates one segment of that," Gabe continued, meaning the situation he and others were "up against," and he turned to face his friend more directly, "the situation of people of color who need and seek work opportunities in the textile industry, an industry suited to the capabilities of those who have had little or no schooling, but one which is entirely closed off from them. Discrimination is everywhere. Everywhere we turn there's a sign telling us we're out of our place, Pa Gabriel. That has to change, but it's not going to change until we change it ourselves."

Gabriel had listened. Now, it was his turn to respond with a degree of respect approaching reverence, "I know, Son. I'm afraid you're right. I know you're right."

"Thanks, Pa Gabe. I'm glad you understand that I have to do this. I had no doubt you would. It's my part, Sir." His eyes looked sad, old for one so young, and apprehensive, but defiantly hopeful, as well.

"Be careful, Son. Be careful," said Pa, as he grabbed him reflexively, protectively, "I don't want to lose you, too."

"Thank you, Pa Gabriel," said the younger one, pausing. Almost sheepishly, he asked then, "Can I tell you how honored I feel to bear your name?" Before the older man could reply, he added, "I'll do my best, Sir."

"The honor's mutual. I thank you, Son," breathed Pa Gabriel in the steadiest voice he could manage.

——————

"On the next Saturday, Temperance and Rhonda, inseparable, best mill hill friends (they were in different grades at school and had other "best" friends there) went to the seven o'clock feature of that week's movie at the Paramount Theater, something they had not done that late in the day until then." It was now time to reprise the dark strip story. To finish it, Temperance decided. "Always before on their frequent trips to the movies, they were getting out and heading home about that time of day. When they walked out of the air conditioned movie house, Temper was mildly taken aback to see how close to dark it was. Still, she wasn't especially worried. The evening's balmy, summer air she had gratefully escaped into, from the chilly theater, warmed and reassured her. And she and Rhonda had walked home along Savage and Blount Streets many times before, though not so late, almost nine o'clock in the evening."

Wasn't that how it had gone? Temperance had dreaded getting to this part of her story, but now she had begun it. And recently she had remembered why they had gone to the later showing of the movie that day. As she had told Fredericka and Jeff Singer, it was Rhonda's idea. She was having her period, the second day of her cycle, and she was cramping and bleeding heavily. They had talked it over and decided to wait until closer to evening when the heat and humidity wouldn't be so bad and the walk wouldn't keep Rhonda out in the heat so long, or something like that. They would decide then, after they saw how Rhonda was feeling. Temperance remembered, now, having had misgivings about waiting until that late in the day to go and she had expressed her reluctance to Rhonda, but after six, Rhonda claimed that she was better and insisted more strongly that they go on to the seven o'clock showing. Both girls hated to miss the movie, and Temper relented. Still, she couldn't recall its title or who the star was they wanted to see so badly that day, but she remembered vividly the decision to go and how it was made.

Temperance picked up the story at its climax:

Instantly, a tall, lean figure crossed the dark street diagonally and dissected the space between the fleeing girls and the men chasing them.

"Hey, fellas, what's got you in such a hurry?" he called out in a loud voice, hoping to alert others within earshot to what was going on inside the dark strip.

The disrupted men stopped, hesitated a few seconds, and turned about, as if abandoning their chase, not wanting to be identified by an unexpected rescuer. Whether Herbert and Morris knew it was Gabriel Laughinghouse or not was uncertain.

For her part, Temper had not seen Gabe's face, but she had recognized his voice. Both girls ran on, slowing up only when they reached the Smith yard. Shakily confident that the men were no longer chasing them, Rhonda kept heading for home, now worried that her folks would be upset that she was getting home past her curfew, while Temperance stumbled up the back porch steps calling,

"Daddy! Daddy!"

As she burst into the kitchen, Stedman arose from the dining table, his breath stopped by the panic in her voice, and banged his chair on the wooden floor as he lunged heavily to his feet: "What is it, Shug!?"

"Daddy, Craven . . . what's-'is-name an', an' Butch . . . that man Butch, followed Rhonda and me . . . !" she wailed long and loudly, and hurled herself inside the fortress of his arms as instinctively as she had done at four, as trustingly as she had done at all times of peril.

Temper howled her outrage and hysteria inconsolably, wildly, unable to talk intelligibly, until she caught sight of Mae's and Pa Gabriel's alarmed faces. Sobered, at least to a degree of normality by concern for them, and afraid that they and Stedman would think she had been raped, she willed herself to calm down enough to talk. It was all right. She could hear Stedman's voice, and behind his, Addie's to him,

"It's all right. It'll be all right. It'll all be all right," he soothed, his hand rubbing her back methodically, as he said repeatedly what he intended to make true. Both consoling and ominous Stedman's voice reverberated. Temper heard it, if Mae and Gabriel did not.

She was home and she had not been harmed, not physically. At length, she was able to tell her folks, coherently, what had happened. "I know the man who stopped them was Gabe," she insisted adamantly, "I recognized his voice."

"And you're sure it was Butch Morris and Craven Herbert . . . ?" asked Stedman. There was no need to supply the predicate. His face was gray and hard, and the edge she had picked up was still there, Temper registered.

"Yes, Daddy, I'm certain of it," she responded, as if swearing from a witness stand and sealing someone's fate. She had some history of something like this, she recognized. An ass-kicking in one form or another would be the follow-up for her victimizers, she had reason to expect. The atmosphere in the kitchen had grown noticeably heavier, more threatening in its portent, Mae and Pa Gabriel finally now saw.

"What are you going to do!?" Temperance shot out, suddenly terrified of what would come next, of what Stedman would do next. Whatever it was, she knew it would be his move. No longer worried about Rhonda and herself, she was afraid of what Stedman would now do. And of what might be done to him in retaliation.

She was worried about Gabe Laughinghouse most of all. So far as she knew, he could be dead in the dark strip. And if not, she knew the Ku Klux Klan would get wind of it all, if they hadn't already. Was Gabe okay?! She knew about the Klan's activities and had heard rumors there were members working in the cotton mill. Gabe was a Colored man, a half-breed Negro-Indian, some saw him, held in even less regard, as ridiculously impossible as that seemed, than a full-blooded Negro. The Klan singled out men like him, especially if they dared tangle with a White man. Gabe had done that tonight. The jumble of thoughts crowding her consciousness made her feel sick at her stomach, like she was going to throw up, maybe. She glanced toward the bathroom but swallowed queasily and spoke again,

"Daddy, I'm terrified! I'm scared to death 'bout what they might do to Gabe!" He knew who "they" were. "And maybe to you, too, if you try to do anything! As far as I know, Gabe might be dead already!!"

The thought of it brought a fresh tumble of tears and wailing. None of them, not just Temperance, could bear to think of that demonic possibility, and each couldn't stop thinking of it, either. Gabe's grandfather's slain image filled their minds, as they imagined and dreaded a like fate for this young prince.

"Pl-ease don't do anything dan-gerous!" Temperance pleaded, sounding more like the meaning of her ancestral name than anyone had heard until then. And, in fact, it was the rational deliberation of temperate thought and action for which she precociously counseled her own father now.

Stedman was headed to the telephone to call the sheriff's office when the front porch screendoor opened and slammed shut again, and Gabe himself walked into the room.

"Gabe!!"

With a bound, Temper threw herself into Gabe's arms, replaying her fear and trauma, and now her sudden reprieve. Crying loudly again, but laughing too, she broke into a dance of relieved joy and thanksgiving for his safety, whirling around him and her family like shouters at New Faith Free Will Baptist had done before the Lord, when she had crawled under the collection table and sat and watched as a child. Like their jubilation, too, her dance of joy was an unfettered shout of reverence and gratitude. Gabe was unharmed! He was okay!!

"I'm so thankful you're all right, Gabe! Thank you for helping Rhonda and me!" she said, weeping and laughing still. "What would have happened to us if you hadn't been there?! And you! I was afraid they'd jumped on you, Gabe!"

Her face darkened instantaneously, fluidly, the frown and pallor as visible and genuine as the color and glee they replaced. It was what Gabe liked most about her. Emotion was natural to her and her lovely face showed it all. He had privately allowed himself to imagine what erotic ecstasy would look like there. And then felt ashamed of his indulgence. Ashamed and conflicted. More than anyone else he had yet known, Temper's capacity to feel and express what she felt abounded. He sensed what he was sure was true. He knew he could not, and would not, know more than that.

Not aware of his thoughts, Temperance grabbed him unashamedly around the waist and hugged him protectively. Then, catching herself, and perhaps absorbing something of the nature and depth of his thoughts, she backed away, realizing she had clung to him. Almost as she had done with Stedman, she added and edited, feeling the need to neutralize other thoughts crowding in upon those. Tonight, Gabe Laughinghouse had qualified for that high status, she focused anew. With Stedman and Pa Gabriel, he now completed a triumvirate of trustworthy humanity, both able and just. Those were the qualities which mattered to her. Softer virtues, like mercy, pity, and kindness, radiated from those strong ones, she believed she had learned. First lessons in values had come when she was much younger and more vulnerable. They had stayed.

"Come on, Shug, let's get ready for bed," Mae crooned, taking her by the arm.

Temperance offered her thanks to Gabe again, gave to each another shaky hug, and let herself be led off to bed. She was bone tired.

Mae said, "We'll leave the menfolk to study the situation out; they'll talk it over and decide what's best."

When fitful sleep drowned Temper's consciousness, the consoling hum of intelligent voices promised to keep the darkness outside the door.

All day Sunday, Temper sat with the men on the front porch, the four of them talking it over, studying it out, and grappling toward a decision of how best to handle what had happened. It was certain they would not drop it or let it slide.

Stedman lit one Chesterfield after the other, igniting each new one with the butt of the cigarette he had finished. While the others talked, he listened mainly. Not because he had nothing to say, but because he had more to think about than talk about. Everybody on the porch knew their input was relevant, but nonetheless largely academic; it would be Stedman who would decide what to do. Gabe Laughinghouse, too, had no doubt Stedman was carrying the ball, now.

When twilight came again, Stedman knew what he was going to do.

First thing Monday morning, he sent one of his first shift men across town to tell Craven Herbert and Butch Morris he wanted to see them in his mill office. Nine o'clock sharp. They appeared at his small, second-floor, overseer's office, shamefaced and apprehensive, guessing the reason they had been summoned, standing and shifting from foot to foot, as they waited before his desk. But not for long. Stedman entered the room without a greeting, sat down behind his desk, and characteristically wasted no time.

"Temp'rance tol' me you two sons o' bitches follered her an' her friend Saturday night."

He gave them no chance to reply. Half rising from the chair he had barely warmed, he pinned them like an entomologist a cockroach with his stare, with his dead-eyed fury,

"I oughta' beat the livin' hell outa' ya right here!"

He paused, considering it, and let them squirm. His adrenaline and rage had surged and boiled so high and hot, he could have shattered their vertebrae on the edge of his desk, or astrap the ribs of his office radiator. He'd contemplated both. And he thought of it again.

"Instead," he strangled out, "I'm gonna' fire your damned, sorry asses!"

His voice dropped an octave, barely audible,

"But if ever I hear tell o' one o'you goin' anywhere in sight o' my young'un again, I'll break ev'ry goddamned bone in your bodies," he finished.

Then loud enough for the whole mill to hear, he shouted,

"Now git outa' here!"

As the miscreants bounded through the door and down the stairs, Stedman yelled after them,

"Send your Klan after a *white* man the next time, you snivelin' cowards! But you damned well better keep yer filthy hands off little girls! Sheets or no sheets! Shit!" he yelled above the din of the machinery as they charged out the mill door, "You hear me?!"

They barely did. Already clambering into their rusted, green pick-up truck, they were soon out of sight, leaving a trail of blue exhaust smoke behind them, fouling the air as they went. The mill hill had seen its last of them. But not the last of their venom. There would be more of that.

"That beats Bobtail, and they say he beat the devil!" Matt White exclaimed when he heard what Stedman had said and done to Morris and Herbert, most of it accurate. A number of folks mouthed the same colloquialism, or one like it, when they got the surprising news. The scuttlebutt, largely true, reverberated around the village. Everyone knew Butch and Craven were no-'count drunkards and sorry, to boot, they said, but they had seen an unfamiliar side of Stedman Smith, a side to which they were unaccustomed. Habitually easygoing with his employees, he treated them all with respect and with deferential regard for the womenfolk and elderly, those who had given their prime years to the mill. Those folks were taken aback a little by the reports of his rough language, especially his taking the Lord's name in vain, and somewhat by his tough treatment of the men, firing them and all, but they thought the latter might well have been deserved. Nobody could blame him for protecting his daughter. Such a pretty, well-mannered girl, and a straight A student she was, they had heard.

"If they come back here and tell you I fired 'em for no reason, remember what I tol' you," explained Stedman to Bill Foster at knock time. "I can't count the times they've laid out drunk, an' they spend about as much time outdoors smoking as they do at their frames. I shoulda' fired 'em a long time ago. Maybe this mess wouldn't 've happened," Stedman said, justifying to himself and Bill his actions.

Bill reassured him that his actions had, indeed, been justified, and there would be no reversal of his decision by him. Stedman thanked his friend and headed home to tell his family what he had done. They had already heard. Temperance waited apprehensively on the porch. Mae shelled peas close by, rocking slowly in the cane-bottomed rocker she'd pulled out on the porch for that use.

"Don't worry," Stedman said to them, "I got it all straightened out," as he pulled himself up the porch steps, one heavy step at a time.

Neither Mae nor Temperance felt confident about what that meant. Besides, the firing story was making the village rounds, and Sally Jenkins had excitedly given her version of it to them just thirty minutes ago, pleased to be getting and "broadcasting" the news, even before Mr. Smith's wife and daughter had heard it.

"What did you do, Daddy?" Temperance ventured worriedly.

"I fired 'em. They won't be comin' near you anymore, I don't 'spect."

Scarcely comforted by his terse confirmation of the firing and the knowledge that Herbert and Morris had more reasons than Gabe's intrusion into White men's business and his rescue of her and Rhonda to mount a vendetta, Temper objected,

"But Daddy, I'm afraid they're gonna' try to get back at you for firin' them, and also at Gabe for stoppin' 'em! They're gonna' be mad, Daddy! I'm worried about what they might do to you! And to Gabe!"

Things were getting worse, not better, she reasoned. Mae's opinion matched hers, but she said nothing and shelled her peas quietly.

"We mustn't give in to intimidation and fear, Temper. And we certainly won't give in t' threats of any kind against you." (That datum had been established a long time ago.)

Stedman paused to light up a cigarette, his last in the pack, and he wadded the empty Chesterfield package, the cellophane cracking sharply like exclamation points to his speech, as he handed it to Mae, the gesture itself a husband's unconscious appeal for understanding of his actions. He repeated, as he puffed the Chesterfield into a glowing appendage,

"We can't give in t' fear, Shug. Just like Gabe can't give in t' what Colored folks are put through. That would play right into their hands." (He thought, ". . . the bastards' hands," but didn't say it.) "It always has, (a cigarette puff). They count on it. Intimidation, (another long draw). You know about that."

Stedman studied a long minute, and then he erupted, "But here's somethin' I'll admit you and I," he glanced at his daughter and his wife, "don't know about, not really. You know that fine, stone water fountain in front of the court house with the flowers carved on it so pretty, with "COLORED PEOPLE" engraved on it and "WHITE PEOPLE' engraved under the fountain at the other end, that's what I'm talkin' about, Temp'rance . . . Mae . . . , that's what we don't really know about. But Gabe does."

Then, realizing he'd merged subjects on them, he clarified, "What happened to you and Rhonda and what's happened all his life to Gabe is all mixed up together, Temper. It's about how we treat people. Right or wrong. Only a fool has real trouble figurin' out which is which."

At that point, realizing the need to ratchet down the intensity, both his and theirs, Stedman attempted a more placating tone, a softer approach. It wasn't easy for him.

"We've got to take the long view, Baby Girl," he said to Temper. "You understand that, too, don't you, Mae? Besides, I don't think they'll do anything."

One could only hope. Stedman himself sounded more confident than he honestly felt in the situation. He was beginning to wish he'd fired Butch and Craven without the cussing and four-letter words. He could've done it another way. He now felt he should've.

Both Stedman and Temper could raise the roof, there was no doubt about that. Father and daughter had difficulty reining themselves in when they were on a high horse. Other figures of speech fit as well. Said another of those ways, one chosen by Stedman himself as motto, they were quick to pick up the big stick and let 'em have it, symbolically, figuratively. If rarely physically, (though Stedman had counseled that to his young daughter for self defense), the big stick landed squarely, nonetheless. The firing had been a big stick. With or without the profanity.

Stedman's thoughts circled back, as he sought to rationalize his actions. Herbert and Morris had deserved the firing on account of their sorriness and laziness, and because they had shown themselves to be a threat to the mill village community. He wished he could take back the profanity, though. He'd poured on more fuel than the fire needed.

There might be the devil to pay.

Chapter Eight

I find myself thinking that somewhere down the line both guilt and empathy speak to our own buried sense that an order of some sort is required . . . . something more fundamental and more demanding, a sense, further, that one has a stake in this order, a wish that, no matter how fluid the order sometimes appears, it will not drain out of the universe.

Barack Obama

Two weeks after the trauma of the dark strip incident and the unsettling events devolving from it, Stedman's firing of Morris and Herbert specifically and most immediately, Temperance had regained enough composure and self-assurance to go to town by herself again, midday, at least. Rhonda had gone on Thursday to visit her aunt in Kenansville and would not be home again until the next Thursday or Friday. No matter, as an only child, Temper had long ago learned to enjoy her own company. Besides, solitary walks to town had never bothered her before; if she was lucky, they still wouldn't. And she wanted to look for a yellow blouse. Yellow looked good on her with her nearly black hair and dark brown eyes. Some said they were nearly black, too. Yellow was a hard color to find, however, something she found annoying, as if fate and circumstances had conspired maliciously to make it so. Temper busied her mind with such thoughts, absorbing their triviality, in part to keep from thinking about what she dreaded she would not be able to hold at bay.

The passage through the dark strip (Temper did not try to avoid it) went easily enough, she was relieved to discover, and she was soon uptown. For once, the ogling men at the Esso station on Blount had seemed entirely benign, curiously watchful now, like a proto-community watch assemblage, (as watchful neighbors would come to be identified), as they had tracked her approach, according to their habit, through the darkened sidewalk bordering Miss Mattie's house and yard. Familiar eyes were watching. But the men had no knowledge of what had happened. They were enjoying the pretty girl's sway and bounce; that was all. Temperance now realized they had never done more than observe: no whistling or commenting (that she could hear), and certainly, no chasing. They stood silently and watched her go by; she marked the difference between their actions and those of Herbert and Morris. And she wouldn't lie to herself that their attention was not flattering; a little embarrassing, but flattering it surely was, nonetheless. She wouldn't deny she liked it.

Meandering in and out of several department stores and a couple of ladies' shops, Belk-Tyler's and Brody's among them, Temper fussed inwardly at the thought that her search had been fruitless again. She felt herself growing tired and irritable by the moment. And hungry. In point of fact, she had buttressed the whole trip with another anticipated end in mind, one unrelated to the blouse hunt and impervious to its success or failure. This was a hot dog, with a few onions, a moderate amount of chili, and lots of mustard, "extra mustard, please," at McLelland's lunch counter. Shopping generally made her hungry; it famished her, she admitted, and around noon, she stopped in at the dimestore beside the Carolina Theater, her old stomping ground since the first grade, to order the hot dog with a fountain Co' Cola and maybe a bag of Wise potato chips. She was now feeling weak, no doubt from a drop in blood sugar, or what Mae called "the weak trembles." Both of them suffered a touch of hypoglycemia now and then, and Mae's name for it described it well. The hot dog and drink were what she needed; they would do the trick, and she had her heart set on them.

Inside McLelland's, she first paused at the cosmetics counter, despite her mounting symptoms, and looked at the lipsticks, a ritual of long standing consisting of opening a few tubes and smelling them, then rolling out the lipsticks to see the color and shade better. That was her method, smelling and then checking the shade, since she was nine or ten. Unobserved, she hoped, of course. But she had never touched the lipstick itself when she was younger. Now, she cheated a little and sometimes wiped a tiny smear on the back of her hand to get a better idea of how it would look on her. She convinced herself it did no harm to whoever later bought it, if she didn't buy it herself. Usually she did, and if she had a cold, she voluntarily deferred her ritual, anyhow.

Temperance had long since decided the dear Christians at New Faith Baptist in Pineboro had had it wrong about the perceived evils of cosmetics, those lovely, sweet-smelling wares. And about movies, too. Stedman had been her ready ally on that one. The lipstick decision she'd made on her own. Mae still didn't wear either lipstick or earbobs. But far be it from anyone who knew her to question the way Mae Smith lived out her faith. Either shame or humility shut their mouths; they all knew they had a long way to go to match her devotion and authenticity, her simplicity and service. Temperance respected her mother's way and defined and claimed her own, a mark of her intelligence and self-assurance.

With growing confidence in her developing powers of thought and analysis, Temper relied less on others' analyses and opinions than on her own, pretty much. To be sure, as a young child, she had been headed that way. It pleased her to know it.

"I'd like this one, please," said she, handing a bright pink Revlon lipstick to the saleslady who approached her with a courteous smile, never a merely incidental behavior to Temper who valued courtesy anytime it was extended to her. With considerate treatment she was nurtured and bolstered, and it made her strong. She was smart enough to see that.

Reaching into her change purse for the quarter she owed, on the rumble of a stomach growl, she thought again about the hot dog in the back of the store. Apologizing to the amused clerk, she commented that her stomach was talking to her and that her weak trembles were getting worse. The clerk signaled that she knew about the weak trembles, too, and agreed that she needed to get something to eat, now.

"Thank you, ma'am," Temper smiled, "thank you for your help," she added, and took the small, paper bag with her lipstick inside it.

As Temperance turned and looked toward the long, green, lunch counter running the full length of the back wall, her eye picked out a single, empty stool. She was glad there was a vacant spot for her. Next, her eye and mind grasped the presence of two men. Her spot was between two men. Two men had chased her. Moreover, young girls chose seats beside women or children, not men, generally. For this complication, she was not glad. Then, her eye and mind identified the two men as Colored. On either side of the empty stool sat a young Colored man. At first glance, on the model of a Rorschach test, her mind had registered only the single, vacant stool. Then, the two men, and the dark strip chase got fused with that. Only afterward, did she see that they were two Colored men. Test complete.

Nothing political came to mind. Just that she'd never sat between two Colored men at a lunch counter before that day. Shit fire! She was too weak, and too hungry, to split hairs and leave without the hot dog!

And then, her good sense told her there was nothing wrong with sitting there. Nothing wrong at all. Indeed, her mind had already told her that. In point of fact, there was something intrinsically right about it. Decent. True. Another test completed.

Temperance sat down. She probably could have taken her own good time deciding. There was no apparent hurry needed to snag it. No one seemed to be thinking about grabbing the last stool. Though two hungry people, to their credit, were quietly seated on the other side of the Colored men, no one except Temper appeared to covet the last, empty stool between them.

Five years later, Temperance would watch passively, but with mounting discomfort, while a college student acquaintance and classmate elected to stand in the aisle beside an empty seat on a Raleigh transit bus, rather than sit beside the Negro passenger in the seat adjoining it. Numerous times Temper had wished she had risen from her own window seat a few rows back and offered it to the classmate. And sat beside the rejected woman herself. She hadn't. She had to have had a failure of nerve that day. She refused to rationalize it now, unless an explanation was itself a rationalization. She knew better because she had already acted better.

That earlier day, no one of the three, Temperance or the two, courageous men on either side of her, said a word, either she to them or they to her. Temperance gave her request to the lunch counter clerk who took her order, and then, she raised her face slowly up to the youth on her left and looked squarely into Gabriel Laughinghouse's eyes. They weren't laughing. They were somber and tentative, but pleased, very pleased, that she had sat down beside him. Not surprised, either, very pleased. Temper would draw on that lingering look of admiration and gratitude Gabe's eyes held for her. On that eternal look.

At the moment, she gasped her surprised recognition and, as instantaneously, she realized that it was important that she not speak to him or draw any attention to the fact that they knew each other. Whether she had ever seen the man on her right or not, she did not know and she dared not look to see. With dispatch, she ate her hot dog and left the store without glancing again at Gabriel.

Now, as she wrote her memories, Temperance did not recollect that she had noticed either Gabe or the other young man eating or drinking anything at all. She would guess they were not. She did not recall that anyone offered to serve them. No one said a word to them, as far as she knew. Gabriel and his friend just sat there, silently. She had no knowledge of how long they had been sitting at the lunch counter before she arrived, or how long they remained seated on the stools after she left, whether they were forced to leave, or chose to go on their own volition. She wished she had more recollection and knowledge of that, but she didn't.

Not until years later did Temperance realize she had witnessed and inadvertently participated in one of the earliest lunch counter sit-ins of a burgeoning Civil Rights Era. What she did realize that day, seemingly instinctively, intuitively, and decidedly and clearly analytically, was that Gabriel Laughinghouse had again put himself in great danger. Though no police officers had shown up in McLelland's to remove him and his friend from the counter, and no media representatives, either newspaper reporters or radio journalists, had picked up the story, or considered it newsworthy if they had, so far as she could tell, she felt certain the Klan found out anyway, maybe before she reached home.

As Temperance walked back through the dark strip, a dread, a foreboding, fell on her which she cleanly identified as related to the trauma of two weeks earlier, yes, but which was connected to the day's lunch counter incident more immediately, and possibly more dangerously. Catastrophe had been escaped two weeks ago. But what about now? Were others likely to read Gabe's actions as innocent, inconsequential? She was afraid not. The mechanics at the Esso station nearly forgotten, she had barely noticed their noticing her as she had passed their workplace again.

Mae was in the kitchen warming up leftovers for dinner when Temperance reached her yard. She had heard the familiar hymn as soon as she had opened the screendoor.

"This is my sto-ry, this is my song . . . ."

Thirsty from her brisk, hot walk home, she went directly to the sink and filled her favorite water glass with water from the tap. Then she poured it out and went instead to the water bucket beside the stove, scooped a half-full dipper of water, and absently drank it, her mind on more than her thirst. Replacing the long-handled, enamelware dipper into the bucket somewhat abruptly, she asked her mother,

"Where's Daddy?"

Mae could hear the urgency in Temper's voice over the crackle of ice cubes as she mashed them from the tray and plopped them into the bucket, adding more to cool the water for dinner. It was Saturday, and Temper knew Pa Gabriel was working at West End Grocery. Stedman generally had Saturdays off, however.

"He's on the porch," answered Mae, wondering what it was she had heard in her daughter's voice. She guessed it might concern young Laughinghouse, so much had involved him lately.

Turning toward the front of the house and preoccupied with worry that the lunch counter particulars would cause trouble for Gabe, Temper walked through the house and out onto the porch where Stedman sat in his customary place astraddle his ladder-back chair. He was then talking to the junior overseers under him who managed the second and third shifts. The conversation sounded curiously animated, she had heard as she neared the porch, not their usual, muted and matter-of-fact shop talk. Reflexively, she wondered if the village grapevine had already relayed the lunch counter news to the hill.

"I'm glad I don't have t' put up with Butch any longer," Marvin Swindell, the second shift overseer, said energetically, "I never knowed 'im to be on time, I don't b'lieve, maybe once or twice, at the most. Craven, neither." Marvin punctuated his announcement with an explosive burst of tobacco spit launched off the side of the porch steps and into the yard.

Gene Brewer lit a Camel. He smoked about as many Camels as Stedman did Chesterfields. Swindell favored Lucky Strikes when he smoked, and alternatively Beechnut chewing tobacco if he had more of a mind to chew, which he did when his breathing got extra short, "like it's done today," he had declared when he arrived. Laying off cigarettes a few days seemed like a good idea, or "idee," to him at such times, and his doctor had advised him to do that.

"That young Colored feller, though," Gene Brewer was saying," there's some that's upsot 'bout him comin' 'roun' the mill so much. It's like he's out'n his place, you know," Brewer adjudicated.

She had held her tongue and listened, but now Temper jumped into the conversation,

"If we invite him here, this is his place," she said. "Besides, who's got the right to say what another person's place is?"

Both bossmen shifted uncomfortably, visibly embarrassed that a girl had disputed with them, interjecting herself into the discussion that way, almost challenging them, it seemed, but they knew

Stedman's girl to be right headstrong. Her behavior now wasn't altogether unusual. Stedman picked up her question; he knew she hadn't intended it to hang out there in the air that way. And that if he didn't answer it, she would herself.

"I guess we've all got to try to answer that question, Shug," Stedman replied with another drag on his cigarette, "and it's a mighty big one. As long as nobody's breakin' the law or committin' a crime, I guess ever'body ought to get to say for himself what his place is."

Temperance wasn't satisfied. "But some laws may not be right; they may be unfair, the laws themselves," she pressed, the color rising in her already flushed cheeks as she saw in her mind the fresh image of Gabe at the legally sanctioned, Whites-only, lunch counter.

"If it's a law, it's a law," said Swindell, with a second from Brewer, neither man especially liking what the two of them had heard from either their supervisor or his girl.

Neither overseer wanted to sort out the messiness Gabe Laughinghouse's presence in the mill community had brought to their work. Clearly, the disdain they held for Morris and Herbert had not translated into increased tolerance for one seen as an intruder. Worse, as an inferior, a man out of his place.

Swindell stood up and announced, "Well, I 'spect it's time I got on back t' the house. I'll see you Monday, Stedman."

Gene Brewer arose, too, and offered some explanation about needing to pick up some dog food for his hunting dogs.

Temperance was glad to see them go. Their rigid views disturbed and annoyed her. Besides, she wanted to talk to Stedman about what had happened at McLelland's. Almost sixteen, she and her father had gradually become, as she grew older, each other's confidant, consultant, and, on occasion, co-conspirator, not to mention baseball buddies and avid fans of the Lenoirville Eagles. Reliably, he had been a solid bulwark for her since her birth, and over time, she had grown up to be a source of strength for him. This pleased them both and welded the bond holding them fast. In that strong context, she told him about the lunch counter episode.

"You did the right thing, Shug. Gabe Laughinghouse is a good human being, good as I've ever known. To refuse to sit beside him would send a message that you consider him to be less than you."

Stedman had mistaken her point, Temper felt. That was unusual. She had no question about the rectitude of her actions and she was seeking no guidance along those lines. She knew she was right. Her concern had to do with the possible consequences following upon Gabriel's new intrusion into what most White persons considered their territory. What might happen to Gabe on account of that? How many times could he dodge the bullet? He had gone where White people like Swindell and Brewer thought he had no business. Again. Wasn't that what they had just heard from the overseers? And they were pretty decent people, not scoundrels like Morris and Herbert, and nobody suspected them of Klan alignment or sympathy. Besides, the matter at hand here was the fact that the Klan would know all about it and probably already did, not whether she had done the right thing or not by sitting where she did, Temper thought with considerable annoyance toward a father who seldom annoyed her. But, after all, she was, as Mae had said, one who would argue with a signpost.

Seemingly oblivious to her impatience with him, Stedman had not stopped talking about the significance of sitting next to a Colored man. He was talking as much to himself as to her, Temperance decided.

"If you'll sit beside a White man, you should sit next to him. Besides, he's your friend."

This was plowing new ground for Stedman, too. His unambiguous words did not honestly match his apprehension, but his logic was faultless, notwithstanding. Despite his "knock-down, drag-out" philosophy, and behavior occasionally exhibiting it, the first clause of his mantra was clearly one of nonviolence and respect for all persons. Temper had gotten that point early. Refusal to sit beside a Colored man constituted disrespect. It was as simple as that to Stedman. This lunch counter new ground wasn't so hard to plow, after all. He had learned early that, if you started with your values and they were just, things fell into place, most likely. He rehearsed those, for himself and for Temper,

"I've always said, 'Never hit another person first.' You're old enough now to know that includes not treating them disrespectfully in any way at all. There's more than one way to knock a person down."

Temperance nodded her agreement and Stedman picked up his cigarette pack off the porch railing in front of him. He pulled a cigarette out and struck a match to it, cupping it with his right hand to keep the breeze from snuffing the wispy flame. Then he blew the match out and flipped it over the banister. Like cigarette butts, match sticks, too, most persons did not regard as litter in the early days of the nineteen fifties.

"Why do you think I invited Levy Butler to come over to our house and play your piano for us? Sure, he could make that thing stand up and talk," he remembered with a smile, "but I had another reason besides music and poker to invite Levy. A Colored man was as welcome here as a White man, if his character was as good, and Levy's was. That's still true; nothing's changed about that. That's why Gabe's welcome at our table, too. It'd be nice if he could play the piano," Stedman joked and grinned, trying to coax a smile from his glum daughter.

He took a few puffs on his fresh Chesterfield, as though testing its flavor, and resumed his narrative about Levy Butler's membership in his Saturday afternoon poker games, a body of a half dozen or so games in the chilly, winter months when it was too cold for birdhunting or going to the dog racing in Greenville, and when those pastimes were out of season, in any event. Stedman's White friends had no objection to Levy's participation in the poker games. If they did, they kept it to themselves. Besides, Levy was no better than a mediocre poker player, good enough to play the game, but not hard to beat, so they could generally win his little bit of money he bet. To put it kindly, he gave them no serious competition at the poker table. At the honky tonk piano, though, Levy was unbeatable.

"Pistol Packin' Mama" and "The Old Rugged Cross" were standards of Levy's and he played one as fervently, as energetically, as he did the other. For "Pistol Packin' Mama," though, Levy added a raucous thump and grind, and it brought 'em to their feet. When Levy played like that, even Mae could not resist a smile and a tapping of her feet, despite her stated objection (to kindred spirits at church) to that kind of music. It rocked the house, literally. They could feel it shake. Like poker playing, such music was the devil's work, Mae believed, and she peeled her potatoes in the kitchen with visible discomfort, commingled with foot-tapping, but without saying anything to anyone at home about it. For her part, Temper flat-out enjoyed it and said so.

Mae liked it better when Levy played "The Old Rugged Cross" and "Farther Along," the first a favorite of hers and the latter a favorite of Stedman's and a standard request of his. Everybody sang along, including her, enthusiastically. A hymn was good whenever and wherever it was played, Mae allowed in occasional, brief commentary. And by whomever it was played, Temperance added, as she recalled those days, and she knew her folks agreed on that, as well.

The poker games dwindled and dried up after Levy's tractor-trailer jackknifed and broke up, sliding and crashing into one car after another, one icy Monday night between Norfolk and Burlington. Several people were hurt badly, and Levy was the first of three who died. They said the superintendent at the cotton mill in Burlington sent his widow an envelope stuffed with twenty dollar bills. Stedman, with Levy's other poker buddies, took up a love offering at his house for Ava Butler and her and Levy's seven, school-aged children, except for the two oldest who had married off by then without finishing school. Temperance and Mae thought four hundred and eighteen dollars was a right smart sum from poor folks; the eighteen dollars were their part of the gift, Mae's and Temper's. They later learned Ava Butler had used most of the money to get their car in good running condition, and she had bought a washing machine with the rest of it.

Stedman's story about Levy Butler was in no wise merely ancillary, but it was a way station on his journey back to another memory and chronicle previous to that one. The lunch counter incident, Gabe's application for a job in the cotton mill, the dark strip assault and the trouble with Butch Morris and Craven Herbert, his firing of them, most dramatically, along with recent conversation between Gabe and himself, had rewound Stedman's thoughts to earlier days and another central struggle not yet talked enough about; he needed to talk about it all. And he needed Temper to hear it all. She had caught him at the apex of this confluence of memories and incidents, and it was time to unwind, time to confide in and entrust with her a part of her family history she did not yet know. She sensed the reality unfolding and settled herself to listen patiently, insofar as that was possible for her to do. Her father's face looked uncommonly tired and drawn, she noticed, now. Not since his kidney surgery had he looked that way.

"Shug, I never told you why I left—we left—Martinville so fast back in '46. You may not remember it, but we were there only two months before we moved up here."

Actually, Temperance did have clear childhood memories of the days in Martinville, including the brevity of time they lived there. Her teacher's response of sincere disappointment over her leaving the school had sealed the memory of that short time for her. She had learned how to tell when a person meant what she said.

"Oh, I'm so sorry Temperance is leaving," Miss Betts had lamented, "I was just getting ready to move her up to the top reading group."

Those were her words to Mae that last day when Mae had picked her up from school.

With visible effort, Stedman pushed onward, "Well, something happened there I never told you about," he was saying, his earnest, hazel eyes clouding with his charged memory.

Temperance's thoughts suddenly launched and spiraled out of control. Had he been in a fight?! Had someone died?! At his hands? Her father wouldn't kill anyone. No matter how mad he got, his threats were more comical than violent. Kicking someone's ass 'til his nose bled sounded pretty bad, but its hyperbole, its excess, was exactly that, she knew. Most importantly, Stedman was just, inherently so by nature, she believed, and justice never included killing anyone. At least, she didn't think so. Except maybe in self defense. Or to defend the innocent. She needed more time to think it out. But she both feared the possibility and believed its impossibility. What had Whitman said about such inconsistency? She knew her father's character.

Stedman's voice halted her wild tumble of thoughts. He was saying,

"A bunch of us decided we needed to start the union up in the cotton mill. A labor union representative, a nice, young fella by the name of Stancil, had talked to us a few times about it, in secret, you see, because Nelson Riggs, the bossman, didn't like him comin' 'roun' there and influencin' us. But Stancil told us how things had improved at other mills where the union got in. Higher wages, more rest breaks, better workin' conditions all roun'."

Stedman paused and lit another Chesterfield. After a long drag on it, he continued,

"Riggs got wind of it an' notified Paul Grant, the mill owner, and a few days later, Mr. Grant came to the mill an' called us all together."

He stopped and adjusted his chair, changing his position slightly, and waved a bothersome fly away from his face.

"I saw his big, black Cadillac when it pulled up in front of the mill office, and I knew it was him," Stedman recalled.

The man who stepped imperiously and a little stiffly out of his long, new sedan when the Colored chauffeur opened his door for him was surprisingly diminutive in height and build, no more than five-five or five-six, at most, "not much taller than you, Temp'rance, if any," Stedman had said. The first thing Mr. Grant did was to run his fingers slowly down the razor-sharp creases of his expensive, gray trousers, almost as if to delay the thing he was hell-bent on doing, or more likely, to burnish his prestigious image. Small-framed and short, with an accustomed Napoleonic air resembling the emperor's look and his mien of command and privilege, Mr. Grant possessed, as well, a thick head of coarse, white hair and small, unremarkable features, hard and stonelike and close to the same color, but otherwise commonplace.

Stedman thought his face looked like maybe it hadn't seen a lot of light. As noticeable as his pallor were the thick, heavy eyeglasses he wore and their magnification of his irises and pupils. When Stedman saw him up close later, inside the mill where his millhands waited quietly for Mr. Grant to address them, he noticed how big the glasses made his weak eyes look, giving the autocratic mill owner, at first impression, the comical appearance of a human bug. Comical, were it not disconcerting to Stedman, and pitiful, he couldn't help thinking.

"Indisputably," Stedman commented now to Temperance, "Mr. Grant was burdened with a problem of poor vision."

There followed a long pause in which father and daughter were silent.

"Wait a minute, Shug," Stedman requested.

He fumbled in his shirt pocket where he'd replaced his cigarette pack, pulled it out of the too-snug pocket, and got the last Chesterfield, a slightly crumpled one which he smoothed lightly with a tobacco-stained finger and lit deftly, as usually, with the butt of the one he'd smoked down to a stub. Temperance had no memory of anyone's discarding a half-finished cigarette, in those days. Hot tips were smudged off and the salvaged remainder redeposited in the cigarette pack when situations indicated a cigarette could not then be finished and the smoker had to wait. But cigarette stubs too short to smoke dotted the ground all over the hill and on the sidewalks in town. Little attention was paid to it. Temper watched as her father flipped the snuffed, spent stub, barely long enough to grasp with thumb and index finger, over the porch railing and into the bushes.

Temperance had long experience of this familiar ritual and welcomed the curious peace it conferred. Quiet attended the ceremony, and a kind of solemnity, a setting straight the order of things, before Stedman resumed his speech. Her father's cigarette smoking was as much a part of her daily life as his parental dependability. They, the smoking and the parenting, were a unified, iconic whole, one interwoven fabric and reality, framing and informing the day's experience and helping in making sense of it all.

Stedman took up his narrative again, oblivious to the cascading thoughts in Temper's mind, lost in his own, intent on telling this story of his, hers too, which he had saved until she was old enough to sort it out with him in thought and discussion. It was difficult to narrate, she could see. Stedman had put on too many extra pounds in Lenoirville, and his breathing had become noticeably labored over the last several months, what with his chainsmoking and the fat meat Mae cooked for them, his earlier kidney disease, and this thing he was about to confide, perhaps with that, most of all. This is what he told her:

When Paul Grant had stood to his full five and a half foot height to address his assembled millhands, his voice had matched his stone face. If his height failed to meet expectations, his voice measured up; it was fully the commanding voice of an authoritative man. He offered no words of greeting. Right out of his belly, he spewed,

"I've found out that some of you want to start up the union here. In my cotton mill. Well, I won't beat aroun' the bush. The day will not come when I let the union come in one o' my mills. Before I do that, I'll close 'em all down. I've got enough money in three banks t' last me the rest of my life."

His commanding voice spiked tinny and shrill, making him appear less self-confident, and rather more distraught and small, as bragging and bullying commonly do to those who practice such, than he wanted to present himself as being. But his pit bull attack had eviscerated its intended victims. Powerless, intimidated "millhands," valued *only* for their hands, shrank visibly under his attack dog assault and its fury. But it had not ceased.

"And I don't need any o' you! Before I turn the labor union in here, I'll fire every one o' you an' put you back to eatin' catfish 'n' cornbread!" he swore apoplectically.

Grant sputtered and wiped his mouth, rocking a little, unsteady on his feet as in his moral bearings, his physiological compass as flawed as his spiritual one, Temperance wrote. In the nineteen thirties and forties, a lot of people believed catfish were unfit for human consumption. This included poor people who of necessity ate almost anything considered clean enough and decent. Catfish were not. Unlike most other fresh water fish, they were known to be scavengers, seeking out and devouring rotting things for their food. Most poor folks considered them "nasty," and anyone who ate them had to be "perishin' t' death," to do so. Paul Grant knew all that.

Grant's threat was more than a job threat. It was a targeted insult and a slap at whatever shred of dignity the men and women huddled before him yet possessed.

The ashen, stone absence of color in his peaked face had heated to fiery red, now. But Stedman saw and heard nothing more, except the hollow sound of his own footsteps on the wooden mill floor and the loud bang of the heavy, outside door, as he departed the Martinville mill for the final time. Grant had lost his best millhand.

"That's what happened, Shug. I couldn't stay after that. I wouldn't stay. So I walked straight to John Hester's grocery store, right through the pourin' rain, and called Bill Foster here, an' he tol' me to come on up. There was a job for me here in Lenoirville, he offered, and as soon as he could work it out, there'd be an overseer's job, to boot," Stedman said before finishing, "We moved the next day."

Temper drew in a sharp breath. She had held it, literally, barely breathing enough to support consciousness. She felt ashamed of herself now for imagining that her father might have injured someone in a fight, maybe killed him. She knew he wouldn't. Her worry over Gabe must have muddled her thought. Addie had loved him, Stedman, too much. People who have been loved a lot, even by one person, anyone, don't ordinarily kill others, she believed. Killers are made that way, carved that way, Pa Gabriel had said, by neglect and mistreatment, by abuse and harsh disrespect, and by exclusion and hate. A killer's soul has already been killed, she and Pa believed, before he kills another. That was not Stedman.

His voice jostled her attention.

"I guess if he hadn't, we'd 'a been in a fix. Out of a job an' nowhere to go," he was saying.

The risk still sobered and imperiled him, Temper could see. Vulnerability and hardship like he'd experienced left a residue. And he had more to say to her.

"But I'd 'a done somethin' to feed us. I'd 'a cut ditch banks, gone to the log woods, somethin'," he rambled, having some difficulty turning loose of the emotions he'd excavated.

It was true. He would have, she knew.

Stedman paused, reflective, unmoving, still. Temper expected him to reach into his shirt pocket for another Chesterfield, but he didn't. Perhaps he remembered he was out. She knew she herself was feeling new pride in him. He had stood up to the dirtiest mouth he had ever heard and refused to listen, laying everything he had on the line. Without obscenity or profanity, Paul Grant had managed to be more profane and obscene, more cruel and unmerciful, than Stedman would tolerate. It wasn't merely about him and Mae. It was about all those friends and assembled co-workers who gave their energy, time, and job loyalty, to Grant every working day and whose contributions he had thrown into the dirt, along with their hopes for a secure job and opportunity to have a better life than mere subsistence and struggle. Not least was the assault on their dignity. If Stedman had wondered where his limits lay, he believed he had found them that morning. And he had acted. He would not support Grant's cruelty by standing by in silence and returning passively to his job, working the long hours, breathing the cotton dust, and giving his best years, to a greedy few who profited at the expense and very soul of so many, and who blatantly, without shame, did the disgraceful act Grant had done on behalf of himself and those few, with impunity. Mr. Grant was half right. He would eat catfish and cornbread first. And he said so, if not in just that way, in exactly that spirit.

"There are times we have to take a stand, Temper. Some things are right. And some things are just plain wrong. A fool oughta' be able to see they're wrong. Plain as the nose on your face, I say."

The catfish-and-cornbread onslaught had stoked old fire, stirred old outrage.

"A smart person can gen'lly tell the difference. You did the right thing, Shug. I'm proud of you."

Then, he responded to Temperance's target concern,

"Gabe did the right thing, too. He's got to do it, Temp'rance. It's his only way. I hope and pray he'll be all right."

Did he realize he had not said that he would be all right? That it all would be all right? Temper noticed and wondered. Still, he'd responded honestly, truly. It was what she had sought from him.

Now, Stedman reached out a tobacco-yellowed finger and pushed her hair off her high forehead and behind her ear. The characteristic, habitual gesture comforted, reinforced and reassured, her. It was like he was saying thereby,

"Let your face show to the world who you are and what you stand for, Temp'rance. Make it plain and clear. And be proud you did."

The way he had done. The way Gabe had done.

What he had said in plain words was,

"There's more than one kind of big stick, Temper, and more than one way to hit 'em as hard as you can. I found mine. You'll find yours. When you do, let 'em have it!"

Chapter Nine

One more devils' triumph and sorrow for angels,
One more wrong to man, one more insult to God!
Robert Browning

Temper spent the evening watching for Gabe, hoping he would come by the house, eager to tell him so many things and anxious to know he was all right. She wanted to be certain he knew why she had not spoken to him at the lunch counter and why she had eaten her hot dog quickly and left so fast. She believed he knew why, but she wanted to be sure of it.

She needed to ask him why he was sitting there, he and the other Colored man. She thought she knew that, too, but she wanted to hear him talk about what he was attempting to do and how it related to his efforts to get a job in the mill. (The term "sit-in" was not yet in America's cultural lexicon and she had not yet heard it.) Most of all, Temperance wanted to know that he was still safe. He had compounded the dangerous risks he had been taking weekly since his arrival in Lenoirville. And she had been the cause for one of those risky actions. Her responsibility in this scenario was not a fact of which she was unaware or innocent. And the scenario itself was taking on an ominous life of its own, she feared. She would come to know she was right about that.

Since he had arrived in Lenoirville, Gabe had done something to raise somebody's hackles on a weekly basis. First, he had visited in an all-White community and eaten at a White family's table, several times. He had applied for a job which was open to White folks alone. He had challenged two White men and interrupted their drunken chase after her and Rhonda. Now, he had sat at a "White only" lunch counter in McLelland's Dimestore and expected a White waitress to serve him food and drink. Colored men had been lynched in North Carolina and all across the Southland for less than that. Just one of those perceived infractions could bring the wrath of the Ku Klux Klan down on him. She had heard Malcolm Burton say that his grandfather had seen a Colored man beaten to death in broad daylight on the main street of Grange City, a one-horse, farming town in Alabama too small to be called a city, where he had lived in the days of the Great Depression. He, the Colored man, had looked too long at a White man's comely sister, it was told by some both alarmed by the violence and curiously proud of the racial vendetta. Temperance could hardly bear to think about it. And she couldn't stop doing it, either.

Around six-thirty, Temper asked aloud, although rhetorically, why Gabe had not come by the house to let her know he was okay. He must know that that question had been on her mind since she had left the dimestore a little past noon. There was no use pretending there was nothing to worry about, if that was what he was doing. Everybody knew there was.

Last time she had waited to learn that he was safe, when he had walked into the dark strip between her and Rhonda and the men after them, separating them from harm; she had worried until he had shown up then, too. He knew that. But he had finally come by, and maybe he would now, she reminded herself in a vain pass at self control and patience.

Still, she had to keep thinking about that. He was busy and hadn't had a chance to get by there, yet. Or maybe he and the other young man went to some kind of meeting they had to go to first. There were always reasons. She mustn't just assume the worst ones.

That "blue time of day" came and passed and the sky grew dark. Stedman turned on "The Grand Ole Opry" out of Nashville and they all sat around and listened to the radio while Mae read her Sunday School lesson and Pa Gabriel whittled a peachseed monkey. Temperance tried to read the newspaper with half her attention and intermittently watched the sky darken, as she followed the hands of the clock with dread and whatever attention she had remaining for anything but sick worry.

Mae tried to comfort and reassure her, "Don't cross a bridge until you get to it, Shug."

Temperance was by nature a bridge-crosser, not a nail-biter, but definitely a bridge-crosser. Where was he?! She looked at the clock again. Ten-thirty! Why hadn't he come about the same time he showed up the last time? About ten o'clock?! She was terrified that she knew why. He couldn't. That must be it. Considerate by nature and choice, he would want to erase her fear and worry. He would want to let her know he was safe. If he could. The circular thoughts tormented her mercilessly now.

And even for him, Stedman had deposited a lot of cigarette butts in his stand-alone ashtray beside his recliner, one of the first such chairs offered for sale in a Lenoirville furniture store. (His doctor had recommended he purchase it for his back after the kidney surgery.) She knew why. He was worried, too, despite his efforts to conceal it and pretend he was interested in Roy Acuff's singing. And Minnie Pearl's cornpone jokes. But the cigarettes gave him away. His words to her had been wise and true and she agreed with them all, the spoken and implied ones. They would uphold her and strengthen her when she needed to draw on them. She could count on them. But right now, she needed to hear from Gabe.

When Temper finally went to bed, an hour after Pa Gabriel and her parents had turned in, she lay awake another hour, listening for a step on the porch, a squeak of the screen door. At last, she dropped off to troubled sleep. Gabe had not come.

On Sunday morning, daybreak awoke her. Immediately, she pushed off the wadded bedspread half covering her legs and hurried into the living room to see if Gabriel had come in after she had fallen asleep, perhaps to spend the night on the couch, as he had done on one occasion. She had left the screen door unlatched for him. Gabe was not there.

Saturday's newspaper lay scattered on the couch and on the floor, exactly as she had left it. No one had touched it. There was no indication he had been there at all. Temperance decided that she would ask Stedman after breakfast to drive her over to the Morgans' house where Gabe had told them he was staying. They would need to ask someone in the neighborhood which house belonged to the Morgans. Maybe Gabriel had gone back there, instead. A glimmer of hope flickered, but faintly. At least, she was doing what she could.

Gabe had not returned to the Morgans' house, either. Throughout the weekend and the early part of the next week, Gabe made no further visits to the mill hill. This was not like him, the Smith family agreed. All except Pa Gabriel joined in the talk about what might account for Gabe's absence. At West End Grocery, it was already becoming the scuttlebutt. Pa was unusually quiet on the subject, morose, it seemed. Temper's distraction over Gabe left her little focus for renewed concern over Pa's disengaged behavior, except a momentary worry and hope that he was not sinking into depression again.

Temperance asked everyone she saw, "Have you seen Gabe Laughinghouse, I mean, since last Saturday?" They had not.

She made another trip uptown to McLelland's to ask at the lunch counter, and throughout the store, if anyone there had seen him. No one had.

Gabe's unexplained absence was all the more peculiar because he had become a member of the Smith family. He knew he had.

"I ain't seen 'im since last Thursday," Mae realized.

Pa Gabriel merely nodded.

Fridays were typically the days Mae fixed salmon stew, or she fried perch or pike from the river, or fresh croakers or, occasionally, flounder from Kennedy's Fish Market, and Gabe tried to be present for those meals, the fish and the boiled, Irish potatoes and homemade slaw, Pa's buttermilk cornbread, and frosty pint jars of sweetened, iced tea, sweeter than he was accustomed to drinking in Detroit, but about the same as he had learned to like in Georgia. It wasn't Friday supper without Gabe there; now, it was that way, and Gabe had missed Friday's fish supper with his friends, with his new family. Still, there was nothing particularly unusual about that.

He was mighty busy. And Temper had seen him at McLelland's on Saturday. Such were Mae's silent thoughts.

Stedman ate quietly, his silence a match for Pa's. He, too, wondered where Gabe was, and reasons for worrying were mounting, though Stedman tried not to let on that he was doing that. His words of consolation to Temperance were words of truth. He was glad he had said them to her. Now, he was having his own trouble grabbing hold of them. Gabe Laughinghouse had given some folks provocation for a lot of resentment against him. The list scrolled by in his head, as it had done in Temper's. Mae would not let her mind dwell on it. First, Gabe had applied for a job in the mill, Stedman tallied, and soon after that, he had rescued Temper and Rhonda, thank God for that. Stedman regretted not having called the sheriff when Herbert and Morris followed the girls that evening. Gabriel had intervened and stopped them, thank God, but that had made enemies for him, and they were not just Craven and Butch. Others resented Gabe for that, fool White men who believed a Colored man should never oppose a White man, on no account.

Hell, it made no sense, no use tryin' to fit a square peg in a roun' hole, Stedman fumed. His mind jumped ahead, resuming the tally. Then, Gabe had sat down at a "White only" lunch counter, for God's sake! Things had snowballed and gotten out of hand before they had seen it coming. Would it have made a difference if they had? It seemed like he was tryin', Gabe was, to get 'imself in trouble, Stedman thought irritably, despite the confidence he had expressed to Temperance about Gabe's having to stand up for what was right. That much was true, but he was wishing Gabe had been more sensible about how he went about it and he was growing angry at him for not having done that. The anger was as much at himself as at Gabe. He recognized that, too.

He was getting himself worked up, Stedman realized. Mostly, though, he was flat out worried. Worried, too, because his handling of the chase episode had made matters worse, more threatening, Stedman feared and admitted. If he'd turned it all over to the law, instead of cussin' the men out an' firin' 'em, things might not have got as hot as they had. He felt certain the bastards were layin' for 'im.

Temp'rance was right about that. They would figure a half-breed, Colored man had no right to meddle in a White man's business. They wouldn't be forgivin' 'im for that, not 'til hell froze over. They were bound to take their grudge against himself out on Gabe, too. Powerless to retaliate against a White man with his relative authority, they would find a scapegoat, and Gabe was their logical choice, if anybody could call it logic. He would be their target. All told, things looked mighty bad for Gabe.

Fishing for a Chesterfield in his shirt pocket and finding none, Stedman rose from the kitchen table and felt through his pants pockets. He retrieved a crumpled pack with a few cigarettes still in it and headed to his spot at the end of the porch, where he straddled his chair and pushed its back up against the porch railing. There, he rested both arms on the worn banister and lapped his smoking hand over the top of the other. This favorite position relieved his fatigue and the strain on his side where the hernia from the kidney operation was located. He could lean forward at a comfortable angle and rest his weight against the railing. It helped the strain on the small of his back, too.

Temper finished her meal and followed him to the porch. Like him, she cut to the chase,

"Daddy, what do you think has happened to Gabe? Are you worried about him? I'm sick to death, I'm so worried. I'm afraid something has happened to him. And Pa Gabriel's so shut-mouthed, I don't know what's goin' on with him," she fussed.

It was not like Pa Gabriel to remain so quiet, she expressed again. Maybe the concern about Gabe had kicked up his worry and depression over Seth, as she had feared it would, she reasoned. Ordinarily, he would be trying to console her, but he had said almost nothing to her. And he had gone back to skipping meals and staying at the river every minute he wasn't working at the store. She couldn't make out his behavior and what it meant.

"Let's not buy trouble, Shug," Stedman said gravely, "he's prob'ly just busy with some of his research. Gabe, I mean. And Pa's all right," he added.

He had spoken his hope, but not what he thought. His staccato puffing on his cigarette gave him away. Temperance knew what that idiosyncrasy meant. The short, rapid puffs signified that he was anxious, and in this situation it meant that his spoken words and true thoughts didn't match. Stedman was worried about Gabe a lot, she could see.

"I heard he borrowed Sam Tate's fishin' boat on Saturday," Stedman said, as though that hearsay explained Gabe's absence, one looking at this point, though he didn't say it, more and more like a disappearance.

The remark did more harm than good, Stedman saw instantaneously. The idea, if not the word, of a disappearance now hung in the air. Gabe had disappeared. If Stedman's clumsy words had not yet sunk into Temper's thoughts, they had served to stir up and agitate his own. Now, the thought of the source of that information and certain peculiarities about how it had been given to him aroused new questions and flagged disturbing innuendoes. Buddy Nelson had been the one who had mentioned that morning in the cotton mill that Morris and Herbert had told him about the fishing boat, about Gabe's borrowing it from Sam Tate. Buddy's manner of telling him had seemed awkward, like he was reciting something he'd been told to tell someone, because they wanted to get the word out and thought the best way to broadcast it would be through an emissary. Buddy had a slight speech impediment, however, so Stedman was uncertain that he had heard him correctly and paid him little mind, in any case, as Buddy dropped the comment into the conversation going on around the spinning frame Stedman was trying to get repaired just then. Now, Stedman wondered privately, why would Morris and Herbert want him, or anyone else, to know about the loan of the fishing boat? Maybe he was imagining Buddy's unusual behavior. Still, something about it all didn't fit.

For Temper's sake, he said more than he believed, "He most likely went fishin' with some of the new friends he's made, and then jus' got busy spendin' time with 'em. He'll prob'ly be back in a few days."

Heavier on Stedman's mind than anything else was the fact that Gabe had told him on July fourth that he planned to make a visit to Detroit to see his folks the last week of the month. Only a few days were left in July, less than a week. Gabe wouldn't leave for home without saying goodbye to the Smith family, for the particular reason that he would not be returning at the end of the summer, but going back to Atlanta for the beginning of the fall semester at Morehouse. Everybody knew that. On those grounds, Stedman was sure he had not gone to Detroit yet, but where was he?

———————

In the cool, dew-damp, early morning hours of July the twenty-fifth, Pa Gabriel had circled his aching body inside the fishing cave beneath his tulip poplar and was trying to doze. The breeze before dawn had stirred up and cooled the air to a chill, and he thought the earthen shelter would be more comfortable until the sun rose above the horizon and the breeze leveled off. He had awakened in the company bedroom that morning about four o'clock, unable to go back to sleep. Like Temper and the rest of the family, he had worried and wondered why Gabe Laughinghouse had not come by to let them know he was all right.

Gabriel had heard about the lunch counter incident at West End Grocery before he left there on Saturday. The news had traveled faster than after Gabe had applied for the cotton mill job, if that was possible. Folks were puzzled by the actions of the two, young Colored boys. Why did they want to eat at a White lunch counter, anyhow? What good would that do? Some said they sat beside a White girl. That was not proper. Colored folks, some of the young ones, were startin' to get out of their place, folks were saying to one another. Tension was already running high. Now, this.

Too uneasy to go back to sleep, Gabriel had gotten up quietly while the others slept and had gone to his refuge beside the river. Now inside the cave, whether he had dropped off or not he couldn't be sure, but the sound of men talking close by aroused him. Their voices were hushed and hurried, and the tone had conveyed to him that something secretive was afoot.

"Push 'im on out. He's got t' be in de deep water, or he'll wash up."

"Damn it! How d' I know I'm not goin' t'step in a mess o' water moccasins?!" another exploded.

"We're goin' to be in a lot worser mess 'n dat if dis nigger washes up. We got t' make shore he stays down, or leastwise, dat people think he drownded natur'l, ef he does come up."

Gabriel had squirmed around in order to position himself so that he could tell what was going on. It was still too dark to make out their faces, but he could see that there were two men crouching over another form crumpled in the bottom of a fishing boat which they had pulled out to the middle of the river.

Hunkered down in his look-out, Gabriel had willed his eyes to see through the dark and early morning fog what he could hardly stomach finding out but knew without sight to confirm it. Damn it, the sons o' bitches had killed him! He was certain of it. Not given to profanity, Pa Gabriel's mind could close itself around nothing so completely as profanity at that god-awful moment. The realization nearly sufffocated him.

They were pulling Seth's grandson's body out to dump it into the river. The old lady's words, the elderly fishing companion's words flooded Gabriel's mind. Dead already, Gabe Laughinghouse's corpse was now only a burden to dispose of and conceal. Gabriel had felt his proximity to the men such that he had been afraid they would hear him breathing, so fast and hard the labored breaths rasped out of him. His skin grew clammy and he became dangerously, physically ill, nauseous and weak. His heart pounded against his breastbone and in his ears, and sweat drenched his body from hairline to knees. Pa suffered from adrenaline surges. They had started when Hannah died, and he recognized the symptoms and knew their danger. He could have a heart attack and die there, in his earthen womb, unborn. But that was not what was uppermost in his mind.

Sick in body and soul, Gabriel had been terrified the men would see him and flee to avoid discovery, before he could identify them. He had to identify them, he knew. Gabe was beyond saving, but his assailants had to be identified. Nothing would do but that. Mercifully, the men were preoccupied and never looked toward the riverbank where he lay. They did not suspect they were observed.

Their sorry business took longer than the felons calculated. It was still dark, but the dawning sky had lightened to cobalt blue, no longer slate, and the faintest gleam of light rimmed the horizon above a dark strip of dense trees seaming the river's edge. They had pulled on Gabe's death-heavy body, but it was nearly too much for them to hoist over the side of the boat. Minutes longer than they could spare, they had tugged and shoved and stumbled and fallen and stood again, until finally, the boat was empty.

At once, a bright stab of first light speared their heads and caused them to jerk their grimy faces upward and toward it. In that vivid burst of sunlight, Gabriel saw them plain as if they had been posing for a picture, sitting for a mug shot. Just as he had suspected and dreaded. Craven Herbert and Butch Morris. The men who had followed Temper. Those whom Gabe had kept away. Now, he could distinguish unambiguously their voices, too, the same voices he had heard lying and bragging at West End. Staring at their blighted faces awash in daybreak sunlight, Gabriel had had to fight to restore his equilibrium, to keep his breath even, and to slow his stampeding heart rate to a survivable pace.

He had done the nearly impossible thing, and perhaps saved his own life, by willing himself to remain almost catatonically still, and prayerfully averting, directing, his gaze away from the malefactors to a scene which, in normal hours, calmed and cheered him. This was a parade of ancient, longleaf pines whose tops touched heaven. Near the crest of the centermost one of those was a bald eagle's nest. Only two days before, he had watched while a regal, white crown ascended out of the nest, and presently, a splendid wingspan of eight or nine feet's breadth arose over the green canopy and hesitated briefly, high above the river, before soaring upstream to another destination. Looking at the trees and thinking about the grand eagle's ascension and flight had calmed his respiration and modulated his heart rate enough to stabilize him physically, and enough to allow him to wait quietly until the criminals had finished their "devils' triumph" and "insult to God" and left.

That early morning, some who lived near the river heard one, long, piercing cry, whether human or animal, they said they could not tell. Others thought they heard something but were not sure and soon forgot about it.

PART THREE

Into Light

Chapter Ten

Greater love has no man than this, that a man lay down his life for his friends.

John 15:13

Temperance slapped at the mosquito whining beside her ear and looked at her hand to see if its crushed body's black smudge meant she had gotten it. With an absentmindedness born of a surfeit of practice, she wiped the tell-tale smear on the Kleenex she pulled from under her pillow and swiped at her temple, all the while making a vague, mental note to wash it with soap and water as soon as she got up.

She looked irritably at the alarm clock on the dresser across the room. Ten twelve, it said. The Jordan's Feed and Seed Store calendar beside the dresser, an outsized almanac page with no pictures, showed July was nearly gone. A prettier, smaller calendar with the little Coppertone suntan girl on it sat on the dresser. July the twenty-eighth. Only a few more weeks of lazy, sleeping-late mornings remained before school started again after Labor Day. Temperance felt a pang in her stomach at the thought. But that dread was a distant second to the worry she felt about Gabe. They still hadn't heard a word from him, or from anyone else who had seen him, or knew anything of his whereabouts.

Feeling a little guilty for sleeping half the morning while both her parents had been at work for three hours, she recently had offered a voluntary penance, and a welcome help, by having supper almost done when Mae got home. Now old enough, Temper had surprised Mae by volunteering to get supper on the stove for her, on weekdays, until school began. She liked hearing her mother say that she was "growing up." Pa's and Stedman's acknowledgments of that fact she had enjoyed, too. A change had come over her this summer. She didn't need her folks to tell her so, and they didn't know the half of it, Temperance mused. She stretched her full, young length under the pink-flowered bedspread, the Belk-Tyler one, and glanced toward the latched door opening directly from her bedroom onto the porch. The inner, wooden door had been left open all night to coax a blessed draft across her bed, one which would not, and had not, come until well past midnight in the dew-pleasant hours before sunup.

A latch on the screen door had offered sufficient security and privacy. Besides, most felt they had to leave the wood door open or suffocate from the heat and humidity. Old folks with heart trouble and breathing problems especially suffered. Temperance had observed the fact that cemeteries were filled with markers with summer dates on them, and both her great-grandfathers had died in August in the same year. There was nothing incidental about either of those facts, she was convinced.

Wondering for a moment where Pa Gabriel was, Temper remembered that the most likely place was his river shelf. Pa's strange quiet puzzled and now annoyed her. Her grandfather who conversed more than anyone else she knew had kept his own counsel since Gabe's absence (she would not allow herself to term it a disappearance). She could think of no plausible explanation for his uncharacteristic behavior except depression. Unless . . . . he knew something he was not telling, it now occurred to her. Why had she been so slow on the uptake? Did he know something she didn't?! If so, why had he not told her?! If he had not told her, he had not told anyone. Of that much she felt certain.

Beyond the screendoor and porch, Temperance noticed a thin stream of people heading in the direction of the mill. Where were they going? She unlatched the screen and stuck her head out to get a better view of the column of ten or fifteen people, most of them men and older boys, hurrying, she could see now, toward the Neuse River behind the mill. There was something about the way they walked and the hushed way they talked and bent their heads close to those near them which made her curious and uneasy. They appeared dreamlike, grotesques in a hurried, funeral procession, or a funereal one. So concerned and solemn their movement, though quick and unchoreographed, it limned a requiem mass, as it joined the chords of dread beating in her heart.

Forgetting the mosquito remains on her temple, Temperance pulled on the gathered skirt and sleeveless, eyelet blouse she had worn the day before and dropped on the stuffed chair beside her bed. She jammed her feet into a pair of ballerina slippers, (not actually, but called that because of their similarity), passed a comb over, but not through, her thick tangle of hair, dabbed on a smear of the new lipstick, and ran to join the quasi-stately procession rounding the southwest corner of the cotton mill and pointing its way toward the Neuse where the river flowed closest to the mill village. She was one of just three females in the line. As she and those marching with her neared the river's edge and the small assembly already crowded there, she heard one of the bystanders answer another's question, or did she imagine that, and the question she thought she heard was hers?

"I don't know, 'cept it looks like a Colored boy."

Temperance felt sick to her stomach. She already knew who it was. Her eyes fell on the bloated, dark body of someone, of *Gabe*, just his shoulder and back, before it was wrapped in a heavy tarpaulin. Feeling faint, she sank down on her knees in the sunlit grass. Then, she prostrated herself face down, burying her face in the grass and burrowing her hands into the earth, raking it with her nails and breathing deep smells of sharp grass and the cooling dankness of river dirt. They alone prevented her slide into unconsciousness.

"Looks like he's been in the river a few days, judgin' from the condition of his body," a distant voice said, floating somewhere above her body and gliding in and out of her hearing.

"What do you think happened? Has anyone gone missin'?" another muffled voice asked.

"Gabriel Laughinghouse . . . . a student at Morehouse College . . . . stayin' with a family across town . . . . He's been missing since last Saturday."

221

The last voice was Pa Gabriel's. Until he spoke, Temperance had not known he was there.

"It is Gabe Laughinghouse," Pa Gabriel stated flatly, authoritatively.

He had been the first person who noticed the body washed up in the tall grass beside the northwest bank. He had watched for it. Already, before Temperance got there, he had made a positive identification to Henry Johnson, the coroner.

With Pa's help, Temperance pulled herself up to her feet. Beside her, someone had laid a fistful of dandelions and wild violets, field flowers, a yellow and purple bouquet, its fresh beauty a stark contrast to the scene of death and violence smothering her. She instinctively picked it up and stuck the violets to her nose. Trembling, she looked about to see where it had come from, who had put it there, wordless and secret.

Then, she saw him. Butch Morris. Elbowing his way through the crowd. He glanced back at her and the flowers she was holding, timidly nodded his head slightly toward her, and disappeared. The look on his unshaven face was serious; no doubt, scared. Without question, she realized later, it had been sober. That way, he had looked younger . . . . confused.

Deep, heart-wrenching sobs tore out of her throat as she dropped the flowers and grabbed Pa Gabriel.

"Let's go home, Temp'rance. I have something to tell you, now," Pa intoned solemnly.

On Sunday, that death morning after Gabriel Laughinghouse was murdered, and after Craven Herbert and Butch Morris had driven away from the river at sunup, Gabriel Lewis had hurried home to get paper and pencil to compose a letter to Sheriff Mac Whitley, which he intended to have legally signed and notarized the next business day with the letter's date, July 26, 1954, certifiably documented. Searching the pie safe and bureau drawers and scanning Temper's stack of books and papers, he failed to find a pencil, but early on

Monday, he went directly to Standard Drug Store across the street from the Carolina Theater and bought unlined paper and a box of envelopes, and instead of a pencil, he purchased his first ballpoint pen. Then he walked the half block to the post office and asked for five, three-cent stamps, two more than he needed, and those he stuck inside his wallet for future use. After that, he went to the Lenoirville Public Library and found his favorite table in the corner nearest the newspapers, glad to see that it was unoccupied, the hour being early. There, he composed the letter to Sheriff Whitley and carefully hand-copied three, exact copies. These copies, he purposed to send, one, to the editor of the *Lenoirville Daily Free Press*, the second, to Gabe Laughinghouse's father, Abraham Laughinghouse in Detroit, and the third copy, he would give directly to Temperance Green Smith when Gabe's body was found, as he was confident it would be. He planned to delay mailing the letters one day, until July 27, 1954.

When Gabe's bloated body washed up on the northwest bank of the Neuse River on the next day, July 28, the timing was perfect. Gabriel knew Sheriff Mac Whitley would be coming by his house, or by West End Grocery, to question him that very afternoon.

Gabriel had taken all precautions to see that the investigation of Seth's grandson's murder would not be mishandled the way Seth's had been. He would see to it. Here is the letter Gabriel George Lewis composed in the Lenoirville Public Library.

It seems to me that we all make a promise when we come into this world and draw breath. And that promise, made to everybody and everything, and most of all, to God who made us all, is that we will take our place, and make our place, in a way which respects all others around us, big and small, colored and white, powerful and powerless. We promise to respect them, and to help them, as much as it lies in our power reasonably to do that.

It's a promise we don't even know we've made for awhile, but we make it anyhow, by taking that first breath and all the others we help ourselves to after that.

The first time we break that promise is when we try to assign a place to ourselves and our tribe that's above and better than the one we assign to others not like us in some way, those of a different color or language or social class or religion, or different from the powerful group, our group, in some other way.

The second time we break the promise is when we tell ourselves and others that it's always been this way and no other.

Worst of all, we claim it is God's way. We take God's name in vain.

Finally, with the promise broken through the lies we have told, we find a thousand ways to shut our brother out, to deny his full dignity, to kill his hope, to defer our sister's dreams and close the door of humanity and hospitality against all her children and their descendants.

When we've stripped our native promise bare, we turn to murderous violence like that which killed young Gabriel Lewis Laughinghouse, my namesake, my chosen son, grandson of my friend, Seth Laughinghouse.

I hereby testify that I saw Craven Herbert and Butch Morris dispose of a man's body in the Neuse River behind the Lenoirville power plant at daybreak, Sunday morning, July 25, 1954. On the grounds of evidence I have witnessed, I am prepared to testify that it was the body of Gabriel Lewis Laughinghouse.

God forgive us all.

Respectfully submitted,

Gabriel George Lewis
July 26, 1954

Below the text of the letter, Matthew W. Wilson, attorney at law, had signed the document in its original form and affixed a seal, written to Sheriff Mac Whitley, and in like manner, to each of the three copies, all of them notarized with his official signature and dated July 26, 1954. At the same meeting at which the letters were signed, Gabriel had questioned the attorney about how he could go about filing a wrongful death suit against Craven Herbert and Butch Morris. He would not leave the indictment of those who had killed Gabe Laughinghouse to the initiative of the district attorney's office alone. Justice must be done this time.

Pa Gabriel had waited one day to mail the letters to Sheriff Mac Whitley, Editor Christopher Temple, editor of the *Lenoirville Daily Free Press*, and Abraham Laughinghouse in Detroit. The envelopes bore the postmark, July 27, 1954.

Gabriel Laughinghouse's battered and bloated body washed up the following morning behind the Lenoirville power plant.

———

On the morning before the trial began, Temperance found Pa Gabriel at his customary place beside the river. He appeared quiet, still, to her except for the etching he was doing. Serene, albeit, somber.

"Pa Gabriel, I have to ask you a question," she started. "Do you hate those men . . . . ?

She refused to finish her question with its implied end, ". . . who killed Gabe?"

Unable to wait for his response, she burst into a fresh torrent of tears, "I do! I hate them, Grandpa!! I hope they kill them the same way they killed Gabe! And with as little mercy!"

She had said it, but it didn't feel any better. Gabriel patted her shoulder and waited for her to calm down.

"I know. I know," he murmured.

He diverted her attention, "See this little monkey? I've about finished 'im. I want you to have him for your collection. I expect it's about time we added another one to *your* collection," he emphasized with tenderness and warmth in his eyes. "The last two or three I've done for others. *You're* my muse and my patron of the arts," he smiled, and touched his forehead to hers with his comical, eyes-almost-touching stare they had enjoyed and laughed about since her childhood.

Then he said, "I've been studyin' over some things, Honey. I wanta' tell you what I've been thinkin'. I want your response."

He took a deep, long breath and began, "You know that dark strip on the sidewalk Gabe helped you get through?"

Temperance nodded, wondering what the relevance was.

"Well, I've been thinkin' about that. There's a dark strip like that inside every one of us, Temp'rance, I believe that's so," Pa said with some authority. "Every decision we make and everything we do, good and bad, brings us to the edge of that place, or lands us in it, I think. Our genuine actions, the actions that are genuine and most express who we are, come out of what we do when we get there. It seems that life is about what we do with the challenges on the journey, all of them, the little ones and the big ones. In fact, we prob'bly journey along the edge of the dark strip most of our lives. I'm ready to say that there may be, probably is, in fact, something both necessary and beneficial about our doin' that. About our bein' right there. On the edge. But it's treacherous, Temp'rance. That's the danger and the adventure. And if it's somethin' of our own doin', somethin' evil, like the thing Herbert and Morris did, we've got to do our dead level best to rise above it. To conquer it and make restitution for it. The way I see it, we can rise over it, or get lost in it. Two choices. That's pretty much what we have."

Neither a philosophical dualist nor a monist, Gabriel Lewis identified and acknowledged dualistic, and monistic, tendencies in humankind, the two, polar errors tripping thinkers up in reductionist mire since the dawn of human history. His own thinking at this juncture tended toward dualism, and he recognized it. Conquer or be conquered. Win or lose. Prevail or succumb. Temperance was having difficulty following his thought. She knew she could trust in his motives and the intellectual rigor of his reflection. Still, she was in no frame of mind to engage in a philosophical analysis, and in no discursive mood at all. He would have to say more to move her there. And he would have to clarify his meaning better, come down out of the theoretical clouds, and touch ground for her. She was too sad and too tired to think with him on weighty subjects. And too angry. But she said none of this to Gabriel.

"We can rise over it like that bald eagle over there at the top o' that tall pine, risin' over the river, and like Gabe did that night on the sidewalk between you and those men . . . . or we can get lost in it."

He stopped and they watched the grand eagle settle into its nest.

"Shucks, Temper! I'm willin' to say that maybe we *have* to go in there sometimes. The dark strip, I mean. There're all kinds of things in there. Not just violence and evil actions. Mae and Stedman went there when your baby brother died before he was born. I nearly died in there myself, when I heard about Seth's murder," he mourned still. "Maybe that's part of the plan. It seems we all do end up there to some degree, one way or the other. The self-righteous and self-deluded think some stay out while some go in. Of course, they're the ones who stay out, according to their reckoning. After all, that defines self-righteousness, doesn't it? That way of interpreting everything as somebody's fault, and not theirs? But that narrow way of thinking is deaf to the wonder of conscious decisions to go there, courageous intentions to go there. Into the dark strip. For a purpose. The way Gabe did."

Pa Gabriel was touching solid ground now, and he had Temperance's full attention. He managed a weak, ironic smile and turned the almost-crafted peach kernel around in his fingers and studied some more.

"It's the stayin' in there that's the work of the devil," he pontificated, sounding more like his daughter than himself, and a little embarrassed about it. He clarified, "When it involves wrong or evil, or self-pity and depression," he added, thinking of his own self-absorption and his struggle to climb out of it.

Where was he going? He was repeating himself and wearying Temperance again.

"If we get lost in it, we may never find our way out again. That's what happened to Butch and Craven, I think. They got lost in it, Temper. And they never got out. Unless . . . ."

Temper waited.

Then he said something startling, hard to digest, impossible to accept, "Butch's flowers, Temper, they were a step out of that dark place, I think . . . ."

She jumped involuntarily and began to disagree, to protest, but he kept talking.

"Maybe we're all, not just Butch and Craven, but all of us, already in there somewhere, Temp'rance, somewhere inside the dark strip, and maybe, jus' maybe, Gabe was trying to show us the way out."

Before she could make heads or tails of that, he started up again. "I don't know which way it goes. We're either at the edge or already in there. But I do think Gabe was trying to lead us out of it, the more I think about it. And he had to make a lonely journey inside it, through it, to do that."

Gabriel was joining his thoughts end to end, synthesizing them, not as though it was the first time he had thought about them, but like they were still forming and he was knitting them together into a coherent whole. She was not unfamiliar with this method of his; in some measure, it was hers, as well. And she knew it was Stedman's, too. He had stopped merely repeating himself; he was going somewhere.

He shifted his back stiffly against the tulip poplar and continued his mental construction.

"I mean, with it all. When you look at it all, maybe Gabe already knew it was going to end this way. Look at it. The job, the dimestore thing, I mean, the lunch counter thing, and particularly the way he took up for you and your friend. For you and Rhonda. Especially that. It's like he gave up his life, Temper. Not like someone took it from him. He could have chosen the easy road, the safe road, but he chose the dangerous one. I'll say it right out. The one likely to kill him. He put his body between those men and you and let you run on home safe. He might'a died right there. That's what I mean, Temper."

Gabriel inhaled and expelled a deep sigh, a breathing of the Spirit, it seemed, a holy wind, and suddenly, an emphatic shout and explosive tone, like an eruptive voice-over, superseded his weary, agitated one and gained stronger, more insistent force and power, and he announced,

"If we step inside the dark strip and land inside hate of any kind, of any person, we're in cosmic trouble, Temp'rance. Stay outa' there. Stay away from it, Temper," he pleaded. "I know it's hard, but try to stay away from hatred. It's worse than the plague. It *is* the worst of all plagues. It goes by other names, Temp'rance—euphemisms (Miss Newkirk had taught him that word), infernal pretences that it's not all that bad, that it's sometimes even justified, not as bad as hate. But they are, Temper. Prejudice, envy, bigotry, greed, intolerance, exclusion, negligence, injustice in all its forms, it's all hate, Temp'rance. Don't let anybody soft-pedal it to you. It's *hate*. Plainly that." He repeated, "And as bad as that." Then he said it again, "I can't see a nickel's worth of difference between them."

Gabriel had reached the place where his thoughts had been leading him from his first word. His eyes blazed with the energy of his conviction. His annunciation was not yet accomplished, but he stood on the brink:

"If we hate someone because his skin is darker than ours, or his eyes bluer and his skin pinker, or he speaks in a different way, or because he's outstripped us in some way, like drivin' a bigger car, or because he's peculiar to us in some way, like finding his companionship with a person of his own sex, yes, I'm talkin' about love companionship, Temp'rance, you aren't surprised to hear me say that, are you? or we hate our brother or sister for any reason *at all*—killin' results. Hate killin'. Like it did with Butch and Craven and Gabe. (Did he notice he had spoken their three names together? Temperance did.) And like it did with Seth. There're places in the dark strip we gotta' scramble outa' just as fast as we can. Places like hate, most of all, no matter what it's called. Even when it looks like there's plenty good reason to hate," he added.

Gabriel slumped against the poplar, fatigued by the energy he had given to his oration. He repeated, "If we stay there, we'll get lost, and we may never find our way out," he said, burdened by the thought of that implacable threat.

Immediately, his mind looped back to Seth's grandson,

"Yes, I *do* believe he was trying to show us the way out of there, Temperance," he said with finality. She knew he had finished.

Gabriel Lewis examined closely the peachseed monkey he had carved, rubbed his right thumb gently over its tiny, funny face, and handed it to Temper,

"I believe I got all the ugly," he said.

Temper's narrative was finished. She laid her pen down and reached for a cigarette. A celebration was in order, she concluded.

"Temperance, I think you've about done what you needed to do in these sessions here," Jeff announced. "Is that what you think, too? Whether you continue writing your story depends on what you want to do with it, but you've pretty much put your guilty struggle to rest, I think, don't you?"

Temperance nodded in half agreement. The old responsibility was an accounting still, but it felt manageable at last. She could go on now without dragging her sodden wedding dress behind her.

"It was that, Jeff, I believe now. The dress I married Carson in . . . . maybe also the dress I never married in," she paused, and pressed onward, "maybe the dress I would have married in, if my story had been otherwise, in another day and time. The pink roses suggest that to me."

Feeling the color rising in her face, Temper kept going, "The dark water was the Neuse Gabriel floated in and the dark mound beside it is his body, I believe."

Swallowing. and aware of her rapid heartbeat, she had more to say, "I neglected Carson. The dissertation had claimed all my attention . . . and sapped my energy."

She needed to say it all, but she had to wrap it up, too. "When I told him to leave, he nearly collapsed. He sank to the floor and sat like a small boy with his back against the doorframe, crying like a baby and pleading with me to forgive him. To give him a chance. I refused." Then Temperance looked at her hands and said, "I applied

Stedman's mantra too literally . . . and spitefully . . . I see and admit that now. Is that also the dark water? And the mud?"

Jeffrey nodded and asked, "Maybe the dark strip?"

She agreed. "Yes."

More for her ears than Jeff's, she said, and embraced the recognition of it with the speaking of it, "Gabriel was a rival Carson couldn't match . . . or see."

————————

Temperance touched the small tombstone with her left hand and tipped the fingers of her stiffened, right hand to the ground to steady her arduous push and pull to her feet. She had taken care to sit close enough to the stone marker to use its support to push herself up again. Years of living and aging and lack of exercise had done their part to make squatting and sitting and standing again hard to do, and smoking had taken its toll. So like Stedman, in this way, as well, she would carry her addiction with her to her grave, Temper knew. And something else. She had not yet had a chance to question Dr. Evans about post-polio syndrome and whether it might explain her extreme fatigue and growing muscle weakness. Was a mild, undiagnosed case of polio in the forties the reason for her lifelong inability to enjoy bicycle riding and other sports needing strong legs? If she had had it, her case of infantile paralysis had been mild, undiagnosed and unknown, and had left her with no discernible impairment like Callie Sanderson's. A diagnosis would help to explain her mounting fatigue and inability to stand comfortably in one spot for more than a few minutes, however. Fredericka had insisted her symptoms were more than simple, old age,

"I tell you, Temp'rance, you're tireder than you should be. I wish you would talk to the doctor about it."

She murmured something now under her breath to Mae. It was an old folks' habit she had developed, her talking to those who had loved her most and who were no longer with her in the body. The thought about helping when we don't know we're doing that came back. She had been a help like that for her mother, and for Stedman, she was certain of it. Others, her parents, Pa, and innumerable named and unnamed others, had done the same for her, no doubt. Miss Lizzy, especially. She was certain of that, too.

Pa Gabriel, whom she talked to regularly, had shown it to her. Gabriel, Messenger of God. Beloved grandfather and friend. It's all one thing, this complex, torn, creation story. Butch's gift of field flowers . . . flowers of the field. Jeff had mentioned them in their last session. It had taken a long time before she was able to accept them as what they seemed to be. As what they were. Gabe Laughinghouse had to be mourned, grieved. Butch had died, too. A peace offering, they were, the flowers. A declaration of regard, most likely. Timid, bizarre, misdirected, not enough. But they had helped. They helped now. It was one. Creation, fall, and redemption are one story, one journey, divine and human. Not three, Temperance knew. Butch's timid gift of dandelions and violets were, even as Pa had said, a step out of the dark strip, despite her rejection of them.

She was confident Mae would have liked the baby's headstone. Stedman, too. Temper had guessed where to instruct the young attendant to place it. She remembered again that he had been a polite, sensitive, young man and had taken a lot of pains with it. It read simply:

Baby Boy Smith
Infant Son of Stedman and Mae Smith
March 5, 1941
Asleep in Christ

Temperance reached into her skirt pocket for the tiny gift she had brought to put beside the baby's memorial and stooped and placed it there. Now, it looked too small, invisible nearly, nestled and swallowed in the unmown grass. Searching for wildflowers growing in or near the graveyard, she glimpsed a patch of color near another infant's tombstone. As she approached the small, heart-shaped marker, she saw that the volunteer blooms were purple violets, with the spent heads of three dandelion wisps dotted among them. A thin row grew at the base of the baby's stone, giving it a ric-rac edging of color, and behind it, a large clump of violets had rooted and flourished a few feet away in a damper spot. These last, Temperance picked a handful of and paused to study a moment. Then, she returned to the small headstone and snipped with trembling fingers the three dandelions, no longer bright flowers, dry heads of seeds, and added them to the violets, before walking back to her brother's marker. There she placed the bouquet tenderly, almost ceremoniously, and whispered a prayer. It made a lovely frame for the peachseed monkey.

On her next visit, she would bring one for the other baby.

Epilogue

*. . . . Like one that wraps the drapery of his couch about him, and
lies down to pleasant dreams.*

William Cullen Bryant

On the Sunday evening before Christmas, Walnut Grove's children
and teens presented their annual Christmas play. Temperance and
Fredericka attended and sat in the middle of the third pew on the
right of the sanctuary. As in so many small churches in the age of
electronic everything, the program's music was canned and the
play itself uninspired. Nonetheless, it harmonized enough with the
Christmas story to qualify as one, if barely, Temperance conceded,
her native impatience squarely on board. Fredericka could do no
other than to agree with her. Her mind was already forming a skit
for Temper's amusement.

Set and scripted as a spelling match competition for the
coveted roles of Mary and Joseph, the play and its actors followed
a script which alternated correct and incorrect spellings of words
like "wonderful," "counselor," "Almighty God," and "Prince of
Peace," with childish, choral renditions of modern-day Christmas
songs few in the congregation had heard before, but enjoyed still
by the kinfolks in attendance. Temperance and Fredericka would
have preferred hearing "The First Noel" and "Joy to the World."
Or "Hark, the Herald Angels Sing," and "Oh, Holy Night," true
Christmas carols, they whispered.

When the competition words had been spelled, or not,
misspelled, the winners emerged as a white, thirteen-year-old
Joseph and a bi-racial, fourteen-year-old Mary. At the start of

235

the spelling bee, it had not been evident to the congregation that things would turn out that way. Still, Walnut Grove Baptist had a racially integrated communion, though with just one black family in regular attendance and, by their choice, not yet fellowshipped into the church as members. The blond, gangly Joseph and his demure, African American Mary might have reminded onlookers of Barack Obama's mixed parentage, but it seemed unlikely anyone in attendance at Walnut Grove would have considered the scene remarkable in any way but that one.

Though no one had anticipated it, there was one person present who was offended. Abruptly, a young man of medium height stood up halfway back on the left side of the room and waved a revolver over his head like a flag. No one had seen him before, they later declared; he was a first-time visitor.

Incoherent but loud, he shouted something that sounded like,

"Mary ain't black! And it ain't right to mix black and white in the church house! This is God's house!"

"Excuse me," Temperance whispered to the persons sitting between her and Fredericka and the aisle. Quietly, almost imperceptibly in the darkened room, she slipped out of her seat and glided to the altar in what appeared to those who saw her, and felt to her to be, an unbroken, unbound movement, not of this realm, graceful and fluid, for she could scarcely feel her feet on the floor and, indeed, they touched as lightly as gravity legislated. To some in the congregation and to Fredericka, she appeared to belong there, as though her entrance was planned, and the light shining down on her silvered hair gave to her the look of the angel in "The First Noel." Thinking of nothing except the fire arm waving wildly in the man's grip, Temperance had stepped inside the nativity scene and stood in front of the holy family.

By that time, Jeff Singer was beside her and spontaneously, in an ethereal orchestration of movement, the two of them spread their arms, looking for all the world like the two crosses on Golgotha on either side of Jesus, or like a living, double crucifix shielding the children from harm.

A loud shot blasted the air and a bullet narrowly missed Jeff Singer's left shoulder. A second blast tore through the screams and alarmed shuffle and found a deadly mark.

———∿∾ѻⱥѻɢⱥѻ∾∿———

"You almost died. Thank God, you didn't."

"I know. Yes."

"Everybody's saying what a hero you are. How you saved the children's lives."

Fredericka nodded her confirmation.

"How are they?"

"They're unhurt. They'll be all right. They're getting counseling, both of them. They'll be okay, and so will you."

Fredericka frowned, not meaning to show her impatience with what was starting to sound like well-intentioned patter to her. They both knew the doctor's prognosis was guarded.

"Where?"

"Where? Oh! You mean, where are they getting counseling? Where else? Southeastern Ministry and Counseling," Jeffrey smiled, attempting light banter.

"From you?"

"No. I'm not the one to do it. Bob and Donna are counseling them."

"Who is he?"

"He? You mean . . . ? He's a boy from Sugar Hill, a very sick young man, alcoholic and drug addicted, too, poor, snatched around. I'm afraid he's deranged, Temper. Don't worry, we'll get help for him, too."

"That's good . . . . I'm glad."

Fredericka leaned forward and said softly, "We need to go now. We don't want to tire you." She bent over her friend and kissed her forehead. "We'll see you tomorrow."

"They'll run us out if we tire you with too much talk," Jeff took the signal and agreed. "But I have one more thing to say before we go," he added with a glance at Fred and turned back to Temper.

"We'll talk about this more later. You walked into the dark strip. You saved two lives. Two innocent lives, young, just starting their journeys. I think you know this story, don't you, Temp'rance?"

"Bye now, we'll be back tomorrow. Have the nurse call us if you need or want us, Temperature. Love you."

Temperance watched them leave the room. Freddie's sure gait and long stride, familiar and loved, a true friend dependable, sustaining, funny. She smiled weakly. Jeff's lean, tall frame, high-waisted but not unattractive, owing to disproportionately long legs, she recognized at last. That and his strong, good spirit mingled with, perhaps became confused with and absorbed into, a memory of another like him. A ghost now welcome. It was all right. It was all, all right.

Temperance looked on, or down; as in a dream she saw herself under the collection table watching herself shout, then floating over the water, and stepping out onto the bank of . . . the river? Which? What body of water? A mere ditch? The one before her grandmother's and Pa Gabriel's old house? Was she under anesthesia? After the shooting?

Voice: "Aren't you afraid? This is where your mother saw the ghost."

Answer: "No, they'll all be there when I get there."

The door stood open. Temperance saw the familiar house, recognized it now; it was Pa Gabriel's; it was full of people and all the lights were on. A celebration appeared to be inside it. People were standing close and talking in the light-filled, front room. The room where Grandma Hannah's body had lain in her pine coffin. A figure in shadow stood in the open door, his back suffused in light from the room he called her into, now with him. At last to be with them. The ditch was shallow and not wide. She could make it easily. There was no dark water in it. She raised her foot to step across.